I0761524

Beyond & Within

WITCH CRAFT

Folk Tales & Horror Stories

Edited by Marie O'Regan & Paul Kane

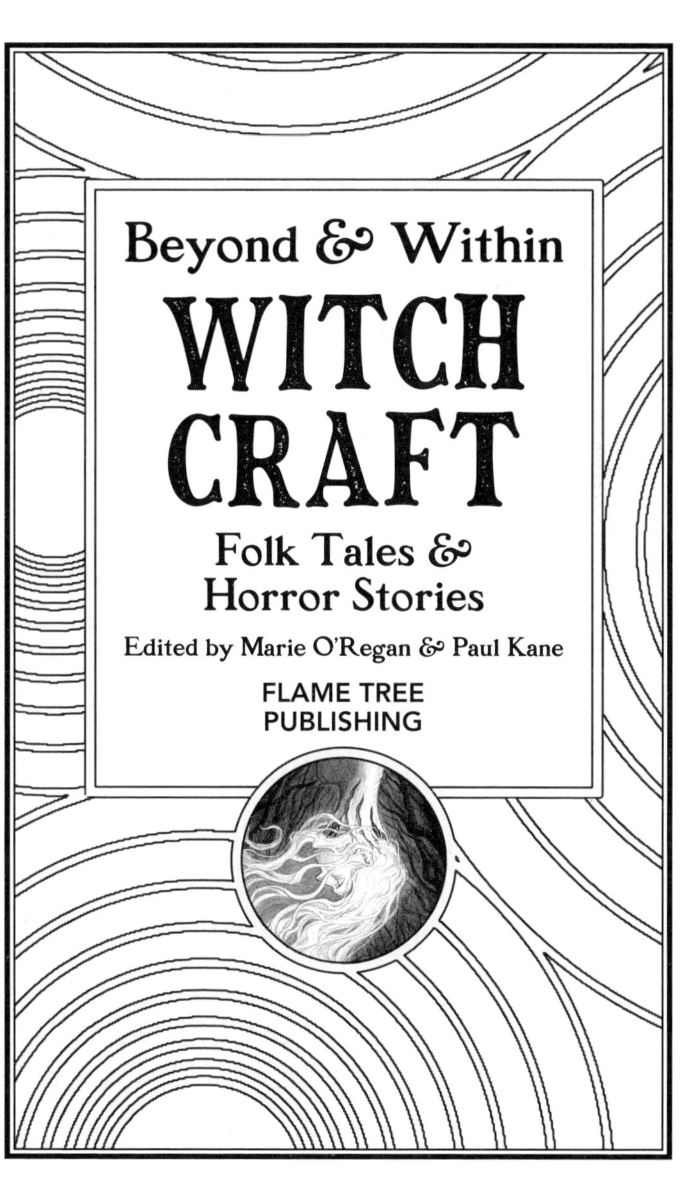

Beyond & Within

WITCH CRAFT

Folk Tales & Horror Stories

Edited by Marie O'Regan & Paul Kane

FLAME TREE
PUBLISHING

Publisher & Creative Director: Nick Wells
Senior Project Editor: Gillian Whitaker

FLAME TREE PUBLISHING
6 Melbray Mews, Fulham,
London SW6 3NS, United Kingdom
www.flametreepublishing.com

First published 2026

26 28 30 32 31 29 27
1 3 5 7 9 10 8 6 4 2

Hardback ISBN: 978-1-83562-597-2
ebook ISBN: 978-1-83562-598-9

Publisher's Note: This is a work of fiction. Names, characters, places, and incidents are a product of the authors' imaginations. Locales and public names are sometimes used for atmospheric purposes. Any resemblance to actual people, living or dead, or to businesses, companies, events, institutions, or locales is completely coincidental.

A copy of the CIP data for this book is available from the British Library.

Printed and bound in China

Represented in the EU for product safety and compliance by Authorised Rep Compliance Ltd., Ground Floor, 71 Lower Baggot Street, Dublin, D02 P593, Ireland. Contact at www.arccompliance.com

Table of Contents

Introduction

Marie O'Regan & Paul Kane

WHEN WE handed in our previous anthology to Flame Tree, the well-received *Beyond & Within – Folk Horror*, and started to think about the next one, the subject matter was right there staring us in the face. After all, we'd been reading a fair amount of witch tales for that book.

Folk Horror and Witchcraft go hand in hand when you think about it, in fact two of the three 'unholy trinity' movies that coined the term back in the '60s and '70s revolve around the subject – *Witchfinder General* (Michael Reeves, 1968) and *The Blood on Satan's Claw* (Piers Haggard, 1971) – draw their inspiration from the real-life historical witch trials and persecution of women, not to mention the publication of the *Malleus Maleficarum* (*Hammer of Witches* – effectively a witch-hunting manual). A topic that was itself reframed by Matilda Joslyn Gage's

1893 book *Women, Church and State*, to show how the hunts and trials had been used to police female sexuality, women's bodies and reproduction.

Of course, we can go right back to Medea in Greek mythology, then on to Morgan le Fay or the weird sisters in Shakespeare's *Macbeth* if we're talking about famous witches in fiction. Or how about the witches who populate those fairy tales by the Brothers Grimm, first published in the nineteenth century? In 1900 L. Frank Baum (interestingly Gage's son-in-law) created the Wicked Witch of the West, who first appeared in *The Wonderful Wizard of Oz*, someone you should be familiar with if only because of a certain couple of recent musicals based on the Gregory Maguire books. And the origins of C.S. Lewis's *The Lion, the Witch and the Wardrobe* – the first of The Chronicles of Narnia, another fantasy take – stretch back to the '30s.

But it wasn't until the 1940s, '50s and '60s that a more 'light-hearted' and less evil version of witches began to appear in films like *I Married a Witch* (René Clair, 1942) and *Bell, Book and Candle* (Richard Quine, 1958) and TV shows such as *Bewitched*, the latter also reflecting Women's Liberation that was bubbling under the surface in society (indeed, some episodes were even written by feminist Barbara Avedon).

With the advent of Folk Horror, Exploitation and Satanic Panic, horror soon claimed witches for its own again, though it wasn't long before we were being given more powerful characters in this respect once more. *The Witches of Eastwick* (George Miller, 1987), *The Craft* (Andrew Fleming, 1996) and *Practical Magic* (Griffin Dunne, 1998) along with Willow in *Buffy the Vampire Slayer* or the main trio of *Charmed*, were all very different examples of 'girl power', before *American Horror Story* took it much darker with *Coven* and the cartoon/sit-com of *Sabrina* got a more chilling makeover for her own live action Netflix series.

From Joseph Conrad's 'The Inn of the Two Witches' and M.R. James's 'The Ash Tree', through to Anne Rice's *Mayfair Witches* (also recently adapted for television), J.K. Rowling's Harry Potter series, Kelley Armstrong's Dime Store Magic books and Grady Hendrix's *Witchcraft for Wayward Girls* – and that's even before we get to comics like Marvel's Scarlet Witch, or Hellboy's *The Crooked Man* (adapted for film in 2024) – it's not hard to see how or why writers have gravitated towards this subject as a source of inspiration. Even in the last few years, we've had novels like *Circe* by Madeline Miller, Katherine Arden's *The Bear and the Nightingale* (the Winternight Trilogy), *The Year of the*

Witching by Alexis Henderson, Lana Popović's *Payback's a Witch*, *Where the Dark Stands Still* by A.B. Poranek and *Weyward* by Emilia Hart to name but a few, showing that if anything the demand is increasing.

All of which makes our latest anthology a no-brainer.

As always, we've tried to gather together a varied mix of writers to illustrate just what can be done with the theme of witches and witchcraft. Ally Wilkes (*Where the Dead Wait*) straddles different time periods for her contribution, kicking things off perfectly, while the author of *Jump Cut*, Helen Grant, and the author of *The Crimson Road*, Angela 'A.G.' Slatter, effortlessly blend crime with the supernatural in 'Remembrance' and 'Murder Ballads by Moonlight'. Eugen Bacon (*A Place Between Waking and Forgetting*) delivers an African-Australian relationship tale you won't soon forget, and Alison Moore (*The Retreat*) flirts with childhood memory and loss for her story.

Amanda Mason (*The Hiding Place*) presents us with a generational predicament, while Lisa L. Hannett (*The Fortunate Isles*) tackles the nature of *growing* and Eliza Chan (*Fathomfolk*) examines different perspectives of certain myths.

Mark Chadbourn (*The Sword of Albion*) focuses on Middle Eastern witchcraft, *Daughters of Flood and Fury* author Gabriella Buba introduces us to some Filipino-inspired magic, Muriel Gray (*The Ancient*) relates the events at a very unusual wedding ceremony up in Scotland, and author of *Scuttler's Cove*, David Barnett, returns us to the location from his novel of the same name: Withered Hill.

As we did last time, we also have an exciting opportunity to present stories from new (to us) authors. So, it's with great delight that we give you Melissa Bobe's reworking and updating of the dark fairy tale 'The Witch in the Stone Boat', Buhlebethu Sukoluhle Mpofu's 'What Bones Remember' and Aveline Fletcher's 'Catharsis' – which pay homage to some of the mythos mentioned earlier on in this introduction – an Irish-infused tale from Damien Kelly, and finally Kay Hanifen takes us into fae territory.

So, there you have it. We're sure you're going to fall under the spell of these excellent examples of the many versions of witchcraft.

They're just, well, magic!

Marie O'Regan & Paul Kane
June 2025

Apotropaic

Ally Wilkes

THERE'S A WITCH who lives on the outskirts of town, a place filled with brambles and dark sentinel pines. When the wind blows from the woodland which crests the hill, it smells of sharp things: needles and salt, the copper-tang of blood. Agnes has been told not to let her siblings go near the witch's house, because everyone knows the lonely old women murder children. They chop them up and boil them down, stirring and macerating, until the greasy fat is rendered. They smear it on their bodies to go riding through the air, and the charm is made up of belladonna, hemlock, and henbane, which smells like unwashed bodies ripening under a harvest moon.

So why, Agnes thinks, *does it smell so much cleaner out here?*

She glances over her shoulder, heart thudding. In the gloaming, the wall which delineates the town limits looks like an old serpent turned to stone. She doesn't think she's been followed; her mother is reluctant to leave the house at nightfall, for fear of evil air, miasma. The invisible ague. Agnes had crept out without even a candle, for fear that Little May would follow her. That child is too curious. And Agnes is sixteen, old enough. Something entirely wonderful is within her grasp – she just needs to reach out and take it.

The witch's house is thatched with clean straw, a marvel when everyone knows how much it costs. There's a fire glowing deep within, seen through the warp and bow of the doorframe, painted black as sin; when Agnes enters, she sees the witch-marks carved into the wood, stark and jagged and utterly unsettling. Witchcraft is in the air.

This is a place that's unholy, Agnes tells herself. She must be on her guard.

* * *

"I need a love charm." Agnes twists her apron until her fingers purple.

The witch stirs her cup once, very precisely, with a teaspoon that has a tiny knight carved into the handle, like the stone statues which rest in the lord's church; man-sized and terrible.

Her expression says: *do you?*

Agnes finds it surprisingly easy to talk to the witch; no one else has listened much in her short life. She explains that it's the lord's son, red of hair and loud of laugh. How these three months have been a maelstrom of confusing feelings, lingering glances, and – finally – trysts in the forest, where animals cackle away in the undergrowth. The lord's son is gentle, and gives her flowers picked from the banks where they lie together. It's like a tale from a tapestry. It's unbelievable that he's chosen her, lifted her out of the sad mundanity of her existence, like he's making her anew. He's seen so much of the world – was a man grown before Agnes ever came into it.

He tells Agnes he's never known anyone like her.

The witch's face puckers at that – but still, she's a bit too comely for a witch. The shawl wrapped around her hair and shoulders makes her look credibly ancient, but there are hints that she's a great deal younger and more beautiful than Agnes expected. Her eyes are bright. As she listens, she pours tea without looking, and it smells of fennel, licorice and sweet.

"He says we'll be together," Agnes explains. "He doesn't care what his family thinks. He'll take me away from here, and we'll go down to London, and ride in a golden barge on the river. He just has to wait until his father dies, and then—"

"I hadn't heard that the lord was ill," the witch says, mildly.

"He isn't," Agnes says.

"Ah." The witch crosses her arms. "And how old are you?"

Agnes doesn't answer.

"Look," she continues gently. "No doubt you think that you're clever; a clever girl, older than your years—" (and Agnes squirms, because that's exactly what he says to her) "—but I can tell you that you'll be miserable. I can give you a love charm, but…"

She stares into the fire a while, her eyes hooded and unreadable.

"You'd do better to break it off. This doesn't end well."

Witches hate men, Agnes remembers with a flash of anger. They mock God's natural order. She should know that she can't trust this woman, living alone on the outskirts of town. Because who would choose Satan over love? Who would want this awful knowledge, and isolation?

As if she can hear Agnes, the witch flushes. "You always think you know best," she says softly, which doesn't make sense, as they've never met before.

Agnes starts to stand, and the room swims a little: it's warm in the cottage. Well-worn. Not entirely frightening. "I don't *care*," Agnes insists, her voice growing desperate. "I have to be sure – I have to be able to count on him, because…"

The witch groans audibly, and puts a slender hand over her face as she steers Agnes to a different, more comfortable chair. Her ring, a single tear-drop of jet black, more wonderful and beautiful than anything Agnes has ever seen, gleams in the firelight.

"How long?"

Agnes bites her lip, looks down at the tea – which she hasn't drunk. She knows better than to taste anything in a witch's cottage. "Two months. Since my last bleed."

Something turns over in her stomach; the faintest suggestion of a baby kicking.

And Agnes could swear that all the things hanging over the fireplace – bunches of tansy, golden-petalled and serrated of leaf, woven circlets of rowan-twigs, and are those *bones*? – seem to sway along with it. Seem to rustle. Agnes clutches at her apron as the dark outside the cottage seems to come a little bit closer.

The witch's eyes contain a question.

Witches kill babies, she's always been told.

"No," Agnes says. "No. He'll take care of me. I just need to be sure of it. I need a love charm. Nothing else. No tricks."

She looks defiantly at the witch, and leaves with the love charm: May Day dew, mandrake, and a candle made of lamb's fat.

* * *

The next time Agnes arrives at the witch's cottage, she's starting to show. Her apron is stretched across a swelling which she's tried to pass off as sickness, the effects of poor diet, eating the cheapest morsels so that her siblings can take the lion's share. She's not sure if it's convincing the townsfolk.

She hammers on the door in broad daylight – or what passes for it. The sky is grey as an old woman's hair, and has been for weeks.

The last time Agnes had been into the forest with the lord's son, he'd been quiet. Preoccupied. She'd asked him what troubled him, and he'd grabbed her arms, stared into her eyes. "You're hurting me," she'd cried. Finger-marks on her skin.

"How do I know?" he'd said. *How do I know?*

"There's no one else, you know it!"

Then he'd kissed those marks away. And the next day ignored her in church.

When the witch opens the door, she's only wearing a shift, despite the chill of the day. Agnes flushes to see the outline of her nipples, her bare feet on the wooden floor. She doesn't ask whether the witch is alone: a witch is always, always alone. As if in confirmation, a cat mewls from the hearth.

"You're back," the witch says simply, and holds out her hands to Agnes.

Agnes scowls. "I need a better charm. Something stronger."

Inside the cottage, it's raining still, with fat droplets falling from the thatch overhead, clanging into buckets like the shrill imitation of church bells. They've barely sat down to tea (the witch insists on it, as if she's here on a social call) when there's a second, louder, hammering at the door.

They look at each other, wide-eyed. Agnes sees that the witch's eyes are almost gold, like a hare's. "Did anyone follow you?" she hisses.

Agnes shakes her head, numbly. She can't be seen. Can't be found here, by the townsfolk, in the witch's cottage.

They both look at the latch with dread.

"Agnes!"

The lord's son.

She's standing before she knows it.

"Stay there," the witch hisses again, and Agnes sinks down into an armchair beside the fire, hidden from the door by a rush screen, to keep out the chill air. She tries to quiet her churning belly.

"Mistress," the lord's son says, when the witch opens the door. "I've come for Agnes."

"She's not here."

"Don't you know where she is?"

"I'm afraid not." Agnes can hear the witch crossing her arms. The cottage is a held breath.

"I promise you, mistress… whatever she says about me, it's not true."

"And what," the witch says coolly, "do you think she's been saying?"

A laugh, curdled. "Oh, this and that. You don't want to pay it any mind."

"Will you marry her, good sir?"

There's an awful pause.

"Where is she, woman?"

His voice is different now. It's the way it gets when he's

denied. When Agnes is reluctant to go to him, spend a soaking wet night in the forest when he gets to go back to his nice warm bed and she's up in two hours, still drenched, shivering through sodden clothes for the rest of the day, so weary she feels like she might die. When Agnes asks him to whisper the right words, that he'll always be true, that the blacksmith's daughter – fair of hair, fair of complexion – is nothing to him, despite the bawdy rumours exchanged, by neighbours, from pigsty to pigsty. When Agnes tries to draw any lines whatsoever between what he wants and what he's getting.

He's chosen her. And hadn't he fallen in love, so quickly, before magic even entered the picture?

"Stand aside." His voice is a growl.

"No," the witch says, calmly.

Then something happens that's more incomprehensible to Agnes than any love charm: the lord's son doesn't force his way into the tiny cottage at the edge of town.

He leaves.

And, as he does, the countless witch-marks carved around the door, from hinge to lintel to jamb – they emit a single fey splash of light, like a warning.

* * *

The old lord remains hale and hearty. Agnes gives birth with no one at her side but Little May, weeping and terrified. No one calls the midwife.

* * *

"You're disgusting," he hisses.

But it doesn't stop him wanting her, does it? Doesn't stop him coming around, to take what she'd promised.

"You want to ruin me," he says, his face twisted in distress.

But it's him that's ruining *her*.

"You're a witch," he mutters, when he's inside her. And twists her hair so hard that it hurts, makes her cry out. "You must be a witch. Otherwise why would I *do* this?"

* * *

"Listen to me. You have to stay."

It's the third occasion that Agnes comes to visit the witch.

The witch is alone, as she always is, and she greets Agnes – and her baby – warmly. There's something almost sanctified about the light that day, streaming in through the cottage's one crooked window like the way the church is lit for Holy Vespers. Agnes is running out of options.

"I need him to stop," she says plainly. "I need to undo it. He's too much, it's too much."

One day she'd arrived home to find a sumptuous wall-hanging placed on her bed, something ripped from the stone walls of his father's mansion, gloriously out of place in the ruin she's been reduced to; none of her siblings are allowed to see her. The fabric had glowed red and gold, and he'd joked that he might as well brand her; lingered a hand on her rump, so she could imagine the hiss and sting of it. Then bitten her ear hard enough to draw blood. She's a pig at market. She still wants him, despite everything, and that's the cruellest part.

You'll be miserable. It might as well have been a curse.

The witch chews her lip, eyes raking over Agnes, and the small bundle pressed to her breast. *I shouldn't have brought a child*, Agnes thinks with sudden fear.

As if in response, the witch gestures at a small bed, little more than a cot, that's been made up by the fireside. A scrap-work quilt and a thin, sad pillow, which Agnes knows will stab her in the night; the prickly needles of the feathers coming through to be all vexation and no comfort.

"You can stay," the witch says, trying – and failing – to sound disinterested. "I don't mind. There's room."

Agnes looks around the cottage. It's warm enough with the fire glowing away, and there's nothing too enchanted about it. The herbs drying from the beams could simply be there to scent the air, the cat curled up under the table merely a decent precaution against rats. She wants it, for a moment, with a hunger that startles her – makes her lash out.

"I'm not like you," she says, cold. "And you won't have my baby."

An ugly twist mars the witch's lips. "Listen to me. If you try to leave, he will find you. And you'll still think you can handle it, that you can manage him. His tempers, his whims, the things he asks you to do to prove your devotion. But it'll all turn to ashes. You've bought yourself a most miserable life."

"With your help," Agnes says, low.

The witch swallows. "Yes."

"Then why did you—"

The words stick in her throat. She thinks of the time the lord's son had pushed her up against a tree and pinned her there by her throat, eyes laughing, face flushed, to steal a kiss that went on far too long, making her head swim from lack of air. It had been early on in their mad month of courtship, back when she'd genuinely thought he would marry her.

"I shouldn't have," the witch says, her voice hard. "But it was what you *wanted*."

She points at the witch-marks around the door, all those concentric circles and jagged criss-crosses, which seem to have been made fresh overnight. Rusty red has been rubbed into the gouges, and it could be blood or it could be madder root, but it makes them look like wounds, or the scratches of dreadful tall animals. "You can stay. These will protect you. He can't enter here."

Agnes draws herself up to her full height. She thinks of all the ways this woman has cursed her life, and she hates her.

"I thought they were meant to stop *witches*."

"They're meant to stop evil," the witch says bitterly. "It works both ways."

"I don't see how he's evil," Agnes snaps.

"You… never do."

Agnes wonders, then, if the witch can leave.

* * *

In the years to come, Agnes will think on that day. But she doesn't have many of them – years, that is.

So-called dark ages turn to light.

And there's still a witch who lives on the outskirts of town.

There's always a witch.

* * *

There's a witch who lives on the outskirts of town, past the playground where tangled undergrowth hides discarded chicken boxes. Not many kids go there: anyway, Jenny thinks, it isn't entirely safe to let children play outdoors these days. They've all seen the headlines. Somehow it always seems to happen in a town like this, where most of the shops are boarded up, and four o'clock in winter descends with the inevitability of the grave. *Missing* posters peel on lamp-posts, bunches of roses create a makeshift shrine, and within months it all starts again in another place where the people have just given up. More troubling are the missing pets: dogs, cats, in what seems like their hundreds.

Who could need that many stolen pets?

They blame the witch, of course, but that's standard.

* * *

The witch's house is a small end-of-terrace with a black glossy door and a sage-green colour to the pebble-dash. It's pleasant enough, but Jenny instinctively thinks of mould, which she scrubs off their bedroom ceiling every morning: it makes her cough and shield her face. She's been told it's poison, creating bad air, lung disease, but try telling that to their landlord.

Jenny checks her phone as she deliberates whether to knock. The lock screen is her sonogram, a little goblin thing at twenty weeks, impossibly enchanting. Beneath it are six, seven, eight messages from the man, wanting to see what she's up to.

A Facebook notification lingers: she's been tagged in a post about Claire's hen night. Jenny had only been to the drinks beforehand, and heard the whispers between her old friends when she'd gathered up her things to say goodbye. She'd seen the concerned looks. One of them had even divulged, with the air of someone staging a fucking intervention, that she'd previously been in a *bad relationship*. But the man in question is someone that Jenny's seen around the town for years, whistling and oblivious with a succession of young girls in tow. So there's obviously a line, an unspoken line. How bad is *too* bad? Because clearly some people put up with it.

The sonogram is a ticking clock sketched in black and white.

Nine, ten, eleven messages from the man. Their tone getting nastier and more insistent by the minute. She doesn't dare delete them.

Steeling herself, pulling up her collar to block the drizzle, Jenny knocks on the witch's door.

* * *

Jenny isn't sure what she'd pictured: her mother had only said that witches were the third option when it was the proverbial rock and the hard place; that they usually wanted something of you in return, but not always; and that the woman living at the edge of town was a witch. The woman in the doorway has amber eyes that light up when she sees Jenny, as if something inside her says: *oh, it's you.*

"You're..."

"Younger than you expected? Yes, people usually say."

The witch cocks her head to invite Jenny inside, a small smile tugging at the corners of her mouth. She could be anywhere from thirty to forty, and she's got the most incredible silver hair, wavy and untamed, crowning her head.

"Who told you about me?"

"My mum." Jenny swallows. "She said there's been a witch here since Gran was younger."

"Oh."

There must be a thunderstorm coming: there's a jolt of static electricity as Jenny steps across the threshold. It makes her skin tingle, and she revels in the momentary feeling of power – of *potential*. The witch, though, has her back to Jenny, showing her through into a living room full of plants; it looks like a café far too expensive for this town. The air smells so beautiful that Jenny takes a deep breath, wanting to drink it all in. To let it clean her lungs.

"Coffee, sorry," she says when the witch asks if she wants tea, and the witch says that's fine, of course, but it's only instant. She disappears into another room, leaving Jenny with a tail-swishing cat which looks like it's on the very last of its nine lives.

Her phone buzzes in her pocket. She doesn't need to check to know it's him: *come home right now or so help me—*

Or, worse, the pleading.

Jen, love, I don't know why you're doing this, you know I can't live without you—

Then why does he do it? Why do *any* of them do it?

"You live alone?" Jenny asks, because she's genuinely curious. The coffee is jet-black and spiked with some sort of sweet, nutty syrup.

The witch nods. "Always."

There's something in the way she says that word. Low, it drops off her tongue like a stone. It makes Jenny feel something, but she doesn't know what.

"Well," Jenny says, trying to make it into a joke. "Sometimes I wish I did."

"Tell me."

Jenny just cups her chin in her hands and raises her eyebrows, rather meanly. She feels that a *real* witch will know without being told.

The witch looks at her evenly, taking in the deep shadows under Jenny's eyes. The small cut to the side of her lip that had bled and bled: the man wears a heavy ring, calls it – with a baying laugh that used to make Jenny's toes curl – his Prerogative. There's the receding hairline on her left temple, because Jenny sometimes sits, paralysed with fear, while he goes through her phone; she plucks her own hairs out one by one to pass the time, time which is thick and treacled with menace.

No real bruises to speak of. But still, she'd woken up and *known*.

The witch crosses her arms, bracelets jangling. "I don't do love charms," she says firmly. "You don't want him obsessed with you." This last part softer, as though she's explaining something to a child who doesn't know what's good for it.

Obsessed. Jenny feels spiders crawling up her spine at the thought.

"And I won't do poison."

The room seems to shudder for a moment: all the plants moving as one, the lazy twitch of the cat's tail, and there's a batter of rain against the window. Jenny flinches, and looks at her hands. She hadn't – not quite – realised that was what she was asking.

Hadn't she?

"I suppose it's too easily detected… these days," Jenny says quickly, to cover the awful silence. The witch just keeps looking at her. A little frown, now, and Jenny is self-conscious. She remembers the tingling *zap* as she'd crossed the witch's threshold.

"So – what can you do?" She tries to say it normally, but her lower lip is quivering and now the whole air is pregnant with anticipation. Tears not far off.

The witch sighs heavily, and Jenny's phone buzzes again.

In her fright, she kicks the table, and coffee washes over the lace cloth, spreading as a coppery stain. "Sorry." Her heart's in her mouth, and in that moment she feels utterly naked.

It's just a text.

It's *never* just a text.

"Sorry," she repeats, and the tears which seep out are so utterly humiliating that she wants to shrivel up and disappear. They're hot, burning hot, on her cheeks, and the *sob* that erupts from her belly is like a physical punch to the stomach. Bare-knuckled. Well.

Apart from (one day) that ring.

The witch reaches out and takes Jenny's chin in her fingers, examining her from all angles. Jenny isn't sure if she likes what she sees, but eventually she hums and sits back, two pink moons of colour in her pale cheeks.

"I'll give you the magic you need."

* * *

Back at her own house, Jenny sits down at the kitchen table to examine the charm. It looks flimsy in the fluorescent light, and when she teases the bundle open, she finds a strange selection of objects: thin pliable rowan twigs, a handful of rusty nails, a pebble with a hole going straight through. She sets them out one by one on the peeling laminate, and can't resist – feeling rather stupid when she does so – the immediate urge to put her nose to them. They smell… clean. Like pine-scented bleach when you've just scrubbed the bathroom, and your hands are baby-pink and wrinkled inside their rubber gloves.

Apotropaic, the witch had explained to her. A set of things to ward off evil, either individually or together. In time, maybe the man will take it into his head to leave. That's the safest way. That's the long-term game. Jenny and the witch will have to take it slow.

Jenny doesn't want the long-term, though. She feels like a new world has opened up to her, and wants to grab it with both hands.

I won't do poison.

The idea roils around in her head, and she presses a palm to her stomach.

Upstairs, the man is snoring loud enough to wake the dead. It's a tearing, mucus-filled assault on the ears. The soundtrack to every night of Jenny's life, from chucking-out time at the pub until she drags herself out of bed the next morning.

Not *every* night, Jenny thinks.

* * *

In the bedroom, he's been sick on the bed again. A spray of pinkish vomit spreads out around his face on the pillow; it's pooled by his right cheek, viscous and reeking. Cider smells worse than anything in the world when it's been brought up again: ask Jenny how she knows.

She thinks of the charm downstairs.

I'll give you the magic you need.

And, sure, she could run. She could put her faith in the law and the shelters. She could take the chance. But she knows – the witch had explained to her – that she's most vulnerable at the point she decides to leave.

And isn't there any room for punishment, righteous punishment, in this world anymore? Hadn't witches once *cursed*?

Jenny places her hand on his left shoulder. For a moment she just lets it rest there, lightly, satisfied it'll leave no marks, not even the faintest outline of a bruise. She's seen the TV shows – doesn't want to admit that she's been squirrelling it away, the knowledge.

Then she gently coaxes him onto his back.

He goes easily.

His hair is crusty with vomit on the soiled sheets, the ones she's washed and dried so many times; the ones she's had yanked off her in the middle of the night, with screaming and invective; the ones he's grabbed and taken to the sofa, to wake sore as a bear and complaining about back pains and *unsympathetic women.*

There's a gurgle, and more vomit spills from his mouth, which is opening and closing, lipping for air like a greedy pink wound.

Jenny rests a single finger on his head, just enough to keep him face-up. Just enough to discourage him from turning over and clearing his airways. It's not murder, is it, if he doesn't feel it happening? If he might have choked on his own vomit anyway, at this point in the night or some other, with Jenny balled up all innocent in misery at the other side of the bed. Who's to say.

It's not as if she'd meant this all along.

Isn't it?

She waits to see him stop breathing, drowned in his own secretions. Never using more than the pressure of a single finger, like the thin bendy rowan twigs in that charm-bag downstairs. Utterly powerful, and self-righteous, and assured.

Is this how the witch feels every day? No wonder she's fucking *immortal*.

* * *

"You're back."

The witch seems surprised to see her so soon. Her hair is like dandelion fluff, caught back in a scrunchie. She's drinking tea at the door, and its sweet-smelling steam curls out of the cup and wafts away towards the playground of missing children.

"You gave me the magic I needed," Jenny says, and reaches out to take the witch's hand. The witch takes an imperceptible step back, *knowledge* crossing her face, like blood spooling out in water.

Jenny smiles.

There are marks around the witch's doorframe, which Jenny hadn't noticed the first time: jagged capital Ms, or maybe Ws, social-media hashtags, circles within circles. They go right deep into the wood, and she notices the witch's eyebrows raising, her lips parting – just a fraction – when Jenny runs her fingertips over the nearest one. It feels like static electricity. Like the colour of the sky before thunder. *Magic*.

A tiny flash, like a mobile phone camera going off, and Jenny's skin scorches, as if it's remembering the worst sunburn she's ever had. Her mouth opens in a silent scream.

When she turns around, the witch is watching with

a wary look on her face. Forehead furrowed. As if she's seeing Jenny – *really* seeing her – for the very first time.

But Jenny isn't the sort to walk away where a debt is owed.

"Well," she says, glancing back at the witch-marks that had – *just about* – let her inside. Less of a barrier than a warning; a hand placed on the back of her neck.

She thinks of the man. He was already dead, she tells herself. There's more work to be done.

So many other women in *bad relationships*.

"That's all I've got in the world," Jenny says, dropping her rucksack in the witch's hallway. "Baby's due in five weeks. Where do we start?"

* * *

There's a witch who lives on the outskirts of town; maybe it's then or maybe it's now, but either way, she's still there.

Stranded

Eliza Chan

Bloody Mary (origins: unknown, European)

It is difficult to pinpoint the exact origins of Bloody Mary, given that the first name is common throughout various time periods and countries. Some speculate it alludes to the English queen Mary Tudor, who executed hundreds of religious dissidents during her reign. Others have pointed towards a Hungarian countess and serial killer believed to have murdered women and girls due to vampiric tendencies. Either way, to invoke Bloody Mary, one must chant her name three times in a mirror lit only by candlelight. When correctly summoned, this will conjure an image of their true love, or in more unfortunate cases, their death.

THE BELL at the front rings. Shrill. Insistent. Sending a puff of dust into the air. A woman in her late forties taps her foot. Her tailored coat is heavy with rain, dripping from a few loose strands of long hair and the leather overnight bag clutched in her hand. Puddle water rings her like a summoning circle.

"Excuse me!" She catches my movement from behind the ajar inner door. "I said *excuse me.*"

There is no apology in her tone. I have not even spoken and already her pursed lips add up the faults. I have been cooking all day and night, trying to recall the old recipes that my grandmother, and great-grandmother before her, never thought necessary to write down. So much knowledge has already disappeared, lost when I was too young and stubborn to listen. I don't have time for distractions such as she clearly is.

"I need a room for the evening."

"We don't have the space." My voice creaks, out of practice.

"I find that unlikely. I can pay cash." She runs a finger along the dusty sign on the counter. *The Strand*, it says in gold typeface. An opulent name for the dilapidated guesthouse I inherited. I push the stiff door open with both hands and she starts, taking a step backwards at the sight of my taloned nails.

"It isn't ready. The rooms are not yet habitable."

"Well, that certainly makes more sense," she mutters. Then she shakes her head with business-like acumen. *Too far down this rabbit hole already, Alice, might as well commit.* "But look, my car broke down and there are no trains until morning. It's miserable outside. All I need is a bed, a sofa even. Surely you can do that much?"

I slide forward, letting her finally see me. My hair hangs long past my knees. White, not as snow but cobwebs. As thick as moth-eaten brocade curtains, it conceals most of my face. I prefer it that way. Under it, I search my belt. Thrust the crooked key out from beneath my hair and drop it into her startled hand. "The attic room. One night only."

"I assure you, I do *not* want to be here any longer than necessary." She is a straight line. From the middle parting of her caramel highlights, down the plane of her crisp white shirt and neatly buttoned coat. The type to lay out her clothes for the week ahead. She will not like it here. And yet here she is, walking in as if she owns the place. The only person to have knocked on my door in years.

I lead her up the winding stairs to the attic room, my hair sweeping the dust from the stone steps before me as I go. In my grandmother's day it had been pristine. The jade ornaments unchipped, the fine bone china in matching sets. Back then I did not know whose bones had been ground into the clay.

"I don't suppose you have Wi-Fi? The reception out here is atrocious but I really ought to give the car hire company a piece of my mind. Imagine renting me that piece of junk? I do not believe it's been driven in years, never mind passed an MOT."

I do not deign to answer her question with a verbal response, simply glaring with my good eye until she comes to her own conclusion.

"Of course not. What else did I expect."

"This is you," I say and let her fiddle with the key in the old lock. The door rattles and refuses at first before recognising her, yielding with a protesting squeak. I peer in behind her. One wall is pastel purple, covered in faded posters of singers. Fairy lights are draped from the metal bedframe and a bookcase fit to bursting with yellowing paperbacks, jewellery and knick-knacks stands in the corner.

"Is this some sort of joke?" she says.

"Pardon?"

"Why does this look like my childhood bedroom?"

"Does it?"

"Stop bullshitting me, it's an exact replica!" She gestures, hiding her terror behind the movement. The room shudders, frozen like the jammed shutter on a camera. And then it changes. Nothing but a perfunctory attic room, devoid of any personality. A divan bed to one side is covered in a plastic sheet, and piles of boxes fill the rest of the space. The warm glow of nostalgia has disappeared entirely. I miss it.

"Well, good night."

"Wait a minute, you—" She reaches to grab me but then pulls back as if burnt. My hair is a shield of static.

"Do you want me to stay and hold your hand?" Ice drips from my voice, my mother's words rising like scum on the surface of water. The question shuts her right up. I can see the teenager she once was. The type who made herself small so that she would fit in. She stopped speaking in tongues at home, abandoning the old language and the old ways for all that was new. Agreeing with friends' suggestions until she was unable to form any opinions of her own. I saw so much of myself in that. Never wanting to stand out despite the fact that my skin always marked me as such.

I leave her to childhood memories and return to the kitchen. The kettle hisses in protest, steam pushing against the ceiling like low-lying clouds. I left the dial too high and there's only an inch of water left. I have to open all the windows, letting the rain and wind streak around me. My hair lifts from my face, the white strands moving like limbs. The wind is deeply dissatisfied by how nonchalant I act. The window slams shut, the panes rattling in the frame. I ignore them, used to the adolescent temperament of the house. Pour the remaining water over the tea leaves and watch them swirl in my cup. They make shapes on the surface like dancers. Leaves cross over each other, separating into the wings of birds, and then coalescing again like the branches of a tree. The pu'er is sweet as ripe fruit on my palate, the smoky depths filling my nostrils. Empty, I turn the cup three times and invert it, letting the leaves trickle down the sides. Right on cue, the woman screams.

"Alright, alright," I say, patting the wall and pull my creaking bones to standing. The woman is sitting in the bathtub, fully clothed, her knees pulled up to her chin. She points at the mirror, shaking.

Through the polished surface, a girl stares back. A youth in purple pyjamas. One side of her hair has been inexpertly curled. She is hosting her first sleepover. The ritual of girlhood that required secrets spilled and crushes dissected. The gift of being a curiosity, a chopstick using, fish eye eating other, when all she wants is to be the same. The room behind her is in darkness, the candle in her hand the only thing there is to see by.

"Bloody Mary?" The question is aimed at me. I do not deem her idiotic question worthy of a response.

Tap.

Tap.

Tap.

Her eyes flicker down to the sink, but the porcelain is dry, taps turned tight. Still the beat continues, somewhere just out of vision. Someone hitting the same note over and over, hopeful the next time it will sound more in key. Louder now, rushing in her skull and trickling down like a nosebleed.

Tap.
Tap.
Tap.

The candle flares brighter each time, fast as the nervous heartbeat in the girl's chest. She cannot move. Can do nothing but gape transfixed at the grotesque hag staring back from the mirror.

Tap, tap, tap, taptaptaptaptaptap—

I smile. She raises the candle higher. It traces my cheeks, sagging and well-worn with age. The ends of my white hair scatter like an unseen wind whirls beneath me. One good eye stares, the other a sunken inkwell. I reach forward, not with a hand but with my tresses. Stretch as if I might step through. The girl is caught, somewhere between helping me and pushing me away. Instead, she does nothing. Always, she does nothing. Coming up with dozens of ideas but not daring to voice a single one. So afraid it is the wrong choice.

It was always the wrong choice.

The girl looks at me once more, searching my face for an answer she cannot find. And then, finally, "I hate you."

She takes the candle and hurls it. The mirror breaks, a jagged diagonal across the centre, thinner cracks like a broken star spreading its arms. My own fragmented face looks back. Accusing.

"You saw her! You saw her, right? A girl. In the mirror," the woman says, demanding my corroboration.

"Mirrors reflect."

"She was about thirteen at most. She looks so scared – I just – I reached out to reassure her. Her hand was bleeding…" Her voice trails off as she points to the place on her own hand. Notices as if for the first time the faded scar on the palm below her thumb. A faint line, long since healed.

"What have you done to me?" she whispers.

I resist the urge to shake her with my hair. Trying to remember if I had ever been so entitled. "You are the one who came to my door, who insisted on being let in. You are free to come or to go."

"I will," she says defiantly. Her chin points upwards as if pulled by strings. The chin they mocked her for, calling her witch, calling her much worse. It had only been a lark, after all. A sleepover, a pizza, a Ouija board and a mirror. Chant a name three times, pretend they had seen their future husbands. *Pretend* being the key word. The shunning after she had smashed the mirror, convinced she had seen someone there.

More than just seven years' bad luck.

* * *

Slit-Mouthed Woman
(origins: Japan, also known as *kuchisake onna*)

This urban legend most likely arose in the late 20th century in Japan. A woman approaches to ask "Am I beautiful?" before revealing a smile that has been cut from the corners of her mouth up to her ears, reminiscent of a Glasgow smile. It is difficult but not impossible to answer in a manner that will avoid the victim also being sliced from ear to ear by her hidden blade.

THE RAIN is no longer ferocious as she steps back into the darkness of night. She senses me watching. The disquiet between us.

"I'll sleep in my car," she explains, although I did not ask. Overhead, forked lightning illuminates the sky. The crooked arms of the trees are spectres. My hair crackles, lifting from my shoulders in a head of snakes. I slide a hand over it, comforting a wild animal. I do not tell her to turn back. I do not say anything because she will come back by herself. She has done before.

The sky brightens again, the belly of the clouds lit with erratic pulses. A nightclub's strobe. Her receding figure moves in juddering motions. First she is on the steps, then she is halfway across the lawn.

Flash.

Figures dancing to unheard music around her.

Flash.

You aren't from around here, are you?

Flash.

Bodies, more of them. Sour with sweat and alcohol. Everything pressing against her as they writhe: clothes damp, hair whipping across her face.

Flash.

Asian girls are so hot.

Flash.

The woman is back by the door, out of breath. She folds in two, noticing for the first time the platform boots pulled high to her knees. The pink of her box-dyed hair stains her upper arms and bleeds into the fabric of her dress. She reinvented herself after high school. Dyed her hair to mask her true self. Wore colours so bright that others were dazzled: the manic pixie girl of their wet dreams.

She made excuses to avoid family dinners. Inexplicably on holiday during Winter Solstice and Mid-Autumn Festival. Busy at work when called on to sweep the gravestones at Qingming. Disdaining the parochial customs.

"Am I beautiful?" she asks, more to herself than anyone else. Desperation rings in her clipped words. She means interesting, authentic, of substance. Someone. Not just a spectre in a mirror.

"Let me read your face," I say. Her fringe masks a strong brow bone, like a breaking wave. Her nose is small. Her mouth wide as that of a baleen whale, indiscriminately gulping down everything without thinking if it will stick in her throat. A dark smudge marks her cheek, like liner smeared upwards. I reach out, brushing at it with the ends of my hair. The line grows. From the corner of her mouth it curves up her cheeks to her ears. The same on the other side. A drawn-on clown smile.

"Am I beautiful?" Desperation tugs at her repetition.

"Not yet," I reply. She has been wearing the mask for so long that it imprints onto her skin like creases from a pillow. The fake smile. The false interest.

Flash.

Give us a smile, love.

"Not yet," I repeat, angry now. All that time wasted pleasing others. I push into her with my thumbs. The corners of her mouth slide open, the skin and yellow fat peeling away. Layers cut through as if under a scalpel blade until the red wet flesh of her mouth lies exposed.

It unzips slowly, all the way up to her ears. Air, hot as an open oven door, caresses my cheek, a sickly exhale, sweet and sour with decay. Behind that thin smile, lie pink gums and teeth sharper than they had any right to be. They are clenched together in jagged rows. Crocodile teeth.

Flash.

Beautiful.

* * *

White-Haired/Prehensile-Haired Witch (origins: Chinese, wuxia, see also *rusalka*, related *Samson* and *Rapunzel*)

The white-haired witch, also synonymous with a prehensile-haired witch, can use her hair as functional extra limbs. Her previously black hair has turned white overnight due to being betrayed by a lover. Her sole motivation is to hunt down and drown or suffocate unworthy victims, usually men. During initial seduction, she may appear to be an attractive young woman, but on closer examination it is evident she is past her prime.

I LEAD HER into the kitchen, throwing her a couple of tea towels for her wet hair as I make a pot of tea.

"Chrysanthemum. How did you know?" She takes a sip, the yellow petals floating on the surface.

"It's an anti-inflammatory. Also good for anxiety." I stare from my good eye, challenging her to deny it.

"My mother used to boil it when we were young, to combat the heat of fried foods." She had rolled her eyes at the old ways, countering heat with cool, everything having a yin to its yang. Yet as she grew older, she found herself turning back to them instinctively. Avoiding the number four, never going to sleep with wet hair, finding books and websites to learn recipes for the restorative soups her grandmother had once made.

I open a jar, sniffing the pungent dried ingredients and taking out a sprinkle of golden needles; a handful of chalk-white yam slices; five dried red dates that I plop into a boiling pot of water one by one. I take bones from the freezer, frozen solid to the drawer so that I have to chip them loose with a blunt knife. The round ball of a joint juxtaposed by the pointed edge where the butcher sawed through the marrow.

She is no longer wearing the glitzy dress, nor the austere suit. She is in a high-collared traditional jacket with ornate knot fastenings. The type I was forced to wear as a child at Spring Festival.

"Why am I here?" she asks.

"You came to my door."

"I'm not certain that was a choice. The car, the rain, you orchestrated the whole thing, didn't you?" She has always been intelligent. Smart enough to know that she stood out in more ways than one. Surviving meant fitting in; but it was only meant to be temporary. Somewhere along the way, she forgot she could take off the mask; that the only thing stopping her, was herself.

"So, what are we doing today?" The tea towels drape on her shoulders like a hairdressing gown and the three-legged bar stool has become a swivel chair. I touch her damp hair. "Just a trim or…?" The room peels away at my words, becoming her regular hair salon as the question lingers between us.

"No, something more drastic."

"Have you ever thought of stripping it all away?" She always alters her hair first. Hoping the external bravado would hide the gaps. It's what she does. Dye it. Change it. It had been decades since she simply let it be.

"I'm afraid it won't suit."

"Trust me." She nods and I seize upon it before she

can change her mind. Dip the ends into the boiling pot of herbal soup, rubbing her hair between my fingers. The heat does not bother me. I am from a long line of women who put their hands into the fire. She flinches beneath my sharp talons but does not voice her discomfort.

I hold the ends of her hair and snip with tiny scissors. Vertical cuts slicing each strand into a split end. Perfection is a lie. I run wire wool over her locks, scouring the surface. The liquid foams with every layer she has used over the years: pink merging into blue, shades of brown like autumnal leaves, even the black oozes off. It wiggles like cursive writing as it moves.

I pick one up, dangling it upside down. It squirms but cannot escape from the tight coil of hair around its tail. Impulsively, I thrust it into my mouth. The creature writhes in panic, pushing against my palate. My tongue pulls it back to the centre and I bite down. The thin membrane resists for a moment then pops, filling my mouth with bitterness. An acquired taste. "They used leeches at barber shops. Bloodletting was believed to cleanse the body of impurities."

I tread on a lever and the chair tilts back with an abrupt thud. The woman is horizontal before me, as if at the dentist's. Her eyes widen. I caress around her hairline, down the column of her exposed neck. Her hair spills off the chair into the void that has opened up beneath us. I cannot see the bottom of it, only her hair twisted like a fraying rope. "Of course they also believed evil could possess people through the hair. And that drilling holes in the scalp alleviated pressure."

Her throat bobs up and down. "Is that what you're going to do?"

"Are you under excessive pressure?" I answer her question with my own.

"Excessive? I've never known otherwise."

I laugh, a hag's cackle that spreads from my belly and spews from my mouth. I don't remember being so funny, but it was never deliberate back then. More armour than anything else. "Why would you crave to be ordinary? To be forgettable, when you can be something else?"

She winces, not at my comments but at something below. Her hair is pulled taut, yanking her head down on one side. The unnerving chitter of mandibles smacking together, the scurrying of many feet. From the depths, something clambers upwards.

"What was his name?"

"What?" She is distracted, hands around her hair as she pulls back, an awkward tug of war.

"His name? I've forgotten it."

She does not ask who I am talking about. She has accepted that much. Tears swim in her eyes as she answers. Beneath us, the named creature shrieks. The pull on her hair resumes.

"You thought he was different. The one. The prince to rescue you from your high tower."

He had glowed with confidence, without the hesitation that plagued her. Swept along in the tide that gave her an answer of who to be. But then it had twisted, hidden tangles matted in the strands. It became how *not* to act. Who *not* to speak to. Where *not* to go. Until her whole world shrank down to nothing.

"No one is perfect." She is compelled to defend him even though he betrayed her. The messages on his phone she had ignored for months. But seeing the other woman in *their* house – as he ran his fingers through her locks – was too much. She aches from forcing herself into a smaller and smaller space. The diamond ring on her left finger, the offer on a suburban house, the company car. All the things she had been taught to covet and yet there is none of the joy they promised. Just simmering rage.

She does not remember where she went after that. Where she even got the rental car that broke down on the quiet country road. Only that the universe compelled her to this place: this derelict guesthouse in the middle of nowhere, the lights blazing when everything else around her was smothered in darkness.

"It was always a warning," she began.

I nod. "Don't end up like those old witches."

"Those crones," she spits.

"Outside of society."

"Free." She looks at me with a question, knowing now who I am. What I am. She is more tired than she has ever been. Bristled antennae run over my feet, feeling for the floor as the monstrous thing climbs up her hair into the light. A giant head louse, its wide carapace pulsing as it sups from the strands of hair as if they are straws.

I say nothing, handing her the scissors. The metal warmed in my hands. She holds them near her neck, throat bobbing up and down.

"Is this right?" Even now she needs to be told.

"What do you want?" She wants the solution. I of all people should know. The crone to her maiden and mother. "It's about you. In this moment. Not who you once were or who you might be. You."

She cuts.

One swift motion with the honed edge of the scissor blade. It hisses like a snake. Her hair falls, cut at a blunt angle below her ear. Beneath us, it cascades into the darkness, the parasite shrieking as it falls. A single long note that echoes up until a satisfying crunch ends it. The floor is firm again.

She breathes hard, looking at her palms as if she does not recognise them. They are wrinkled now, filled with lines of possibility and the myriad routes she could choose to take. I righten the chair so she can see out of the darkened kitchen window. Her reflection gapes back. Her lopsided cut is painted through with silver. Wiry locks in two wide streaks like curtains. I rest my chin gently on her crown, my own white hair framing her face. The white-haired witch that I have always known I was; denying it only hurt myself.

"Is it worth it?" she asks.

I have been lonely in this rundown house, dealing with the never-ending repairs, tending to the temperamental roots and herbs in the garden. Sometimes I venture into the nearby city, as a free-spirited tarot reader, a judgemental old auntie ubiquitous in every dim sum restaurant, a foul-mouthed crone, a jovial grandmother armed with boiled sweets. I am none of them and all of them at the same time.

I lost so much to obstinance. By refusing to listen whilst the old ways were still there to be learnt. But I cannot spend all my days regretting. I might never have taken this path without those mistakes.

"If you want it, it is." My hair reaches out as it once had through the mirror when she was but a girl. Offering her a hand. I have always been here for her. My hair a lifeline; an embrace; a noose or a guiding rope. Alone, a strand is weak, easy to snap; but braided and twisted together, there is nothing we cannot do.

Murder Ballads by Moonlight

Angela Slatter

SHE'S NERVOUS and every step has been a regretful one since she left home.

A moonlit night, sure, but night nonetheless and she knows that, no matter what, the darkness is still a threat to her as a woman even though she's a witch too. Learned some of that from Grandma Molly who went missing one stormy eve and left behind a husband who couldn't even be bothered to hide his satisfaction. Didn't matter, he soon got his just reward, sleepless and gibbering about how the room was so cold at night, how the bed froze over whenever his ghostly wife slipped in beside him.

Erica would like to have stayed rugged up under a blanket, fire crackling, Romeo curled beside her, snoring and snuffling. Instead here she is, big coat, two sweaters, scarf and beanie, boots, tights beneath jeans – half her actual size again to ward off the cold, looking like a red panda trying to puff herself up to appear more dangerous. At least Romeo's here even if it's not a terribly good idea, but if she'd left him at home there's no guarantee he wouldn't have spent however many hours she's out howling at the door. All she needs is for the neighbours to hear that – 'coz this dog, this damned black and silver-frosted dog with that streak of wolf in his blood, can make a noise and a half that travels on the cold air for kilometres. Her nearest neighbour's not even twenty metres down the road and god knows that old bat is already suspicious of Erica and her ways and her family background.

But it has to be this night, when the doors in-between are open.

Romeo's got a muzzle on, one that can be released in a moment should it be necessary; he's leashed, too, because she really doesn't need him running off. He keeps giving her reproachful looks. *Why did you do this? Don't you love me?* She stays strong. He'd bark at the worst possible moment. It's happened before, and he doesn't like the weird things that lurk in the woods around the house let alone the ones deeper in, the little sprites of twigs, the squirrels with eyes that burn too bright in the night, the four-legged things that aren't quite as canine as they should be, and certainly not sufficiently so to guarantee Erica's safety. She feels better with Romeo there, but it brings its own anxiety: she doesn't want him getting into a fight – that's happened before, too, and it had been no fun nursing him through recovery. She'd felt so guilty. And he's older now, every year reminds her that he's lived seven to her one, that he'll be gone before her, and she does *not* want to think about that. He trots along next to her, thick fur keeping the cold at bay, head swivelling left and right, and that's enough for the moment; besides, she needs the guidance of his senses when the time comes to get off the road, to find that particular spot…

They'd been taking an afternoon stroll three weeks ago when he'd picked up the trail and led her to…

Romeo had been *so* good, apart from that initial bolt when he caught the sudden scent and jerked the lead out of her hand, and she'd had to run hard to keep up. Truth be told, she hadn't kept up, only found him because he'd stopped and was sitting quietly, panting, in a clearing of oaks and alders, looking pleased with himself. When she'd finally caught her breath, she scolded him, but not very much; had never been able to do so, and his behaviour had never been *that* bad. *Baby*, she'd puffed, *worst baby*. Never *bad dog*, though. Never that.

"Sit, Romeo." He does.

Erica shakes her head, pulls herself back to the moment, this night, and pauses at the edge of the tree line, before stooping to grab a handful of dirt. Taking a moment to work up some saliva, she spits into her hand, onto the dirt, and uses her fingers to mix a muddy little concoction, which she rubs on the nearest trunk, bark rough beneath her palm. Eyes closed, she takes a deep breath and begs the woods to hide her and keep her safe. It seems to Erica there's a moment of consideration from the darkness ahead of her, then a begrudging sort of sigh through the leaves above. *Oh alright*.

She steps into the trees, a bit more confident that roots wouldn't be tripping her up just for the fun of it, that the earth will be smoother beneath her soles and anything lurking in the darkness won't see her unless she wants it to. Romeo speeds up, straining against the lead. Nothing in the darkened landscape looks familiar, but last time she'd been through here she'd been running, not really paying attention. It had seemed to take so long that day, forever, but tonight? Maybe ten minutes, tops, to walk briskly. It's far enough off the road to be hidden, not on a well-trod path and folk are unlikely to stumble upon it. A place someone can reasonably expect not to be disturbed.

Unless a big old dog with a striking sense of smell catches a whiff of something dead and decaying… Her mind flips back to the sight of Romeo that day.

He was *so* good, just sitting there, not digging. Waiting for her. He'd known something wasn't right, that it wasn't his time to look for bones. That any bones to be found weren't for him. She'd thought, at first, that he was sitting in a little garden, until she'd gotten close enough to spot the laminated pieces of cardboard sticking out of the ground, pretty maids all in a row, like they were there to remind the gardener what had been planted. Name, genus, hue…

Or in that case, girls' names, their licences or student IDs depending on circumstance. Addresses. Ages. Height, hair and eye colour.

Erica had cried before she'd done anything else, clinging to Romeo's neck, kneeling beside him, letting the feel of his thick fur ground her – so real, so solid, so secure. And she didn't dig, no more than he had. She didn't call the police either.

Even if they could've caught the killer, what hope was there for justice? *Maybe* find them, but what then? Someone sitting in prison for days and months and years before they got a trial date, living off state resources in not-exactly-comfort-but-not-exactly-squalor when four girls lay dead. And those girls would be pulled apart, their lives autopsied as surely as their bodies would be on steel tables, the dirt washed away, the flesh picked over by gloved hands instead of sharp beaks and blunt blind worms. Lies would be told, and truths twisted to look sinister, reputations torn. Twelve good men and true would decide that somehow these girls had all asked for it; put themselves in bad places, dangerous places, encouraged the wrong person. Wore the wrong thing.

She was asking for it. What's a body to do, faced with such temptation?

No, she hadn't called the cops. Had thought about it, but in the end decided she could do better. Better for these girls. Could help them do better for themselves. So, she'd taken photos with her mobile of those IDs (careful to not leave prints) and then put them back where they'd been planted by whoever, so no one would know things had been disturbed (just in case *someone* came back).

She'd spent the weeks since researching, in between shifts at work. She'd used the county library's internet rather than her home computer, looking for articles about missing persons in newspapers, local and further afield. In the interests of her own mental health, Erica didn't watch or listen to news, only consumed the bite-sized morsels that snuck in via a heavily curated Insta account, so she hadn't seen anything before about missing girls. The moment she started looking, however, she was inundated by a river of the vanished, and had to discipline herself to stay focused on her four. She checked their social media profiles to ensure she'd got the right girl with that name, that no one was updating their statuses after they'd supposedly been gone for months.

Soon, her list was confirmed.

Sara-Lee Biddle, seventeen, went missing from her night job at the local Services coffee shop. Finished up, swapped gossip with the lad coming on for the next shift, headed to the car park and then *poof*. Disappeared. Only her car keys on a pink crystal heart keyring remained, splayed out like a spider on the gravel; her wallet was missing.

Corrine Smith, twenty-six, single mum, working part-time during the day and studying at night to finish a degree while her dad looked after her two little kids. Left the uni library to walk to the bus stop and catch the campus security shuttle – a thirty-metre stroll, yet she never made it. Her backpack opened, her wallet taken out, only her student ID absent.

Larissa Waters, nineteen, receptionist at the local radio station, snatched during broad daylight when she went to the toilet block located out the back of the ancient building. Her handbag left behind, a scattering of tampons and lip-glosses disgorged on the tiled floor, her licence taken.

Anna Baines, twenty, waitress at the Swan & Dandy pub… well, no one had any idea how and when she went. One moment serving behind the counter, the next lost. Satchel gone – a ballsy move, given that staff personal items were left in lockable drawers in the office during shift – and Anna Baines gone too.

They all looked a little alike, with pretty, round faces and long dark hair, all about the five-foot two mark – easy to overpower. Not all from the same place – indeed, all from different villages – but in close proximity. Far enough, though, that maybe no one would make the connection, at least not for a while, not for another ten missing girls or so. Someone had given that due consideration, she was sure. And no one else knew where they were.

Except Erica.

She had to admit she'd gotten a bit obsessed with their families, searched the web for soundbites and clips of parents and siblings and friends offering recollections of the girl in question, begging for her to be released, begging for her to come home (in the unlikely event she'd run off under her own steam). Like Erica's family when her older sister had disappeared fifteen years ago. The parents sounded just like hers, like they all sang from the same song book, voices falling naturally into identical tunes of grief, cadences of disbelief – *How could it have happened to them?*

No one had ever found Celia. Not a whisper of her ever heard. She was ten when Erica had been born, so they were almost strangers, except for the fact that Celia had changed her nappies, fed her mushy food from the little bottles when their mother was working late, when their father couldn't find time. Good old Celia stepping into the breach, like every firstborn daughter ever. There every day of Erica's life until she wasn't; until Erica was five and then Celia was gone, without warning, without fanfare, leaving behind their parents' matching howls that eventually tore them apart. Erica and her mother stayed in the council house, her father finding a tiny flat in which to eventually drink himself to death at the age of forty. Her mother…

Her mother had moved north three years ago, to an island off the coast, deciding that crofting was the perfect way to isolate herself or punish herself or both. Erica heard from her every few months, but they had so little in common the calls were brief and stilted. Some days she wondered if things might have been different if Celia hadn't gone; if her sister's presence might have formed a strand to keep the warp and weft of them together, as a family, or if her taking had simply accelerated a deconstruction that was always going to occur.

And Erica… Erica had inherited Grandma Molly's two-storey Victorian 'cottage' with its many rooms, even more books, and everything in a perfect state of very slow decay – it was all a goth girl could ask for. The house had been in the family for three generations, passing to the oldest daughter except in the case of Erica's mother (the mutual dislike between her and Molly was intense). Erica's grandfather had been positively apoplectic to realise that *he* would not be inheriting after his wife vanished, that it would be going directly to his granddaughter and that, in addition to his wife's ghostly cold feet, may well have contributed to his swift demise.

The fact that Erica's family had been touched twice by tragedy – indeed four times if you counted her father and grandfather – made the people around her wary and sparing with their sympathy, so no one made any great efforts to be kind, lest some of that terrible luck rub off on them. She wasn't lonely because there was Romeo, and she had a life she didn't hate, a job at the local Co-op that required very little brainpower and only part of her time, a comfy home and all the books she might want. She could be offhandedly friendly with customers and make a point of not knowing their business. Goth clothing and makeup, always clutching a book in her red-nailed hands, didn't encourage familiarity, but she was efficient, smiled vaguely and didn't have her phone out doom scrolling at the register, so no one had anything specific to complain about. She didn't get to know customers by their names so much as their regular groceries: Mrs. Four-Bottles of Prosecco, Mr. Kipling's Best Patron, Vegan Burger Boy, Captain Microwave Meals, Private Incontinence Pads and so on. It was a quiet town, quiet county, not much going on.

Except, apparently, murder.

When Erica had established the girls were (a) real and (b) actually missing rather than just part of an elaborate prank or the graves part of a film set, then she began her preparations for All Hallows' Eve…

And now here she is, armed with nothing more than a small backpack, a large dog and hopefully the best will of the woods and some of the things in it. Erica didn't begin as a witch, or she didn't think so, at least. Her mother had committed no acts of magic and showed no interest in it, but Grandma Molly had more than a few habits. She'd read the tea leaves without provocation; leave small pyramids of salt in the corners of rooms for cleansing (and Erica replaced them regularly); wove tiny dollies from weeds and wildflowers and stuck them in little Erica's pockets whenever she left after a visit (her granddaughter would keep them until they turned to nothingness); she'd light candles on the full moon and hold scraps of paper scribbled with wishes and intentions to the flame so the words were taken upwards; burn bundles of smudge after any visit by her daughter (who, she told Erica, carried despair with her like a high-priced handbag); and sweep from the gate to the open front door, muttering for wealth to flow to *this* home. Erica didn't know if her grandmother simply lacked the audacity or ambition to ask for anything greater, but whenever Molly performed this last ritual, money would arrive unexpectedly, just the amount needed for the gas bill or the groceries or a new pair of shoes.

Grandma Molly had never overtly taught her granddaughter these things – lest her daughter complain loudly and forbid further contact – but she'd noticed the girl watching and always made sure the view was clear. As she grew older, after her grandmother's death, Erica began to buy books and read whatever she could about magic and witches and what they reputedly could do, what they did do, what they didn't and how they were punished for it no matter what.

She started trying things out: small rituals, tiny spells, Grandma Molly's little prosperity enchantments first of all and sure enough supplementary amounts would arrive. Erica wasn't greedy, didn't want to attract attention with some gigantic lottery win, just liked that whenever she came up short, she could *will* enough to cover the shortfall into being. As time went on, she became proficient at making herself hard to notice, occasionally invisible if she really put her mind to it, and then to seek patience and protection from whatever spirits ruled in woods and trees, streams and lakes, even cities and towns. Even places like that, the godlings hadn't entirely fled, just became different, harder to spot and please and a little more demanding in their bargains. Erica was grateful she didn't have to do too much negotiation with the urban sprites. Eventually, she began to experiment with tarot cards and Ouija boards, other divination, with summonings and sendings. So far, it had all gone well; well enough to make her think that tonight's work might succeed.

Up ahead, the trees part and this spot she recognises. Hard to be certain, in the darkness, but the moon's bright when she steps out from under the leafy canopy, and Romeo gives the tiniest whimper around the muzzle. Another reproachful look; *Mother, however can I warn you of squirrel danger with this monstrosity affixed?* Romeo's voice in her head is, she admits, a good deal better bred than someone who regularly rolls in mud and eats assorted shit at the first opportunity.

And this *is* the best night for it: All Hallows' Eve, Samhain, Halloween. The doors in-between are open, and the dead can more easily pass through, back and forth, back and forth.

Standing in front of the row of graves, Erica pulls the plastic container from her backpack and opens it, placing an iced cupcake beside each laminated ID. Soul cakes were traditional for All Hallows', an offering to the spirits; vanilla cupcakes from Fancy Fran's Bakery are the closest she can get. Next, a can of cider, of which she figures most teenaged girls have, at some point or other, taken a swig or two; she pours out four drams into the earth, then gulps the last of it herself. The can's returned to the pack and replaced by a box of salt. The circle she makes with it is mostly round, and she does the circuit twice more, just to ensure the line will be unbroken around her and Romeo.

Next, Erica sticks four short black candles (each one carved with a girl's name) into the ground, and drips fragrant oil on them before she strikes a match and touches it to the wicks, then carefully steps into the protective circle to sit, cross-legged.

"Romeo, stay still, and stay quiet," she tells the wolfdog at her side, and his head lowers to the grass with a whimper. She pats his head, the spot between his ears, between his eyes, is glad of his warmth. "Good boy."

She'd thought long and hard about the murder ballad to use as part of tonight's calling. There are plenty of old ones: 'Tom Dooley' (too frivolous), 'The Two Sisters' (not very feminist), 'Pretty Polly' and 'The Wexford Girl' (apologist cant, the both of them) – and a bunch of others these girls are likely too young to know. Even Nick Cave's 'Where the Wild Roses Grow' has cobwebs on it by now. She's pleased with what she'd chosen, what had hit her like a bolt of lightning: Taylor Swift's song about how the lack of a body denotes a lack of a crime. It fits perfectly, and the dead girls will most likely recognise the tune, heed its call. She's made sure she knows the words by heart, but by the time she sings it all the way through four times, her faith feels a little wobbly…

Until, at last, the candles and their tiny flames start to waver and the ground begins to shift as if breathing. At first a little tremor, next, kind of a shudder up and down again, until twiggy fingers with shreds of meat attached poke through the dirt and the grass that's grown over resting places and their unwilling occupants.

Erica feels dizzy, tastes a little bit of sick in her mouth because she's never done *this* precise spell before. She knows all the theory, has read those books forward and back until it seems like she's engraved them onto the squiggly surface of her own brain, but this sort of practice? She couldn't bring herself to try it, not even a test run on a dead animal because what if something went wrong? What if she'd fucked up and unleashed a plague of zombie squirrels or zombie cats, biting people, making them turn into things that licked themselves and shat in boxes? No, no, that wouldn't do.

While her mind's off on this little tear, chasing itself around the hamster-wheel of her skull, the dead girls manage to heave themselves out of the earth and onto it.

They sway like drunkards, and it makes her heart threaten to stop. *How is this better than zombie squirrel-cats?* But she remembers they've not walked in months and it's a habit that needs to be relearned. In various stages of decomposition – white bones showing through split skin, dried blood and withered flesh, eyes all gone, toothy grins, sunken noses, hairstyles with just a hint of how carefully they once were coiffed – but a consistently terrible smell wafts off them on the cold autumn breeze. She dreads to think how bad it might have been had she done this in summer, then reminds herself it would never have been summer because the doors in-between didn't open then. But it's already midnight and they need to hurry – she doesn't know how much longer this will take. Erica had carefully woven a spell within the spell, a failsafe, to make sure the girls had an ending: 'til dawn or their vengeance was done, whichever came first.

They're looming over her now, or as close as they can get and she's very glad for that circle of salt. Romeo's not making a sound, which is unusual for any dog because unlike cats they've got no affinity for creepy things – she remembers the joke about the cat going to hell who walks up to Lucifer on his throne and says, "You're in my spot". Erica gives a nervous laugh. The girls, she realises, are just waiting to know why they've been summoned, why they've risen from an unwilling grave. What they should do. Erica clears her throat.

"Welcome home," she says, her voice all aquiver. "You have a chance to make things right, to find the one who did this to you. You have until dawn."

At first, she's worried they're too far gone, that the ability to hear has disappeared, ears filled with worms and dirt and maggots. Then she notices that they're sniffing – that what's left of their noses, cartilage, a tiny meaty tip barely hanging on by a thread, are twitchy as they seek for a scent much like Romeo does, like he had when he'd found them.

All four turn at the same moment and set off into the woods. She gives them a decent head start, rises, hastily repacks her bag, and snatches up the laminated IDs from beside trampled cupcakes, dropping them and the snuffed candles in her pocket – again, careful to touch the edges only – then sets off after her shambling, staggering girls.

Erica wonders who they'll find; she's got her own list of suspects. Creepy old Thom Jenks whose wife and daughters all wore consistent and mysterious bruises? Alexander Fitzgibbon, up at the big house, whose girlfriend had tried to get a non-molestation order against him, except the magistrate said it might 'blight his future' and she should stop provoking him? Harold McIntyre, whose wife left him, apparently, and hadn't been heard from by anyone in over a year? Or even that woman, reputed to be an ex-nun, who never returned any toys that found their way into her garden, balls over fences, frisbees on roofs? That one might have been stretching it and disliking children didn't make you a monster, no matter what the papers said.

Nearly two hours later and Erica's almost regretting her decision to do any of this. Romeo's dark eyes haven't left the little wavering band, he's not even growled once. Erica's kept the girls in sight while also keeping her distance as they shuffle through the trees. She was heartened when one of them had tripped and caught her foot somehow, the other three turned back and helped her. *Good girls.* But that feels a very long time ago, when she was younger and full of hope. The weight of doubt sits firmly on her shoulders now. How far will they have to go to find the killer? Is it the same killer of them all? Did said killer even live in the local area or was the dump site chosen because it was a drive of days and days from where the murders had actually happened?

They'd left the woods a while ago, walking across several fields, past farmhouses where dogs had been eerily silent, as if sensing the little parade wasn't one to interfere with. They'd skirted far around bonfires where groups danced and sang and laughed and leapt over flames. No one had looked up, no one noticed their passing by.

And then, as Erica's about to give up, a caravan comes into view, on the edge of an open field but wedged back into the flank of another tract of woods.

Dingy and small, peeling paint. No light shows inside because it's after midnight and apparently only a goth girl on a mission and her posse of heavy ghosts are awake. No one's coming to this place asking for sweeties and dressing up in costumes. No one except her band of unsteady girls who, as she watches, wrench the door off its hinges with very little effort, and pour inside like a flood tide.

Still keeping her distance, Erica listens carefully as the screams begin. No neighbours nearby so no chance of interference. There's a moment when the man inside tries to make a break for it, the top half of him darting out the door like a Jack-in-the-Box. The full moon peeks from behind the clouds, so she recognises his face, very vaguely, as someone who's been in the Co-op on occasion, then he's gone again, so quickly, dragged back into the dark maw of the caravan.

Nothing distinguishing about him. So ordinary. A packet of cigarettes, milk and bread and a box of cereal, once or twice a month, perhaps? Not a talker, never a smile, but often a starer, from somewhere off in the aisles, sneaking around corners when he thought she wasn't watching.

Erica touches her long straight dark hair, feels at her face to confirm its roundness, the soft features; her resemblance to the dead girls who are taking the man apart like he's a Ken doll to be dissected.

And Erica's powerfully struck by how he is *nobody*, yet he thought it his right and privilege to deprive these girls of their lives, to remove all their hope, all their potential from the world. To burn all their possibilities, to inflict wounds on parents and siblings and friends that will never heal, to create holes in the universe that these girls were meant to fill. To snuff out four bright lights.

She waits until the noises stop before she moves forward, slowly, quietly just in case, keeping a now-whimpering Romeo on a tight leash, and holding up the torch on her mobile, half terrified that something will swoop at her out of the darkness.

But no.

The light spills across a scene of carnage. The man in four pieces – both arms and left leg pulled off – blood spattered over the meagre furniture and some sizable pools of black-red still leaking from him, eyes wide and disbelieving. She hopes his terror was at least as great as those girls suffered. The girls who lay around him now like puppets without strings, draped on benches, the stained carpet, one angled against the sink, their deed done, their revenge had. Erica whispers a final blessing over them for a peaceful rest.

She sweeps the beam of the torch across the room one last time. Nothing noteworthy. Carefully she reaches into her pocket, gathers the IDs, and sets them on the top of a cabinet. Easy to see, should someone happen to come along.

Erica wonders if, one day, she might find her sister's final resting place. If, some day, she might wake Celia in the same way and watch her sniff out a killer. If she'll be able to make herself do the same spell again. Still without an answer, Erica turns and walks back into the woods, Romeo at her side.

The Smokeless Fire

Mark Chadbourn

THIRTEEN PEOPLE watched him step off the Seventh Avenue subway platform in front of the southbound train en route to Brighton Beach. He didn't run. Didn't hurl himself to his death. His face glowed with a beatific expression as if he'd just been visited by an angel, so one of the witnesses said.

The police report had some discrepancies. Three people insisted they saw not one but two people go over the edge onto the tracks, though the details of that second person were too vague for any of them to recall. The team that spent the next hour cleaning up the tangled, bloody mess disagreed. One person. One set of body parts. Basic maths.

How long had I been waiting for this moment? Months? Years? Scouring the news websites, tracking the downward spiral of a life through career humiliation, relationship breakdown, financial woes, the kind of stuff that you chalk up to bad luck.

Only it wasn't.

She warned me what the future held, for him, for me, that night in the cramped clay-brick hut with the breeze sweetened by the sticky scent of roasting lamb from the village fires.

There was a price to pay.

But these days it was a constant struggle for survival, on a battlefield where none of the rules were clearly defined. Fight and deal with the fallout or be defeated.

I chose to fight.

* * *

Most of it feels like a dream. A nightmare, maybe. But the details are strong. The burnt rubber smell of the jet fuel afterburners and the heat haze wavering over the concrete runways under the merciless sun. The gritty dust blasting from the distant wilderness like hot needles ramming into my skin. The Hindu Kush turning crimson in dawn light.

The betrayals, the injustice, the cruelty.

Most of all I remember that light, deep in his eyes.

The light of the smokeless fire.

Bagram Air Base was America's last stand in a country it never understood. The military arrived with high-minded ideals, Stars and Stripes fluttering alongside the twenty-first century sheen of the finest weapons technology the world had ever seen.

But ultimately Afghanistan defeated them, as it had defeated every outsider before.

I was working for a tiny NGO providing humanitarian support for the people who'd been caught up in the endless factional war between the zealots of the Taliban and the coalition trying to keep them out of power. Little Ellie Smith, the smart kid in the class, who swapped rainy Manchester for sweltering Kabul in the hope of using her knowledge of Pashto and Dari to do some good in the world.

The NGO I signed up for was one of the smaller ones. Six of us, heading out into the villages to offer medical support or aid to keep starvation at bay.

My small team was headquartered at the air base. That meant it was impossible not to come into regular contact with the American service personnel. Most were respectful, ma'am this and ma'am that. Some were arrogant and swaggering. The men, of course. The women were just fine, fighting their own private battles in special forces and intelligence gathering.

Some thought every *bitch* was an opportunity for easy sex and some were just plain rapey. You quickly identified those and kept well away.

And we'd always cross paths with the counter-insurgency patrols out in the villages when we were doing our work. There was a sense of order to it all, however fragile. That fell apart when the news came out of the Pentagon that the US was finally withdrawing. There was a small window to leave the country and the pressure of that hectic pace seemed to knock a lot of the service personnel off-kilter.

But the real panic came among the villagers who'd become my friends. With the US gone, they knew the Taliban would be back in power in no time, bringing with them a new age of terror. Repression. Beatings. Enforced disappearances. And for the women, the removal of all their hard-earned rights. My heart broke when I heard them cry that they'd become little more than possessions, locked away in the dark.

America didn't care. They just washed their hands of it all.

On the day the news broke I was in a tiny village in the hills just outside Bagram, a sun-baked crescent of mud-brick houses where the locals eked out a hard living from the land. As we distributed medical supplies I watched the horror leaping from face to face when the word spread, the men standing in silence, shoulders slumping, the women huddled together, crying.

The contrast with the counter-insurgency patrol was stark. The men were laughing, joking, unusually at ease, excited to be going home.

When raucous laughter rang out, punctuated by a distressed cry, I found six men from Special Forces gathered around an Afghan boy. He was only about eight, eyes wide with terror. He was dancing from foot to foot as the men took it in turns to level their weapons at him. I heard one of them say "Al Qaeda", the terrorist group they were supposed to be rooting out, and the boy responded with another cry of denial.

"Stop tormenting him."

The one in charge was Staff Sergeant Clay Trainor, six foot three of gym-hardened muscle with grey-blue eyes that looked like chips of ice.

"You wanna talk to us now?" he said with a smirk.

Trainor was one of those men all the women on the base learned to avoid. He'd get right in your space, trying to frighten you into submission with his sheer physicality. The first and only time he tried it with me, I put both hands on his chest and shoved him so hard he almost fell over.

He didn't like that. He really didn't like it when all the men around him started laughing.

"He's a kid. Leave him alone. He's frightened."

Trainor turned to the boy and started to raise his weapon again. "Gotta be sure he's not a terrorist. They start 'em young out here."

"You know the rules," I barked.

Trainor glowered at me. "You gonna report me?"

"If I have to."

He muttered something under his breath, and when all the men around him laughed, my cheeks burned.

The boy thought this was a good time to get away. As he started to run, Trainor lunged and kicked the child's heels together so that he went down hard.

He didn't move and I could see a dark stream of blood leaking from his head into the pale dust.

"Ah, he'll live," Trainor said dismissively. "C'mon, we got work to do."

Immediately, a woman strode over from the doorway where she'd been watching the incident, her black *kamiz* swirling around her like a pool of ink. She was in her fifties by the looks of it, long hair streaked with grey. What struck me the most was her eyes, which were big and dark and burned with a fierce intelligence.

"Bring him," she said.

Her house was barely more than a single room with a pot bubbling over a few red embers in the hearth. An odd smell hung in the air, something herby that I couldn't place.

She waved a hand for me to lay the boy down on some blankets in one corner.

"Let me fetch my team," I began. "We have some medicine—"

"I will deal with it."

"But—"

"I will *deal* with it."

The woman plucked up a clay jar from one corner and when she opened it my nostrils wrinkled at a sour odour, like dirty washing left out in the sun. Dipping three fingers into the creamy unguent inside, she smeared it on the boy's head wound.

Sitting beside him, she cupped his small hand in hers and began a low chant delivered with such a strange intonation I could only make out a few words – fire, blood, spark; it sounded like some older tongue mixed in with Farsi.

When she was done, the only sound was the whine of the wind through the door, whipping up whorls of dust. She lowered her head until it was almost resting on the boy's forehead and stayed that way in silence for a long moment.

The boy's eyes flickered open.

I clapped my hands together. "Oh, thank God. But, y'know, I should still get my team to check him out."

"The boy will recover. It has already been willed." She looked at me askance. "I have seen you in the village before. You help those suffering. You heal. You feed."

"It's my job."

"A job you chose to do."

I nodded.

The woman returned her attention to the boy, gently stroking his forehead, but I could feel her attention was fully on me. "What is your name?"

"Ellie."

"I am Shazia Husaini."

Her surname told me she was a Hazar, one of the Turkic people who'd drifted into Afghanistan from the north many years ago. Afghanistan was a melting pot. A lot of people didn't realise that; different traditions, different cultures.

"The man who did this. You know him well?" she asked.

"I know him."

"A friend?"

"No."

She nodded. "I have seen him in the village too. He does not help. He harms." She looked up at me now and her stare was intense. "You must beware of him."

I tried to laugh it off, but her face was graven.

"If he tries to harm you, come to me."

Outside in the oppressive heat, I blinked through the glaring light after the dark of Shazia's house and as my eyes cleared I noticed a group of Special Forces gathered around something on the edge of the village. Trainor wasn't one of them so I went over.

They were all looking down at something, their expressions uneasy. I pushed through and found myself staring at a dead body. It was an Afghan man, late thirties, heavily bearded with a claret scarf wrapped around his head. An old-fashioned rifle lay across his chest. Looked like Taliban, possibly a scout.

The man's mouth was pulled into a broad rictus grin and both the eyes were missing.

There was something in the expression that suggested he'd seen the most amazing thing at the instant he died.

"Who did that?" I asked, trying not to sound accusatory.

"Fuck knows," someone replied. "That's the creepiest thing I've ever seen."

"You think a vulture took the eyes out?" another asked.

"And left the rest of him?"

"What, then?"

No one answered.

That image troubled me on a level I didn't quite understand, so I left them coming up with increasingly wild explanations and made my way to the *bujra* where the men socialised. My village contact Umar, from the *jirga*, the council of elders, was listening intently to a visiting mullah from the nearby mosque. Umar was a wiry man with a mass of silver-grey hair. He had a sly sense of humour and he always loved teasing me. I waited respectfully until the mullah had departed, and went over.

"You have heard? The Taliban are coming. Everything will change." Umar looked me up and down. "You will not be able to visit with your head uncovered like this."

"I'll follow whatever rules are laid down so I can do my work."

"Of course, of course. We are grateful for all you do."

I told him about the injured boy.

Umar looked past me towards Shazia's house. "She will be dead soon."

"She's sick?" I thought how vibrant she appeared, as if there was a furnace burning inside her.

"The Taliban will execute her."

"What's she done?"

"Shazia is no *Wali*, no friend of God. She walks with the Jinn. They do not fear her. They serve her."

My face must have shown what I thought about the region's supernatural traditions, for Umar sternly wagged a finger at me.

"Do not dismiss these things. The Jinn are all around us. Invisible. But they can influence this world for good or evil." He glanced back over towards the house. "Shazia Husaini practises *sihr*."

"Witchcraft?"

He nodded. "The Qur'an, as you know, warns against such a thing. The practising of magic, healing, the evil eye. The scholars in the *madhahib* consider it a serious crime, punishable by death."

Now I understood why Umar thought the Taliban would kill Shazia. During their last time in power, they used accusations of witchcraft to execute *difficult* women. Educated women, strong women. Those who would speak out against injustice. It was a way of control that had been used for centuries and not just in this part of the world. The Puritans in England and America used to love nothing more than stringing up and dunking and burning any woman who stepped out of line.

"But the *jirga* have allowed Shazia to live here freely."

Umar steepled his fingers and gave me that slyly humorous look. "I am a godly man, as you well know. But look around you. We are far from the cities and *madhahibs* with their learned debates. The strict rules of those places do not hold here. In the villages, in the fields, we have traditions that existed long before my father's father's father's time."

"So you've been okay with the witches," I said wryly.

Umar shrugged. "We live and let live. Shazia is a wise woman. She heals. Sometimes she helps the crops grow or warns us when there is a storm on the horizon. I have heard tell that some go to her to hear their fortune. Not me, of course." He held his hands wide. "I am a godly man. And a wise one too. A wise man does not anger someone who walks with the Jinn."

* * *

Back at Bagram, the furnace heat was pressing down on the low-level buildings and the F-16s were booming overhead. It wasn't a big place, not one of those showy bases with their huge hangars to justify Pentagon money. Just a couple of runways steaming in the wavering light and the sense that it had been hastily carved out of an ancient land to show some kind of impressive modernity. I showered the dust off me, ate some lamb kofta and then headed to the bar to unwind with my team. I didn't drink alcohol, didn't like how it took away my control, but I was happy for my guys to kick back with a beer, especially after the hardships they regularly endured in this country.

Beyoncé was blasting out from the speakers on each end of the bar and there was the usual mix of sky jockeys and grunts trying to out-swagger each other around the pool table.

We always had a table in one corner where we could keep ourselves to ourselves, two other women and four guys; caring people, smart. I liked them all.

All but one of them got up to dance and I was left alone at the table with Jens, a big Norwegian guy who everyone called the Viking. He had long white hair and tattoos that covered his entire body from the neck down, arms so thick you could easily imagine him wielding an axe. He'd been working across the Middle East nearly all his life as far as I could tell, hard labour in the NGO mines in Iraq and Kuwait, and finally here. Embedded deep in the culture; he loved it. There wasn't anything he didn't know about the region.

After he'd clinked his beer bottle against my glass of iced water, I said, "Got a question for you."

"Go on," he rumbled.

"About the Jinn. You heard of them?"

Jens pressed a finger to his lips. "You don't want them to hear."

I laughed, but he gave me his deathly serious Viking stare.

"The Jinn are all around us, you just can't see them usually. It's like they're on…" He wafted a hand. "… another plane that overlaps with ours."

"So, magical beings."

Jens swigged back a mouthful of beer. "And pre-Islamic, too, though they're mentioned in the Qur'an. Ancient. As old as the world. Always here, always with us. But not like angels. They're created from light. Or humans, which are created from clay. In the Qur'an it is said the Jinn are made from smokeless fire."

Over at the bar, a group of raucous men were throwing themselves at each other, clashing their chests and bouncing back like boys in the playground. One of them was Trainor. When he saw me looking, he made his fingers into a gun that he pointed at me. The others looked round to see who he was targeting, and though he laughed along with them, his eyes were cold.

Killer's eyes.

"So Jinn are invisible, right?"

"In their true form." Jens drained his beer, flicked the bottle up into the air and caught it. "But sometimes you get to see aspects of them. They can take human form too, or animals. They can be good or evil, depending. You don't want to get on the wrong side of them because they can cause physical or mental harm. Drive you mad. Torment you. Then kill you."

"Lovely."

I could sense Trainor still staring at me. He was the kind of man who carried a grudge, one of those weak guys who always overcompensated because their psychology was so fragile that if they ever revealed a fragment of their weakness they'd shatter into a thousand pieces.

"*Don't ever cross Trainor*," one of the female intelligence operatives had once told me when we were listing the men we needed to avoid. "*He's a psychopath.*"

Jens tapped his bottle on the table to get my attention. "Why the interest in Jinn?"

I told him about Shazia.

"Ah, the witches!" Jens laughed. "They are everywhere in this country, in the rural areas. No one ever talks about them, but they're there. Don't get on their bad side, either."

One of the women on my team, Sophie, came over and dragged me onto the crowded dancefloor. I protested, but there was no resisting her. If truth be told it felt good to move, just that sense of releasing all the shit of the day and giving in to your body.

As we bounced around, I kept catching glimpses of Trainor through the bodies. Always watching. A creepy, not-enough-blinks stare that felt like it was cutting into my brain.

Eventually, I sensed him pushing his way towards me.

"How about a dance?"

I showed him a too-polite smile. "No, thanks. I'm with my friends."

"Not good enough for you?" He loomed over me, smiling back, but like a shark.

"I'm with my friends."

He pushed his way into my space, trying to intimidate me, so once again I thrust my hands against his chest and shoved him away so hard he spun into some of the other dancers.

"I said no!"

Trainor came back at me, fists bunching like he was squaring for a fight. A couple of my guys jumped in front of me and Trainor smacked them aside. He didn't get a chance to advance any further. Jens stepped right into him, so close they were almost touching, but Jens was a good head higher, the big slab of meat, and he looked down at Trainor like he was dealing with a naughty schoolboy.

"Ellie said no. I suggest you be a gentleman and back off," Jens told him.

"Or?"

"This'll get messy. I might get a few bloody knuckles, but you'll get disciplined and you don't want that."

They held each other's eyes for a long moment and then Trainor shrugged and wandered away.

I felt angry, but it wasn't the anger of passion; it was cold, diamond-hard, the emotion that arose from the knowledge that Trainor had showed he didn't consider me a person. I had no agency. I was there simply to bend to his will. There was nothing about me that mattered.

I kept dancing for ten minutes longer, determined not to cede my space, and then I went back to the table and swilled down my water.

* * *

I woke naked on my bed. My head was throbbing and my throat felt like it hadn't experienced moisture for days. I couldn't remember anything of the last few hours.

With a queasy panic, I dressed and staggered out into the heat of the day. Jens was waiting by the jeep.

"Hey, where've you been?" he began. "The others have gone ahead—"

"What happened to me last night?"

Maybe it was the tears of anger flecking the corners of my eyes, but Jens instantly grasped the seriousness of the situation. I'd sat for a while and then complained of feeling unwell, he said, and I staggered away like I was drunk.

"I don't drink!" I snapped, then felt guilty that I'd taken it out on Jens.

I cried off work for the day and went straight to the base hospital to get checked out. The medic did a few tests and confirmed what I thought.

I'd been spiked. Roofied. A splash of Rohypnol in the water I'd left on the table.

It had to be Trainor or one of his henchmen, a psychological punishment beating for daring to stand up to him.

The medic and the nurse checked me over and said there was no sign of sexual abuse. That didn't make sense to me, as relieved as I was. Why go to the lengths of dosing me?

Two days later I was called in to see one of the men in the base commander's office. He was an older guy, white hair, red face from the sun. He seemed uncomfortable and somehow sad.

Sitting me down, he made lots of compassionate noises and told me how much everyone valued the work I did. Then he revealed that nude photos of me had been found on some grunt's phone. I looked unconscious, he said, and I heard a hint of judgement behind it that somehow I'd got myself so drunk I couldn't look after myself. The subtext was clear; somehow it was my fault.

That cold anger came back again.

He started to bluster that the guy was being reprimanded, but he had to let me know there was more to it.

The image had been shared widely across the base.

All those men, staring at me nude, unconscious. Powerless. The aim was to show that I was so weak they could do whatever they wanted to me.

"Staff Sergeant Clay Trainor is responsible," I snapped.

Sitting back in his chair, he folded his hands together. The compassion had mysteriously vanished. "Do you have proof of that?"

"I know it's him. He's got it in for me."

"That's a big accusation to make. Career destroying. I'll need some evidence if I'm going to launch an investigation."

I felt like crying, not out of sadness or desperation, but as the only way I could release the fury that was churning inside me.

The commander's right-hand guy must have sensed my mood because his tone softened. "I'll have a word with Sergeant Trainor. See if we can sort this out quietly. I'll let you know—"

I was out of my chair and out of the room before he'd finished his sentence.

* * *

I probably should have left it there. If I could have, I would, but it was eating away at me like bacteria growing in uncooked meat left out in the sun. It wasn't so much how Trainor's abusive act made me feel. It was that he believed he had the right to do it to me. That I had to take whatever he chose to mete out because his pathetic ego was so wounded by a woman daring to stand up to him.

I fantasised about taking a gun and shooting him, but it was an insipid response. I wouldn't feel any better for it and I'd have demeaned myself in the process by lowering to his base level.

Three weeks later, the order came down that we all had to get out of Afghanistan fast: the military, the NGOs, everyone. The measured withdrawal had become a disorganised scramble. Afghan intelligence operatives were getting abandoned because there was no protocol to remove them. That was such a betrayal. They'd all be left to the brutal punishment of the Taliban, who were even now sweeping in from their tribal areas to take control of the government in Kabul.

Get out. Forget everyone there. We never understood it anyway.

In the chaos, I took the jeep and thundered over the rutted roads until I reached the village and Shazia Husaini's house. She must have heard the roar of the engine because she was standing in the doorway when I fishtailed to a halt in a cloud of dust.

"You have to get out," I gasped. "The Taliban are on their way."

She smiled. "And where will I go?"

"Anywhere. Another village—"

"The Taliban will be everywhere. They are like rats."

I slumped across the steering wheel. Of course, she was right. There was no safe place for Shazia, or the women who would lose every freedom they'd gained over the last twenty years. A new Dark Age was coming for them.

Hammering on the wheel, I threw my head back and howled like a wounded animal, thinking of what the women would have to endure, the death that was inevitably coming for Shazia. Thinking of what Trainor had done to me.

"I'm so sick of it all!" The words blasted out with such emotional force it felt like it was ripping me apart. It was a curse. It was a prayer, to gods that I could never bring myself to believe in.

Shazia put her slender arm around my quivering shoulder and led me into the warm dark of her home. Sobbing, I slumped on the rough blankets while she brought me steaming green tea flavoured with cardamom and sugar, and then I was spewing out all that I'd endured, caught up in the rage and the tears, snot streaming down my face. She listened to every word and passed no judgement.

When I was finished, she stroked my hair and said, "You understand, then. The struggle."

"I don't understand anything."

"You do. In your heart. The path I follow is about finding balance in this world. In Egypt, they used to call it *Ma'at*. It lay at the core of everything. Truth. Justice. Balance. Order. It must be achieved, whatever the cost, for only then will there be peace in this world."

My head slid onto her shoulder and in that moment I felt I was with my mother, in the happy times before she succumbed to the illness.

"My time here is drawing to a close," she continued. "I will not survive the Taliban. They will find some excuse to kill me. Not for practising *sihr*. Simply for being."

"There's no justice." I choked back a sob.

"There is the struggle. And if we do not fight it, we lose." She paused. "You have it in you to continue the fight."

Shazia held my flickering eyes as I tried to make sense of what she was saying.

"There is no time to teach you what I know," she continued. "But the Jinn will accept you. You can walk with them."

* * *

We talked for a long time after that. Most of it I don't remember now, as if it was in a dream, hovering on the edge of my consciousness. I do recall her warnings, though. When you welcome the Jinn into your life, there's no going back. They'll do your bidding, yes, but they'll demand much of you in return.

I should have turned her down, but her words reached deep into me, about the balance, the struggle, the need for justice in a world where the powerful had no qualms about using their strength to bend people to their will.

I agreed.

She smiled at me and nodded as if she knew that would be my answer all along. There was a ritual after that, involving a candle, a flame that seemed brighter and hotter than any I'd ever seen in my life. It gave off no smoke, I remember that.

"When you see the Jinn's face, the bond will be forged," Shazia said to me as I stared into that flame, "but you must never look into their face again for it will drive you mad."

She whispered something, and I saw the face. All I can recall now is the eyes, almond-shaped and golden, like the flame, and then the world fell away from me.

When I came round, Shazia was gone. No one in the village knew where she was.

I could sense the Jinn with me. Feel their power, their intent. Sometimes I could even glimpse them from the corner of my eye, like smoke drifting through the world. That power was mine too – I walked with them now –

although I wasn't sure how to use it. I'd learn though. I knew I would.

Back at Bagram, the panic had whipped up into a frenzy as everyone prepared to pull out. Weapons were being abandoned, those poor Afghan interpreters sent off to fend for themselves.

The last time I saw Trainor he was stumbling towards the C-17 Globemaster for the final flight out. Only he was different somehow, twitchy, frightened, and it wasn't because of the frantic situation.

A glow lit his eyes, one only I could see, and I knew then that Shazia's parting gift to me was to ensure Trainor got the punishment he deserved. It wouldn't be pretty. I knew the torment the Jinn inflicted.

But this was war. It had been going on for a long time, yet it had got more brutal and now there was only one choice. Fight and deal with the fallout or be defeated.

I chose to fight.

Wedding Planner

Muriel Gray

"WILL THE LOG FIRES be lit? On the day?"

Mr. Connolly gave a nod.

"Yes. Of course."

"The weather. You know?"

"We know."

They smiled. Ben was meandering, hands in pockets looking out of windows. Chloe called him to heel.

"Anything you want to ask?"

He wandered back.

"Nothing comes to mind."

He resumed his seat, chin resting on hand, surveying the menus and paraphernalia scattered before them. Toying with a small pink net bag containing sugar hearts, swinging it back and forth and tapping it on the tabletop, he pondered on the age of the confectionery in the sample bag and if it was still edible. The child in him wanted to test it by opening the pouch and popping one into his mouth. Mr. Connolly, however, exuded a manner of quiet control that suggested such an act would be discouraged with practised elegance and he decided against it.

"Well, in that case shall we head up to Killie Caomhnóir now? We'll return here to finalise everything."

Chloe smiled and patted her fiancé's hand. Mr. Connolly closed the leather-bound folders.

"And for a light lunch."

Ben looked up.

"Is that extra?"

"Included in today's tasting visit, Mr. Fanshaw. As per the quote."

"Lovely," said Chloe.

* * *

The tiny church appeared to grow from the top of the hill, its dressed stones merely formalising the natural feature it bestrode. Chloe sat in the back seat of the hotel's Range Rover as Mr. Connolly bounced up the bumpy dirt track and, as he drove, pointed out things to Ben in the front. Ben appeared unmoved by the view, a vista that boasted an unbroken ridge of mountains on the other side of the glen, staring ahead and holding onto the door handle as though they were in peril of rolling into a ditch.

"And how are we going to get people up here?"

"The guests will have been taken from the car park up this road by our own vehicles. And then the bride will, of course, arrive by our horse and carriage." Mr. Connolly turned in his seat to look back at Chloe. "The horse is called Stan. He's incredibly sure-footed."

She laughed and found herself clasping her hands together in delight.

An elderly man was waiting for them by the door, a lanyard of keys dangling from his hand. Mr. Connolly introduced him as the caretaker Donald and everyone shook hands.

"It's been wet, so maybe a wee bit cold inside," he said as he attempted to unlock a plain wooden door, scoured by the weather into a beautiful grey striated arch, pitted with square bronze studs. "Sticks sometimes," said Donald as he struggled with the lock.

Despite the light drizzle that had started on their arrival, Chloe left Ben standing impatiently behind the fumbling caretaker and took the opportunity to walk around. Mr. Connolly had returned to the car and was looking at his phone. The church was exquisite. Smaller even than the kind of new-build brick houses currently sprouting in estates round the edge of every city, it had a grandeur that outweighed its diminutive size. There was no transept, merely a rectangular structure with plain arched windows lining each side.

The picture she had seen in the travel magazine didn't do it justice. It was magnificent, jutting like the prow of a ship from its rocky advantage over a landscape of endless wild beauty, proud in its stark simplicity.

This was going to be so very different from all those weddings their friends had organised, each almost identical to the other, in the fashionable registry offices across London, theming them to be 'original' without realising how uniform they were in their smug stylishness. Going with the fashion, Ben suggested they book Old Marylebone Town Hall, though rather than him being charmed by its chic she suspected he just wanted an easy life and a relatively inexpensive day.

"A church?" he'd said with a touch of scorn when she showed him the article on unique venues. "Since when did we get religion?"

"It's deconsecrated. A protected ancient A-listed monument bought by the nearby hotel. They do the occasional secular ceremony."

"In Scotland?"

"I believe things have moved on since John Knox."

So here they were. Only two months away. Chloe excited. Ben, compliant, resigned and penny-pinching.

Hearing the creaking sound of the stubborn door being opened, she rejoined the men and followed them into the gloom of the building. Donald was talking Ben through some history.

"Built in 1623, although allegedly it was on the site of an older structure, it ceased being used as a place of worship in the late 1700s."

Donald sounded as though this was a regular and rehearsed speech, probably one accompanied by a leaflet and a polite request for a donation. Chloe was already designing in her head the pew-end flowers that would line the simple aisle. The glass letting in the murky light was plain, with no colour, so she would bring in their own. Hydrangeas, perhaps. Big colourful blooms, and bunches of fragrant heather.

"And why was that?" Ben broke in.

Their guide looked peeved to have been interrupted. "Why what?"

"Did it stop being used for worship."

Donald side-eyed him. "Well. That was quite the thing."

Ben crossed his arms and put a finger to his chin, the respectful listening gesture, nodding to encourage him to continue.

"Possibly local gossip? Superstition of the age."

"Oh!" said Ben, now genuinely intrigued.

"They believed that the minister, a Reverend McPherson, had made a pact with the devil."

"What's that?" asked Chloe, suddenly focusing.

Ben took her by the hand. "Listen to this."

Donald looked uneasy but continued. "The congregation were afraid of something he had conjured and stopped coming. McPherson left and there was no minister willing to take on the post."

"Goodness!" said Chloe. "Did he just disappear?"

"Yes."

Ben laughed. "I hope he got a good bargain for his soul. No Ferraris or Dubai penthouses back then. I wonder what he wanted so badly?"

"Wasn't it usually pleasures of the flesh?" Chloe contributed. Ben coughed and looked at the flagstone floor.

"We should probably go outside now," suggested Donald.

"In case the devil hears us laughing at him?" Chloe smiled. Then she lit up, remembering something. "Oh, of course, there's that famous church on Islay that's completely round. It was built to stop the devil hiding in corners. I love that!"

"My wife-to-be has a passion for all things strange and wonderful, Donald. I imagine if she had been a parishioner back then and the corrupted reverend had stayed in post, he'd have had an enthusiastic congregation of at least one."

She chuckled. "Legends just make it even more special and exciting."

Donald nodded without smiling as he gestured to the doorway. "There's a few dusty corners here and there, but it'll be swept and cleaned like a new pin for the day, I can assure you." He looked at Chloe with a seriousness it was hard to tell was genuine or mockery. "Nowhere to hide."

Ben halted. "Oh, and just one last question. How many people can we squeeze in here?"

Donald gestured again to keep them moving. "There's a maximum capacity of sixty-six persons in total. Including your minister."

"Celebrant," corrected Chloe.

"Aye. Well, not a soul more than that. The insurance."

"Oh-oh," said Ben, looking comically at Chloe. "Guest list trimming carnage ahead."

While Donald wrestled with the uncooperative door lock, Chloe and Ben took a walk around the ancient graveyard set some distance back from the church, nestled in a mossy hollow with no view of the landscape from its dank enclosure.

She took his hand as they wandered between the tumbled and lichen-encrusted stones, their long-since engraved words now barely legible.

"Are you ok with all this, darling?"

Ben squeezed her hand. "Here to please. And most of all pleased to be marrying you."

They carried on, Chloe delighting in every new discovery. Ben less so, as he found his mind drifting away from examining the intricacies of Celtic knots and wyverns carved on granite to the painful repayments on the mortgage in Muswell Hill, and whether there really was a video of him tongue-kissing Aditi at the office party last week.

He could do with a drink.

* * *

Mr. Connolly looked at his watch.

"All this will be emailed in detail to you both, so unless there's any specific issues you need cleared up right now you can take your time over it and get back to me when the deposit is paid. I just want to make sure we get you both to the station in time."

Chloe was outside phoning her mother. From her extravagant hand gestures and broad smile she was clearly enthusing about the trip, as his mother-in-law to be was the one paying for some of it and was still smarting about not having been invited to tag along. Ben was running his finger down the list in front of him.

"I'm obviously pleased you've given us this discount on the welcome drinks, Mr. Connolly, but can we still meet somewhere in the middle over these canapés? King prawns?"

"We can certainly look at a thriftier option."

"Oh, and there's this," said Ben, tapping it with a finger. "£250: Church Guardian? Surely the caretaker's duty is already included in the hire of the building?"

Mr. Connolly adjusted his tie. "No. This is something entirely different. It's a respected and important tradition connected with the hire of the church."

"A tradition?"

"Yes. Now we currently have three qualified Guardians. Margaret and Sheila who are local, so that's what this fee is based on. But if neither is available Emily is also extremely good, though she lives in Inverness so would have to charge mileage. And that would of course incur a small extra payment."

Ben sat back in his chair, his mouth curving into a half smile. "Sorry. What exactly do these people do?"

"They're..." Mr. Connolly looked to the invoice, deep in thought. "They... come with the venue hire."

"Yes. I'm understanding that bit. I'm just not clear what 'Guardian' means. What exactly are they guarding? Are they cleaners? Ushers? What?"

Mr. Connolly clasped his hands on the table, just as Chloe entered breathlessly and rejoined them. "As I say. It's part of the tradition that they attend before, during and after the ceremony. They remain seated until all the guests have departed. We find it's particularly important at events like this."

"Weddings?"

"Yes."

"So, with the limited capacity we've only just discovered, one of these Guardians takes up a seat?"

Mr. Connolly looked across at Chloe, presumably as a potential ally. Ben was clearly beginning to try his professional patience. "No, not at all. There's a small wooden bench you may have noticed on the wall just behind the main door. It has rather interesting carvings on it. The Guardian sits there. Very discreet."

Ben smiled and nodded. "Well, I think we can save ourselves £250, thanks Mr. Connolly. No Guardian required. Thank you."

The hotelier's face changed. A glint of something Ben could not quite unpick.

"I understand fully your desire to keep such a special day within budget, Mr. Fanshaw, and indeed as you've seen we've made every effort to keep costs down while maintaining an exemplary first-class event. But I feel I would be doing you a great disservice if I failed to caution you that cutting this particular service would potentially be..." He paused. "A mistake."

Chloe raised her eyebrows at her fiancé. "Oh, then shouldn't we just...?"

Ben cut over her. "Thank you for your concern, Mr. Connolly, but I think we'll be just fine without Janet or whoever sitting up at the back."

"Margaret, Sheila or Emily," said Mr. Connolly coldly.

"Whatever. We'll be fine."

Mr. Connolly looked at Chloe again. Ben put his hand over hers, and she reluctantly nodded in agreement.

"We have fifteen minutes to get you to the station. I'll fetch a driver." Mr. Connolly stood up, shook their hands and left.

Ben made a comedic face at Chloe. "Oo-er."

She smiled. Then looked at the door which their host had closed behind him rather too firmly. "Let's not be late."

* * *

Aboard the Caledonian Sleeper Chloe lay on the narrow bed reading a book. Finding she had read the same paragraph three times without taking anything in she lay it on her stomach and allowed herself the pleasure of planning the bridesmaids' dress colour, and wondering if they should have a musician to entertain the guests during the photos.

Ben, in the bar carriage, was finishing his fourth whisky, running his finger around the rim of the glass and thinking about whether inviting Aditi would require asking other colleagues from the company to make it seem less peculiar.

But with only sixty-six places Chloe would most likely have already mentally filled it with her larger family and loud friends. Not a chance. It's only a day, he thought. An expensive day. A necessary day, given they were much too far down this path to question whether it was the right thing to do anymore. Chloe was sweet and loving. So what if other women had begun to excite him more over the last year and a half? They'd been a couple for so long now. A man in his position, and at his age, was expected to have a family. It was just a day.

"Same again, please," he said pleasantly to the woman in the garish tartan waistcoat behind the bar.

"You'll sleep well tonight, sir." She smiled as she poured.

"Here's hoping."

* * *

If there was anything more exciting than the joyous chaos surrounding a two-day wedding event in a distant and romantic location, then Chloe didn't know of it.

The collecting of friends from the quaint West Highland line station, the envious faces of hikers in the carriage windows looking on as these exotic people stepped off the train, waddling in city shoes across the single-track line in front of the train to get to the opposite platform and be swept up in a sea of hugs and screams.

The fussing over clothes, and flowers. Parents being parents, looking at flowers in the grand gardens. The constant questions from the staff regarding details of the loveliest kind. Where champagne glasses should go. Where the fiddle player should stand. When was the piper to begin? Then there was the bumping into family and friends in unexpected places in the hotel or its grounds. And of course, the bar.

Ben was mostly to be found there, as indeed he was when Chloe went searching for him, laughing raucously with his best man, Milo.

"You say anything like that, mate, and I mean anything! I *will* kill you. No, eviscerate you first."

Milo laughed and waved away the threat. "It's the finest speech known to man. It will live on longer in history than those feeble attempts by Churchill or Martin Luther King."

"I know for certain that Dr. King never said the words 'He liked tits you could hang a bath towel on.'"

"How do you know? Were you ever present when he was doing a best man's speech?"

Chloe could hear their laughter even before she walked through the door into the oak-panelled room.

"There she is!" said Milo, holding out his arms. "The world's most beautiful woman just about to come off the market. Absolute tragedy."

"And how is your own lovely wife, Milo?" said Chloe, kissing him on both cheeks.

"She sends you all her love and totally understands about the limited numbers. The London version of this will be at ours and whole suckling pigs are already being slaughtered in anticipation. The twins would have destroyed the day in any case."

Chloe looked at Ben with love. "Nothing will do that."

He smiled back and kissed her.

"Now," she said, "I believe it's time you gentlemen repaired to your separate lodgings. The next time you see me I'll be walking down that tiny but beautiful aisle."

They drank up and made to leave. Chloe hugged Ben. "I love you."

He held her close, looking over her shoulder to the window where swallows were swooping and diving. Free. Soaring. Mocking gravity. Nothing tethering them to earth.

"You too."

She watched the men go, then, spotting her friends laughing round a parasol table in the garden, went to join them.

As she walked through the foyer a small, middle-aged woman who had been sitting in an armchair stood up. She had poorly-dyed hair, grey roots showing through a much too vivid red, and despite the warmth of the day was layered up in several cardigans of varying states of deterioration.

"Ah. Are you Chloe?"

She stopped. "Yes. Yes, I am. Hello."

The woman didn't appear to be staff, young and liveried as they all were in smart white shirts and kilts. And she was most certainly not a guest.

"I'm so glad to have caught you. May I have a word?"

She indicated the chair she'd risen from, there being two arranged around a coffee table. Chloe looked at her curiously but did as she was bid.

The woman sat down and offered a hand. "Margaret McKay. I'm pleased to meet you."

Chloe shook her hand, a chubby affair bedecked with an astonishing variety of rings. "Yes. Thank you. Hello."

"I hope you won't mind this intrusion, but Mr. Connolly told me... he's the manager of this hotel."

Chloe interrupted, irritated at being kept from the table of friends. "Yes. I know who he is."

"Of course. Well, he told me about your wedding tomorrow at Killie Caomhnóir, and most importantly that you and your fiancé had decided to decline the services of a Guardian. Is that correct?"

Chloe stiffened and immediately understood. So, this was to be a plea for money. She was disappointed that a man as smart and professional as Mr. Connolly would even have suggested that this scruffy woman should be part of their elegant event, and wondered what kind of scam was being performed. She was glad now Ben had made that decision, despite secretly disagreeing at the small saving at the time, and rather charmed by the idea of following a local tradition that would have doubtless been a talking point at the reception. But now? He was so obviously right.

The frost in her voice was tangible. "That's correct. We didn't think it was necessary."

The woman fumbled in a bag and brought out a cotton hanky to blow her nose noisily and with gusto. Chloe looked on in disgust, noticing the unusual necklace peeking over her cocoon of cardigans. A small silver hand, its fist clenched around a twig, suspended on a leather thong. It added to the impression that this was some aging hippy, the sort who may well live in a caravan. What was he thinking, having someone like this sitting in on their wedding?

"Well, I've spoken with my other colleagues, and I've come here to say that I'm willing to do this one without any payment at all. If that was the consideration."

Chloe shuddered at the thought of this strange woman watching her from the back of the church. "That's very kind of you, Margaret, but we really don't think it's a custom we'll follow in this instance."

Margaret sat up straighter, tucking her hanky into a sleeve. She cleared her throat. Her tone became serious. "It's not so much a custom, Chloe. More of a prevention. And we – actually all three of us – feel, very strongly in fact, that one of us really needs to be in attendance. Emily even phoned me in the middle of the night, which is very unusual as the cut-off is midnight. As most people would agree, unless it's an emergency, of course. My brother's the worst for that. Won't be told. Once called at quarter to two just to say the cat hadn't come home. I mean. Honestly."

"Attend without payment?"

Margaret nodded solemnly. What was the script here? Clearly since it wasn't money, was it the shame or indignation of being excluded from something they were always expected by the community to be present at? She was obviously an eccentric, and one that Chloe had already firmly made up her mind would be nowhere near their wedding.

"Well, that's very kind of you and thank you for coming but I think we'll be fine as it is."

Margaret sat back in her chair, then looked around the foyer as though following an invisible butterfly.

"I wouldn't normally have done this. But you see, this time we can feel, all of us, that it's very strong. Not good at all."

"What is?" asked Chloe.

"It's when there's a sadness. Or an unspoken lie. Or something not right. It ignites it, you see. Feeds it, I suppose you might say. Makes it strong enough to do mischief. And we can't have that, now. Not on your wedding day. Or indeed in your married life ahead." She leant forward. "And very bad indeed for the church and the hotel."

Chloe was properly annoyed now. "I can assure you whatever the 'it' is you're talking about will have nothing to feed off on what's going to be the happiest and most glorious day filled with love and celebration. But thank you again for coming. And please pass on my gratitude to your colleagues for their concern."

She stood up and left without shaking hands and went to join her friends outside as the sound of a cork being popped preceded howls of laughter.

Margaret watched her go. A young waitress approached with a pot of tea, two cups on saucers and a plate of expensive-looking cakes. She placed them gently on the table.

"She's gone I'm afraid, dear. Wouldn't have it."

"Oh, I'm so sorry, Margaret. Please at least eat the cakes. Tommy made them specially when he heard you might be coming."

Margaret smiled and, opening her bag, loaded the four cakes into its depths. "I'll just take them with me. Tell him thank you. And send your mother my best."

The girl beamed and returned to the kitchen.

Margaret looked around again and slowly, sadly, shook her head.

* * *

Stan the horse was a handsome beast as promised, if not perhaps the youngest, and as Chloe was helped up into the carriage by her teary father the beast stood firm, merely flicking a fly off with his tail.

The weather was fine as predicted though low, grey clouds had appeared on the horizon, only beginning to peek above the mountain tops.

Chloe's father had already attempted to make friends with the horse and cart owner, George, in the embarrassing way fathers do, and kept shouting unheard and unacknowledged encouragement to the back of his head as they slowly clopped up the dirt road.

Just as they rounded the first curve in the road George bellowed "whoah" and shook the reins, bringing Stan to a stop.

Margaret was standing on the grass verge at the side of the road. George waved at her, but Chloe looked at the woman with horror.

She approached the carriage.

"What do you want?" shouted Chloe.

"Who is this?" said her equally disquieted father.

"Please, Chloe. Reconsider. There's still time. I can walk ahead."

Chloe felt tears welling. This woman was ruining everything. She turned her face away. "Tell her to go away, Dad. Please."

Her father stood up in the carriage, making it sway a little. "You heard my daughter. Now off you go." He sat back down again. "Please carry on, George."

The driver glanced back at them, then turned to Margaret. He gave another limp wave, shook the reins and carried on. Chloe turned her head once to look back and watched as the woman walked away, slowly downhill.

As they carried on, Chloe dodged all the questions, assuring her curious father it was nothing, and collected herself by fussing with her bouquet and flattening her veil. They travelled on in silence.

Stan stopped suddenly. They were still some distance from the church. They could only just see the edge of the dry-stone wall that enclosed the grounds a few hundred metres above them.

George shook the reins again. “Come on, boy.” He made a clicking noise with his lips.

Stan’s old head was suddenly erect. He let out a whinny and staggered slightly as he stamped his two front feet.

“What’s up George?” asked Chloe’s father.

George didn’t reply and shook the reins again. This time the horse attempted to rear up on its elderly legs and stumbled back, pushing the carriage a few feet downhill behind it.

George jumped off and grabbed the animal’s bridle.

“Calm down, boy. Shhhh. Calm down.”

But there was no calming Stan. His eyes rolled and he tried his best to break free of the shaft, whinnying and now baring his yellow teeth.

George gestured at his passengers. “Get out. Now! I’m not sure what’s got into him. Just get down.”

Chloe’s father grabbed her by the waist and hurriedly helped her down, making sure her dress didn’t touch too much of the dusty road.

“Oh Dad!” she wailed.

"It's alright. It'll be alright."

Horse and owner were wrestling, until George made a decision and uncoupled the troubled animal from his harness and the cart. The moment he was free the horse reared up, then turned and galloped off downhill, leaving behind the tipped carriage and three stranded people staring in horror at his retreat.

George held his face in his hands. "I don't know what to say. This has never happened before."

"Will I run up and get help?" said Chloe's father.

Chloe grabbed his arm. "No! No, Dad, it's ok. Let's just walk. We're so nearly there." She was holding back tears. "It'll just be a hilarious story. People will laugh."

Her father looked at her with pride and offered up his arm. She took it gratefully, lifted her skirts and threw a look at the distraught George. Father and daughter made their way uphill on foot towards the waiting congregation.

* * *

"Here they come!" Ben's ushers looked confused at the sight of the bride and her father walking through the gates, instead of arriving as planned in the pretty carriage. They organised themselves and opened the door.

"Tell the violinist to start."

A signal was made, and music began, prompting the waiting guests to rise to their feet at the hand gesture of the celebrant.

Chloe was beautiful. Her father beamed as they slowly walked down the short aisle, now bedecked as planned with the brightest of blooms and prettiest of ribbons, and they passed row after row of admiring glances and eyes dabbed at with hankies. Ben waited as rehearsed until the very last minute to turn and look at his bride.

She smiled widely at him from under the veil. Her father let her arm go, stepped back and dabbed at his own eyes.

It would all be ok, Ben thought. Look how lovely she is. If passions for other women aroused him, as they already did and he knew they would continue to, he could be discreet. She would never know. What would be the harm? He could make this work.

They turned to face the celebrant and with dignity and grace they took their vows and became man and wife.

The end had come, the readings, the song, the signing of papers was complete, and now Ben was the one taking the arm of this beautiful woman as they turned to walk out of the church and begin the celebrations.

All the familiar faces were wreathed in smiles, and Ben returned every one of them.

And then his glance caught sight of a solitary figure by the door. On a bench against the wall.

It was hooded, head down, hands clasped in respect. Chloe was looking to the left and right, but Ben was fixed on this person. This yet-to-be identified guest.

Slowly the head was lifted. From beneath the hood a pointed chin began to emerge, sliced across by a mouth too wide for its face, and as Ben stared a long black tongue, the length of a snake, slithered out and lasciviously licked a pair of cracked lips. Neither of the cheery ushers standing on each side of the door seemed to notice. And as the couple moved through the doorway Ben remained transfixed by this horror whose eyes were hidden, but were undoubtedly staring back at him from beneath its hood.

Slowly, its arm lifted and a clawed and bony finger, tipped with blackened talons, raised up and pointed at the groom. The shoulders of the creature started shaking. Shaking with a silent laughter that made Ben grateful he couldn't hear.

* * *

Graham Connolly looked out of the French windows and saw Stan galloping faster than he had ever seen him move on the path behind the west side of the walled garden that led to the stable.

Connolly closed his eyes and took a long, deep breath. Dear God. He guessed what that meant. Was there time for damage limitation?

He straightened his tie, cuffs and jacket and walked slowly to the dining room.

It looked magnificent. What, he wondered, would a little respect for tradition and £250 extra have bought in this array of opulence?

He turned and left the room.

From inside the three-tiered cake a scratching noise began as the rat nestled within began to gnaw its journey to the light.

The pictures of the bride and groom as children and youngsters in love, pinned on an easel by the cake, had already started to change into obscenities. Ben performing with his conquests. Chloe, naked, watching on in unspeakable pain.

The iPad on the best man's seat had rewritten its speech, with words and stories too grotesque to be read, far less be spoken aloud. The champagne had turned to vinegar and maggots squirmed beneath the smoked salmon on the canapés.

The darkened sky outside began to deliver its threatened rain, light at first but growing heavier with every minute.

A few miles away, Margaret and her two exhausted companions decided it was hopeless. Time to stop their complex task and have a cup of tea.

Sheila shut the book she was holding and blew out the candles. “Too strong this time, Margaret. Way too strong.”

“We tried, Emily. We really did.”

They nodded sadly and decided it was time for a biscuit.

What Bones Remember

Buhlebethu Sukoluhle Mpofu

The night they sealed away the Bone Witch, the fog ran red.

ELINA'S GRANDMOTHER had told her this story a hundred times before she died, each telling different yet the same. How the village's children had started disappearing first, their small bones found weeks later arranged in complicated patterns in the deep woods. How the dead began to walk, not as mindless creatures but as terrible puppets with too-bright eyes and voices that spoke of things no living person should know. How Yaga, once the village's most respected healer, had transformed from protector to monster, her power growing until she could command armies of the dead with a single gesture.

"But why?" young Elina had always asked, and her grandmother's face would tighten, the scar along her throat gleaming silver in the firelight. The scar that all the women in their family bore was a mark that appeared on their sixteenth birthday like a brand from within.

"Power," she would say, "is like hunger. The more you feed it, the more it wants." Then she would touch her scar, a gesture Elina's mother Raina made too, though neither would ever explain its meaning. The last time Elina's grandmother told the story, the night before she died, she had said something different. Her eyes had been fever-bright, her words urgent. "She is still there, in the circle. Waiting. The stones hold her, but the stones crack. Blood calls to blood, and power to power." She had gripped Elina's wrist with surprising strength. "Promise me you will stay away when the calling comes. Promise me you will not answer."

But Elina had not promised. And her grandmother had died that night, her last breath carrying a word that made the candles flicker: "Yaga."

Ten years later, Elina traced her fingers over the worn carvings in her mother's grimoire, remembering. The candlelight cast strange shadows across the ancient pages, making the ink appear to writhe and shift. Years ago, she had memorised every page of this book, helping her mother with simple healing spells and protective charms. But tonight, the book had fallen open to a page she had never seen before, the parchment darker and older than the rest.

The writing was different here – not her mother's neat hand or her grandmother's flowing script, but something older, the letters sharp and angular like broken bones. Diagrams showed human figures with their skin peeled back, revealing intricate patterns of muscle and sinew. Notes in the margins spoke of death, resurrection, and power drawn from marrow and bone. One word stood out clearly, repeated like a chant: Yaga.

"You should not be reading that."

Elina slammed the book shut, her heart hammering. Her mother, Raina, stood in the doorway, her face drawn with the same worry Elina remembered from her grandmother's tales. The lines around her eyes seemed more profound than usual, and her ordinarily steady hands trembled as she gripped the doorframe.

"I want to understand," Elina said, lifting her chin. "Why do they call us witches behind our backs? Why do you pretend we are nothing more than herbalists when we both know there is more to our power?"

The memory of last week's incident hung between them unspoken. How a young Thomas, barely six, had fallen from the mill roof and stopped breathing. How his mother had screamed and screamed until the sound drew half the village. Elina had pushed through the crowd, drawn by something she could not name, and placed her hands on his chest.

She had felt something answer, then – a pulse of power that had nothing to do with the herbs and poultices her mother had taught her to use. For a moment, she had seen Thomas balanced on a threshold, his small spirit wavering between here and elsewhere. She had reached out and pulled him back, but not before glimpsing what lay beyond – a vast darkness filled with hungry eyes and reaching hands. Not before feeling something in that darkness notice her in return. The boy gasped and opened his eyes, but the village's gratitude was tinged with fear. When they thought she could not hear, they whispered about how no one should have such power over death, how it was not natural, and how Yaga had started the same way.

Raina crossed the room and took the grimoire, her fingers brushing against Elina's as she did. A spark of energy passed between them, making them both flinch. "Because some kinds of power come with too high a price." She tucked the book into her apron pocket. "Yaga learned that too late. She was like us once – a healer, a protector. But she wanted more. She thought she could control death itself."

"What happened to her?" Though Elina knew the story, she had never heard it from her mother's lips. Had never dared to ask about the scar they would share.

"The village elders sealed her away, but not before—" Raina stopped, her hand going to her throat where the thin scar traced its way down to her collarbone. The same scar Elina's grandmother had borne, the same scar that would mark Elina's own throat on her sixteenth birthday. "Promise me you will stay away from the stone circle, Elina. Some doors should not be opened."

"But what if I need to know?" Elina pressed. "What if the power is already in me? Last week, with Thomas—"

"That was different," Raina snapped. "That was healing. What Yaga did... what she became..." She shuddered. "The power to heal and corrupt come from the same source, child. The difference lies in how far you are willing to reach and what price you will pay."

That night, as the fog rolled in thick enough to blot out the stars, Elina entered the forest. The trees seemed to lean away from her path, their branches creaking in the stillness. Shadows moved between the trunks, and more than once, she thought she saw pale faces peering from behind the bark, gone when she looked directly at them. The stone circle lay behind a thicket of thorns which had not been there that morning. The brambles tore at Elina's dress and scratched her hands as she forced her way through, drawing tiny beads of blood that seemed to sink into the hungry earth. Each drop made the ground pulse with a sickly light, like a heart beating beneath the soil.

The stones themselves were ancient, half-buried in earth but still standing. Nine of them, arranged in a perfect circle, each carved with runes that pulsed with a faint, unholy light. Elina recognised some from her mother's grimoire – symbols for binding, sealing, and holding back what should not be freed. But others were stranger, older. Their meanings lost to time.

As she stepped into the circle, the air grew thick and heavy, tasting of copper and rot. The fog swirled around Elina's ankles like hungry tongues and she could have sworn she heard whispers in a language too old for any human speech to utter.

Something gleamed at the circle's centre – a delicate and translucent bone pulsing with its inner light. It called her with a voice that bypassed her ears and spoke directly to her blood. She had been looking for this all her life, though she had not known it until now. The bone sang to her of power – not the gentle healing magic Elina sometimes felt when helping her mother, but something more profound. Older. It promised answers to questions she had not even known to ask. About why her family's women bore the same scar, generation after generation. About why the villagers came to them for healing but crossed themselves when they passed. Why, sometimes, when she touched a dying thing, she could feel the moment when life became death, and she could sense the threshold between worlds.

Elina's hand trembled as she reached for it. The moment her fingers closed around the bone, power surged through her body – ancient, hungry, and absolute. It felt like being cut open from the inside, like something was trying to hollow her out to make room for itself. Like death was trying to wear her skin. The bone burned cold in her palm before rising of its own accord, floating upward to her neck, where it pressed against her throat and began to sink into her flesh, forming a macabre pendant. "Foolish child." The voice was everywhere and nowhere, a whisper that spoke of grave dirt and forgotten things. "You have opened what was sealed. You have claimed what was never meant to be yours." The power burned through her veins like ice, and Elina screamed. But the fog swallowed the sound until it was lost in the hungry dark. When she opened her eyes again, she was no longer alone in her mind. Something old, patient, and terribly aware had awakened, and it wore her grandmother's scar around its throat. In the village below, the long-dead stirred in their graves, remembering what it was to hunger. And in the darkness behind Elina's eyes, Yaga began to smile.

The changes came in whispers at first. Dreams plagued Elina's sleep – memories that were not hers, of power that turned healing into corruption, life into death. She saw through Yaga's eyes as villages burned, as armies of the dead marched across fields that withered at their touch. She felt the intoxication of such power, the way it had transformed Yaga from healer to horror. Worse, she felt how right it had seemed, how natural the progression from preserving life to commanding death.

"They never understood," Yaga's voice whispered in her mind. "The dead are more faithful than the living. They do not question. They do not betray. They simply serve."

Elina would wake to find dirt under her fingernails, her feet muddy from walking in her sleep. Her bed sheets were stained with earth and something darker, and she tried not to examine them too closely. Sometimes, she found herself in the graveyard at dawn, unsure how she had gotten there, her hands raw from digging. The dead called to her now, their bones singing beneath the earth. They remembered Yaga, remembered how she had pulled them from their rest to serve her will. Now they stirred again, reaching through soil and stone toward her presence. She could feel them all – every corpse, every skeleton, every fragment of bone in the village grounds. They whispered their names to her, begged to be awakened, to serve once more.

Young Thomas had also been changed by his brush with death. Since the day Elina had pulled him back from the threshold, he sensed things others could not. He would stare at shadows where no shadows should be, his eyes tracking invisible movements. Sometimes, he would speak in a voice that was too old for his years, describing things no child should know.

"The dead lady says you are changing," he told Elina one day, his small face serious. "She says you are becoming like her. But different, too. Stronger." When Elina asked which dead lady, he pointed to empty air and said, "The one with the bone crown. The one who wears your face in the other world."

Her mother noticed the changes first. Raina watched with growing horror as dark veins spread beneath Elina's skin, pulsing with a sickly green light. Early, the scar that should have marked Elina's sixteenth birthday appeared, carved from within by unseen hands. It wept black blood that moved of its own accord. "Fight it," Raina whispered, pressing sachets of protective herbs into Elina's hands. The herbs blackened and crumbled at her touch. "You are stronger than she is. You have to be."

But Elina was not sure who 'she' was anymore. When she looked in mirrors, her reflection showed two faces superimposed – her own and another's, beautiful and terrible, with eyes that held centuries of hunger. Her hair had begun to streak with white, and her teeth ached as if trying to reshape themselves into something sharper.

A sense of profound dread settled over the village. Fear did not begin to describe it. It was deeper – older – a kind of terror born from an instinct too primal to be understood. The villagers pressed themselves into their homes, hearts thundering in their chests, bodies trembling with a cold sweat. Livestock began to die mysteriously, their bodies twisted as if they had tried to reshape themselves before death. Gardens withered overnight, the earth turning black and corrupt. Children woke screaming about fingers tapping at their windows, about dead relatives calling their names, about a woman with white-streaked hair and burning eyes who visited their dreams and offered them power. The villagers felt the presence of something *other* that did not belong, and they knew, without being told, that this was not the kind of fear they could outrun.

The first to rise was old Marek, who had died these two months. He pulled himself up from the grave like a marionette with knotted strings, skin stretched taut over stricken bone. Yaga's power – now also Elina's – drew him from his rest, gaping mouth wailing a wordless scream. More came – men, women, children, their bodies writhing in ways the living were never meant to.

The dead did not simply rise; they were transformed. Birds flying over the village suddenly had their wings twisted and broken, plummeting from the sky as they fell. Feathers and bone fragments rained down upon the ground below. Horses dragged themselves on shattered legs, their bodies contorted into impossible shapes. Even the smallest creatures were not spared – mice and rats with exposed bones still scurrying, cats with rotting flesh still stalking their prey.

To the villagers, Elina had become nothing but a living curse, a walking reminder of the Bone Witch's dark reign. They discussed her in scared voices, considering what should be done. Some said she should be cast out or executed, that just by existing, she was a threat to all of them. Others were wary, having no desire to incur a wrath that would outstrip even the severity of their punishment.

And so, the villagers did nothing, paralysed by fear and uncertainty. They avoided her when they could, their gazes dropping as she walked by, their bodies stiff with the effort it took to suppress their trembling. To speak to her felt like inviting doom. To touch her was unthinkable.

Elina began to lose time. She would find herself in strange places, surrounded by evidence of things she could not remember doing. Once, she woke in old Martha's cottage to see the dead woman teaching her how to read the future in scattered bones. Another time, she became aware in the church that the holy water was boiling in its font, and Latin prayers were reversed and reformed into necromantic chants. The bone fused to her neck grew warmer and hungrier. At times, it pulsed beneath her skin, sinking deeper before emerging elsewhere on her body, reshaping her from the inside out. Her teeth fell out one night and were replaced by sharper ones. Her fingers lengthened, joints appearing like new branches growing on a dead tree.

"Beautiful." Yaga spoke in hushed tones as Elina examined her changing reflection. "We are becoming what we were always meant to be. A perfect fusion of death and life, of ending and beginning."

The dead themselves began to change as well. The first risings had been simple reanimations, but now they showed terrible creativity. Old Marek's body sprouted new limbs made of grave moss and bone. Martha's form became a twisted sinew lattice housing a poisonous fungi garden. The dead animals merged into chimeric forms that defied natural law.

But what happened to Sara, Elina's childhood friend, marked the point of no return. Sara had been dead for three years, taken by fever, and Elina had thought her grief long settled. Then, one night, Sara stepped out of the shadows in Elina's room, her body a masterwork of death's artistry. Fungal blooms sprouted from her eye sockets, spreading patterns like delicate lace across her skin. Her bones had reformed into spiral patterns visible beneath translucent flesh, and when she moved, it was with a dancer's terrible grace.

"We have missed you, Elina," Sara said, but it was not only Sara's voice. Other voices spoke with her, a chorus of the dead. "We have been waiting for someone like you. Someone who understands that death is not an ending, but a transformation."

Elina's mother found them at dawn, surrounded by a court of the dead. Sara was braiding Elina's hair with grave flowers and bones, whispering secrets of the tomb, while other corpses danced in slow circles around them. Raina's scream of horror broke the scene, sending the dead skittering back to their graves – all except Sara, who smiled with too-sharp teeth before melting into the shadows.

"What have you done?" Raina whispered, her hand at her throat where her scar pulsed in sympathy with her daughter's. "What have you become?"

But Elina did not have an answer. She was not sure there was an 'I' anymore to become anything. She was a vessel for something older that remembered when the boundary between life and death was more permeable, when power flowed across that threshold.

The dead brought her gifts now – secret things they had taken to their graves, forgotten magics, and ancient knowledge. They taught her how to read the language of decay and reshape death into new lifeforms. Under their tutelage, guided by Yaga's whisperings, she learned to craft beauty from corruption and to find power in putrefaction.

"Your mother's teachings are half-measures," Yaga told her as they worked. "She heals the body but ignores the soul. We understand deeper truths. Life and death are clay in our hands, waiting to be reshaped."

The village became a gallery of their artistry. Beautiful, terrible things bloomed in the shadows. The dead rose and fell like tides, each resurrection more elaborate than the last. The living walked carefully, knowing they were no longer their home's dominant species.

But power, as Elina's grandmother had warned, was like hunger. And hunger, given time, consumes everything – even the one who feeds it. As Elina felt herself slipping further into Yaga's embrace, a small part of her – the part that still remembered healing Thomas, still loved her mother, still grieved for Sara – knew that soon there would be no turning back. Raina found her in the graveyard that night, surrounded by her court of the dead. Raina carried the grimoire in her hands, her scar blazing with silver light. "There is still time," she said. "The choice is not made until you let it be made."

But Yaga's laughter echoed in Elina's mind. "Choice? There was never any choice, child. This power is your birthright. Look at your mother – she bears our mark but cowers from her true nature. Will you be as weak?"

The dead stirred restlessly around them. Sara's skeletal hand rested on Elina's shoulder, her touch both comforting and terrible. Through the fog, more shapes approached – every corpse in the village cemetery rising to witness this moment.

"You are wrong," Raina said, her voice steady despite her fear. "There is always a choice. Why do you think we bear these scars? They are not Yaga's mark – they are wounds from fighting her. Every generation, she tries to return. Every generation, one of us must choose to stand against her."

The truth hit Elina like a physical blow. She saw it then – her grandmother's last words, her mother's constant vigilance, the power that had always flowed through their bloodline. They were not Yaga's descendants; they were her wardens.

"Lies," Yaga hissed through Elina's mouth. "They are jealous of our power. Together, we could reshape death itself. Make it beautiful. Make it serve us."

But something had changed. In Raina's words, Elina found an anchor to her old self. She looked at her creations – the twisted dead, the corrupted earth, the darkness she had thought so beautiful – and saw them through unclouded eyes. She reached for the bone at her throat, now fused with her flesh. With a scream that shattered the headstones, she tore it free. Blood that moved like quicksilver poured from the wound.

"No!" Yaga's voice was thunder and breaking bones. The dead convulsed, their forms twisting as the witch fought to maintain control. "You cannot deny what you are!"

"I know exactly what I am," Elina said. She took the grimoire from her mother, her blood staining its pages. "I am my mother's daughter. I am a healer. And you have corrupted your last generation."

The final battle was fought in blood, bone, and memory. Elina felt Yaga trying to hollow her out, to take complete control. But each assault, she countered with memories of healing – Thomas's first breath, her mother's gentle teachings, even Sara's genuine smile before death had claimed her. The bone in her hand grew hot, trying to burrow back into her flesh. She fought through the pain, through the seductive whispers of power, through the grief of letting go of what she could have become. With her mother's help, she spoke the words her grandmother had used that every generation of their family had passed down.

Yaga's scream echoed across the world. The dead collapsed, truly lifeless once more. The fog lifted, and the moon shone down on a graveyard where nothing stirred. When it was over, Elina knelt in the cold earth, her mother's arms around her. Her throat bled from a new scar – not the mark of Yaga's power, but a badge of victory, of choice.

"It is not over," she said, touching the wound. "She will try again."

"Yes." Raina helped her daughter stand. "But that is why we are here. To make the choice, repeatedly, until the world forgets her name."

Together, they began healing what Yaga's power had corrupted. It would take time, but that was what their family did best – heal, protect, remember. And if sometimes, in her dreams, Elina still heard Yaga's whispers, she knew now how to answer. She was a witch, yes. But she had chosen what kind of witch to be.

Jackie's Dust

Alison Moore

WHEN WE SAID Jackie's name in the playground, we felt the air change. It seemed as if, by saying her name, we might be summoning her, but she never came. I used to think her story kept shifting, like when I can't keep track of my lies. She was Jackie from the women's prison, and she was Jackie from the hospital, which might have been the prison hospital or she might have been a nurse. And she was Jackie from the big house where she'd done the worst possible thing. But maybe all these things were true and these stories were like puzzle pieces, and Jackie was like a jigsaw that you had to put together. They said she got life, which ought to be a good thing because life is birth and growth and sunshine, but for Jackie it meant something bad. The way they said *life* made me think of the river, the murky depths, the unseen weeds in which your limbs might get tangled and you have to be careful not to drown. Life meant punishment, it meant long years of the walls closing in and not enough daylight. But when you'd done it, when it was over, you could get out again, and just carry on.

Jackie was seen picking mistletoe in her garden, and walking past our houses at night. Claire had seen her in the Post Office, and got told off for staring. We were supposed to stay away from her, as if she might contaminate us.

I'd heard my grandparents talking about her in the kitchen. My grandmother called her a witch. Grandad said she was just a hippy. I looked up *hippy* in the dictionary: *a young person*, it said, *who believed in peace*. It was written in the past tense, as if there'd been a purge. Anyway, Jackie was old. She was old when she died and I couldn't even imagine her young. They *had long hair*, said the dictionary, *and wore brightly coloured clothes and beads*. She did have long hair, even though she was old – too old, said my grandmother, to have such long hair hanging loose – but her clothes were black until the day she died. I'd heard them referred to as widow's weeds, as if they'd grown out of her body, out of her grieving, out of the darkness inside her. She never went to church, and even though I hated church, I knew you had to go.

I didn't remember her wearing beads or not wearing beads, but even my grandmother wore pearl beads, and I had a string of plastic beads I'd not yet worn. I wondered if wearing them would turn me into a hippy, but I knew from the way my grandad had said it, it wasn't something good. Perhaps the beads could corrupt me, the way the ring corrupted Gollum, who hated it and loved it and could not get rid of it. I lifted the lid of my jewellery box and wondered when I might wear them.

They *often lived in groups and took drugs*. A family, I supposed, was a group, but Jackie died alone. I asked my grandmother if Jackie believed in peace, and she shook her head of short hair and said, without even looking at me, "You know as well as I do what happened to those children," but I didn't, not really. We all told each other the stories we knew, and added a little bit too, so we could see it more clearly. Grandad said that Jackie didn't believe in anything but getting out of her mind. And *self-expression*, he added, as if it meant something nasty. I watched my grandmother taking her pills and asked, "Are they drugs?"

"They're for my heart," she said. "They're to make my heart better."

Jackie, I thought, must have had a bad heart.

When Jackie died, they burnt her. *Ashes to ashes, dust to dust.* If I came home from school with a new story about what Jackie had done, my grandmother said not to think about her, she was dust now.

I left primary school that summer. On the last day of term, I walked home as usual with Claire. We went slowly, and stopped on the bridge to watch the river flowing under our feet. The brown water was high and slow-moving. It looked peaceful but it was full of life. There were fish in there, and frogs, even if we couldn't see them. There were frogs in the long grass too, where you could catch them. There were newts and grass snakes, small enough to put in your pocket, and, if you were lucky, you might see a water rat going into the water to hide.

Where the river passed Jackie's house, there was a willow tree. In the summer, the cascade of leafy branches looked like long, green hair; in the winter, they were more like bony fingers trailing in the cold water or scratching at the ice. When the tree was pollarded, it looked brutal, but it had grown back stronger than ever.

Claire wasn't allowed to go down to the river, but she was eyeing the bright yellow ragwort and the pink and purple foxgloves growing all along the bank when she said, "We should pick some flowers."

"We should go swimming," I said, peering down, trying to see something moving. There were parasites in the water, which could get inside you and make you diseased.

"Maybe your dad will take us to the pool," said Claire, but we both knew he wouldn't. He'd be working, or else with his new girlfriend, who I'd never seen and knew little about. She was from out of town, from some place I'd never heard of. She was less real to me than Jackie was.

Claire reached down to pick a daisy that was growing between the slabs, pulling it out by the roots, and we dawdled home.

The summer seemed like a giant doorway: on one side was my primary school, full of bowl cuts and knee socks and thumb pots, and on the other side was secondary school. I wasn't sure what to expect. I supposed there'd be a lot of work and things I didn't understand, and children who were bigger than me, bitching and bullying. But it didn't seem real. The summer was only just starting, and I couldn't imagine its end.

All summer, I wore my swimsuit under my shorts, in case we went swimming. It was *baking*, we said, it was *stifling*, but I was the only one who wanted to jump in the river. You had to know where the weeds were, though, and there were rocks on which you could crack your head open. I didn't want to go there alone.

I don't remember who suggested walking to Jackie's house, but it was me who said we should go inside.

"We aren't allowed," said Claire.

"No one will know," I told her. Except Jackie, of course.

The house was set back from the road and partially obscured by the overgrown trees in the front garden, and by the ivy that clung to the house itself. The windows, peering through the ivy, looked black. It was big enough for a family, but now we just called it Jackie's house and didn't think about the people who had lived there before. We called it Jackie's house even though Jackie was no longer there, or she was there in the same way a deep, dark hole is there and you have to be careful.

I set off down the driveway and Claire followed, worrying aloud about what might happen to us if we were caught. "I want to see the altar," she said.

"What altar?" I asked. "Who says there's an altar?"

Claire shrugged. "Everyone says so. For sacrifices." We'd find pentagrams drawn on the floor, she said. People used to hear chanting.

“What were they chanting?” I asked. I was thinking of the playground, the chanted taunts at breaktime.

“Mantras,” she replied, uncertainly. “Mantras to summon the spirits.”

I knew about mantras. I had heard my grandmother’s mantra, when she did yoga in the spare room in her turquoise tracksuit. The Om was supposed to be the primordial sound of the universe, reverberating through her body and connecting her with all living things or with divine consciousness, but my grandmother’s Om was perfunctory and self-conscious, the sound of hesitation before speaking, barely audible through a closed door.

I told Claire about my grandmother’s mantra. “I think Om’s all right,” she said. “I don’t think it’s one of the bad ones.”

“What are the bad ones?” I asked, but Claire didn’t know.

The air was thick with heat and when we reached the shadow of the house I pressed myself into the cool stone. Claire stood on the front step, looking up at the door’s peeling face, as if we had come for our tea. Someone had taken the house number off, leaving little holes behind. The house had once had a name as well; I didn’t remember what it was. The letterbox said *Welcome* and Claire tried to push her fingers through but it must have been sealed to stop the hate mail and worse getting in.

"Ring the bell," I said, and she stabbed at the doorbell with her pointing finger, quickly as if it might hurt her, as if she might get a shock, and then did it again. If it worked, we couldn't hear it. She twisted the door handle.

"Why's it locked," she asked, "when there's nobody living here?"

I guessed it was to keep the squatters out, and kids, and anyone else who might be drawn to this place.

"Why don't they just sell it?" she asked then, as if it were an ordinary house, as if someone might want to live there, as if Jackie would have nothing to say about that.

I followed the thinning strip of shade along the front wall of the house. When I reached the corner, I looked back at Claire, who was still standing on the front step, as if someone might yet let us in. I turned the corner and heard her running after me; I heard the shifting of the gravel, heard her calling my name. When she came around the corner, she would see my bare legs slithering through the gap in the sash window, the black soles of my shoes.

The gap was only just big enough, like a lukewarm invitation. My shins scraped against the frame, and I fell awkwardly onto the hard floor. I picked myself up, took a deep breath. The air was nasty, like nothing you'd want in your lungs. The house smelt of damp and rot.

"Which room is this?" asked Claire, coming in behind me, landing gracefully.

There was no way of telling, except it was big. All the furniture was gone.

"The living room," I said. There was none of the warmth of the day in there. The house was as cold as stone in shadow, as cold as mud at the bottom of a lake.

"I'm going to watch TV," said Claire, miming sitting.

"What's on?" I asked.

She pointed an imaginary remote control to change the channel.

"Nothing good," she said.

I went through a doorway into the hall, and Claire called for me to wait. I imagined her having to turn off the TV, set the remote control down on an invisible coffee table and get up off the dirty old sofa before she could follow.

The hallway was huge. Nobody knew how Jackie had been able to afford this big house. She didn't work. Her children had been fathered by men who belonged to other women. Nobody knew how she brought these men to her door. She was nothing to look at, but they speculated, of course. What my grandmother called witchcraft, my grandad called womanly wiles, and my grandmother looked at him long and hard.

I was standing at the foot of the stairs, with Jackie's bedroom in mind.

My mum used to play a game. At bedtime, when it was time for me to go upstairs, she would reach through the banisters to grab at my ankles as I ran up. I hated this ritual at the time; those reaching, grabbing hands had terrified me.

Now, in Jackie's house, I hesitated on the bottom step before climbing slowly up. I was halfway to the top when something touched my leg. It was something cold and barely there, like the shadows of Jackie's fingers, and I waited for them to wrap themselves around my ankle, holding me there. I couldn't speak, and what would I have said to her anyway? I heard the creak of the stairs below me and Claire went by, breaking the spell. Our shadows swam along the wall, over the faded paper and the picture-hook holes, as we climbed towards the landing.

The upstairs was even danker, as if we hadn't been climbing at all but going down into a hole. Claire did cartwheels along the landing and ended up at the bathroom, which was gross, she said, going in. In front of me was a room that had once been a bedroom, judging by the remnants of furniture: a headboard without a bed, a chest without drawers. The room was a disgrace. There were stains on the walls and in the uncarpeted corners. I went to the window and looked out. There was the willow tree, and, beyond it, the river. The water was lower now, but still deep enough. It looked calm but I knew it was not, beneath the surface.

I heard the door close behind me, and crossed the room to find that the handle wouldn't turn. I said quietly, "Is that you?" but she didn't reply. There was no lock, but still the handle wouldn't turn. It was like the letterbox, stuck fast so nothing bad could get through. "Are you there?" I asked. I remembered waking in the dark when I was little, wanting my mum. When I called for her, it was my dad who came, to tell me my mum wasn't there. *Remember?* he said. *Now go to sleep.*

I tried the handle again and it turned; I opened the door and there was Claire, her smug face looming in from the hallway. "Were you scared?" she asked, gawping at the room from the doorway, disappointed by the empty walls, the bare floor. "Did you think it was Jackie? Did you think she was coming to get you?"

I told her I wasn't scared. Her eyes swam over my face, trying and failing to read me.

"Let's go down to the river," I said. "Let's go swimming," but Claire shook her head.

"There's nothing good here," she said, withdrawing from the doorway. "Let's go."

We went from the gloom of the landing, down the shadow-streaked stairway towards the cold light of the living room. The gap in the window looked even meaner than before.

Later, I found red marks on my skin, like whip-thin burns, where all that nothingness had tried to hold onto my legs as I pulled them outside, as Claire pulled me away.

When my dad saw the marks on my legs, he was worried I'd been seeing my mum – he checked the palms of my hands, my back, my belly.

"I wouldn't," I told him.

"Good," he said. "Don't."

He made me tell him where I'd been, and he made me promise, to swear on my life, not to go there again. I didn't go back for weeks.

I met Dad's girlfriend on a Sunday. She came round for lunch, arriving in a little car, wearing a nice dress. She smiled at me and said, *Aren't you pretty* and *You're bigger than I expected*. Her name was Amanda. She was nothing like I thought she'd be. She was nothing like my mum.

She took careful little bites, keeping her lips away from the fork, keeping her pink lipstick intact, and said, "When does she go back to school?"

"Not for weeks yet," said Dad.

"It's a long time," said Amanda, poking her tines into a small piece of white chicken. "What is there for children to do around here?"

"There's the pool," said Dad.

"Claire's mum's too busy to take us," I told him.

"Just stay away from that house. And stop playing with your food."

"Before you know it," said Amanda, "you'll be in big school." She smiled at me like she was promising something nice. I looked away; I went back to my mash.

It was Claire who told me they were pulling down Jackie's house. "Where will she go?" I asked, as if Jackie might need to move in with family or friends. But she had to go *somewhere*. "She'll be furious."

I thought Claire might suggest going to see the demolition site, but she didn't. I wanted to see it, even though, at the same time, I really didn't. I went alone.

It was the end of the summer, the final weekend of the holidays. I was still in my swimsuit and shorts but I could feel the chill in the air. You could tell autumn was just around the corner.

I took a cold chicken leg from the fridge and ate it on my way to Jackie's house. It was a big drumstick: I felt less like a kid with a lollipop than a caveman with a club. I was still gnawing at the bone when I got there. I stood on the boundary of the property as if at a cliff edge. *That's close enough*, my dad would have said.

I was shocked by the speed with which they'd worked, the thoroughness of the demolition. I imagined a wrecking ball slamming into the side of the house, the walls crumpling, crashing down. It was strange to see space where the house had been – where the stairs were, where the bedrooms were – and only rubble in the place where it had stood. I imagined all the nasty air escaping, mixing with the fresh air outside. I thought about Jackie and what she might do now.

I was starting to feel bad. There was so much dusty air in my lungs, so much old meat in my stomach. I felt fingers wrapping around my innards.

Someone was calling my name and I turned. Amanda was standing there, next to her little car. She was wearing a floaty dress, floral gauze that lifted in the breeze. She looked like an advert for something nice. "I was just on my way to your dad's house," she said. "What are you up to?"

I shrugged. "Nothing." I could feel shadows in my heart.

"You don't want to waste a lovely day like this." She looked up at the blue of the sky through her Jackie O sunglasses. "Listen," she said, "I'm early. I don't think your dad will have finished his work yet. Let's do something fun together, then I'll take you home." She was holding the passenger door open for me. I wondered what she thought was fun. I walked to the car and got in.

Amanda walked around to the driver's seat and we strapped ourselves in. She looked at me, and then at the bone, which I was still holding – a nasty old chicken bone in her lovely clean fresh-pine-scented car. There was nowhere to put it. She made a face and looked for a tissue. I knew she didn't like me, but she wanted to take my mum's place, to become Stepmother. "What do you want to do?" she asked.

"I want to go swimming," I said. My indigestion had begun to settle down.

"All right," she said, looking pleased with herself, "I'll take you to the pool."

No, I said, there'd be too many people at the pool. The river was better. I knew the perfect spot. I told her about the willow tree, and the flowers, and the frogs.

"That sounds lovely," she said, "except for the frogs. Unless we find a prince." She smiled, as if we really might, as if she would like that.

There were concrete steps leading from the bridge down to the river.

"It would be nice down here," said Amanda, as the long grass engulfed her white cotton shoes, "if someone would just mow it, and pull up all these weeds." My hand skimmed the heads of the waist-high ragwort and foxgloves as we walked along, and Amanda watched warily as if she could see the poison coming off them.

Rain had filled the river up. There was no bank now; you could not see the edge, just the water lapping at the long grass. We walked along as far as the willow tree, which stood at the end of Jackie's back garden. There was no fence, no boundary marker; it was hard to see where her land started and ended.

"Are we allowed to be here?" asked Amanda, and then, seeing the demolition site, she said, "Well, I guess no one's going to complain!" She stared at the ruins, seeing them from the other side now. "Is that the same place?" She was trying to put it together, like a puzzle.

She turned to peer at the brown river water. "You don't want to swim in there, do you? Maybe we'll just sit on the grass and enjoy the sunshine." She looked around for a nice place to sit. "We should have brought a picnic."

There were rocks at the edge of the river and under the willow tree, but none of them were big enough to sit on. They were all fist-sized or head-sized. I squatted in the grass and lifted one up to look underneath it, looking for worms and beetles and frogs.

"Your dad's been telling me about your mum," said Amanda.

It was cold and nasty underneath.

"Your poor dad. And poor you, it must have been difficult."

I lifted the edge of another rock.

"I like your necklace," said Amanda. "It's pretty." I looked down at my yellow beads and gripped them as if she might try to take them. She took off her sunglasses and put them on me, tucking my hair back as she hooked the arms over my ears. The world grew dim and rosy. "They suit you," she said.

She started looking around again as if she expected a nice bench to materialise for her. "I wish we'd brought a picnic." She looked through her handbag as if she might find one in there: my favourite sandwiches, two nice green apples, a bottle of lemonade for me and a flask of sweet tea for her. She found nothing but a boiled sweet and gave it to me with satisfaction. "You should probably wash your hands, though, before you eat that." I put it in the pocket of my shorts for later.

"I think I'd make a good mum," she said. She waited for me to reply and then turned to squint into the distance. She took a deep breath, filling her lungs with the smell of river water. "Your dad said you don't see your mum much now, not since… Well, I don't know how much you remember. You were so young." She watched me with a sympathetic expression on her face.

I bent to lift a bigger rock.

"What are you doing?" asked Amanda.

I had to stop to tell her, "I'm chanting."

Amanda's mouth twitched, like she didn't know whether to smile.

She turned back to look at the wide-open fields beyond the river, and said to the horizon, "We should probably be going." There was some movement in the river, something breaking the surface. Amanda looked down but it was too quick for her. She went into a crouch, balancing her body above her ruined shoes. "I don't know how *anything* can survive here," she said, peering into the water, regarding her own face. She turned her head and looked at me. I was holding the rock. I was standing in the shadow of the willow tree, considering life. The bugs that had been in the darkness were squirming or scuttling in the sudden light, while the river, and everything darting and slippery within it, flowed quietly on.

Oro, Plata, Mata

Gabriella Buba

1895 Nueva Ecija, Philippines

CRIMSON AND BLACK rosary peas scattered across the banig mat, where Seberina sat under the shade of swaying coconut palms. Flies lazily circled her other wares: bundled water spinach, knobbly bittermelon, and tart calamansi piled high. But the *tok-tok* of falling beads from the man's hand was not the clink of pesos, so she did not appreciate him interrupting her hawker's call of, "Gulay! Prutas!"

Seberina looked up into the goldenly handsome and smiling face of Loreno Yumul, the youngest son of the richest sugarcane haciendero in the province.

"I begin to think you're breaking my rosaries on purpose," Seberina snapped, tacking on a belated "-po" of respect.

She was getting far too familiar with him if she was forgetting such important formalities. After all, she was a roadside hawker, past twenty-five without prospects of marriage to lift her from poverty. Most of the local men were deterred on account of the rumor her grandmother had been a mangkukulam, a jungle witch dealing in curses. And maybe her lola had gone to live up in the foothills of the Sierra Madre. And maybe she'd been good with herbs. Most albularyo were, but that didn't make someone a mangkukulam.

Loreno pouted very prettily at her. He did everything prettily. It was easy to do if one were as well-off, well-dressed, and well-educated as the Yumul sons. She ironed the lifting corner of her mouth flat.

"I need you to make me another, Manang. It's not my fault they keep breaking," the young man wheedled. He'd tried the more familiar address of 'Ate' once, but she'd retaliated with increasingly formal addresses for him. So he'd settled on manang, like she were any other hawker. As he should, because she was.

The glittering sugar dust clinging to him from the mill was probably worth more than all her produce combined.

"Dapat po— You should buy rosaries elsewhere. Why not silver? It will last you longer, Señor Yumul," Seberina demurred with reinforced formality.

"I don't want silver. I want your rosaries. Everyone knows they ward off the devil."

Seberina frowned; she didn't like such a rumor spreading about her. "Nothing special about rosary peas except their pretty colors."

And deadly poison.

Nonetheless she flicked the broken beads away, reaching into her bag for new, measuring out golden jute thread around the browned backs of her hands.

Broken beads had absorbed all the ill luck they could.

"No good reusing rotted thatching," Lola Banta would've said.

She'd normally sell one of her pre-made rosaries. But they lasted longer if she made them knowing the wearer. She strung the beads, muttering psalms for health and protection. Loreno had gone through six that month. If he wasn't breaking them as an excuse to see her... maybe there *was* ang masamang mata, the evil eye, focused on him.

Loreno squatted before her, not put out by the delay, or worried road dust would sully his fine clothes.

She eyed him suspiciously from under her eyelashes while she knotted each bead in place as if they were precious pearls, not common seeds.

* * *

She shouldn't be here. Not at night, not alone, and most definitely not alone *with* Loreno. The Yumul aviary was ill luck. Though the eccentric 'naturalist' Yumul – prone to assuming everyone a poacher and shooting first – had died decades ago, no one but family and trusted keepers entered. Currently it housed a swarm of jewel-toned songbirds Loreno's mother was often gifted.

Seberina wouldn't be here if Loreno hadn't ambushed her after a late evening mass. During the harvest, the priest offered special services so the cane workers need not neglect their souls.

She'd almost refused to go with him, the way his eyes rolled in panic, and sweat poured down his brow. But she hadn't wanted to make a scene. His lurching gait worried her.

Loreno's grip was clammy as he pulled her along by the light of a shaking lantern. "It was an accident! They shouldn't have been there. I didn't mean— you have to help me."

She had to jog to match his stride.

"Help you with what, Señor Yumul?"

"Please, Seberina!"

Her heart skipped a beat. But he wasn't making very much sense. In the distance, Seberina could see Hacienda Yumul, warmly illuminated windows outlining its sprawling wings in many architectural styles. The oldest traditional bahay na bato, to Spanish colonial, even a distant turret, the narrow black spire reaching up into the starry sky like a claw.

"I slipped. You'll see." He was suddenly grim, so unlike the golden, good-humored usual Loreno. She wished she hadn't gone along.

Then they were through the double entry to the aviary, and into the center clearing. The full moon cast the miniature jungle in silvery-blue light, making Loreno's sweat-darkened shirt seem black with blood.

"Tabi tabi po," Seberina whispered, though it wasn't duende she trespassed on.

Then she saw the bodies. Small, feathered, they littered the ground: five, ten, more. She bent. At last, Loreno released her. The songbird was still warm with life, but trembled in her hand. She took the lamp from Loreno's unresisting fingers to better see. Signs of regurgitation clumped its vivid purple and yellow breast feathers, clawed feet spasming so it'd fallen from its perch.

"Your rosary, did it break here? Did they eat the seeds?"

Loreno's hand went to his neck, like he'd just noticed it gone. He swayed, catching himself before he fell. "No, it must've broken inside. My mother brings the birds in to enjoy their singing, but some escaped their cage. I was helping the keeper… I slipped. It was an accident."

His explanation made no more sense of the situation. And she didn't like his swaying, how his hands shook and sweat poured down his face. He was ill. What if Loreno had eaten the seeds, too? But why? The birds, fine. Loreno knew better.

"I must be cursed." Loreno's voice had a terrible timbre as he fell to his knees, arms curled around his stomach. He groaned and collapsed entirely.

Seberina rushed to his side, peering into his face twisted in agony, feeling his cool, clammy skin. Was he dying because of her rosaries?

Her own stomach knotted to think what his family would do if anyone found out. They couldn't. No one could.

Clarity like calm cool waters washed over her. She wouldn't let that happen. She wouldn't be driven into the hills like her lola. She gathered the fallen birds, piling them beside Loreno.

She sensed her lola's warm guiding touch on her wrist as she wrapped her rosary around her right hand, laying it over Loreno's furrowed brow, the other on the dying songbirds.

Her lola had said that how much people believed in words gave them power. She'd made Seberina memorize the bible. It had at least convinced the priest she wasn't a witch when she'd returned from the jungle at thirteen, after her lola passed. She prayed, reciting Isaiah.

"Because you are precious in my eyes, and honored, and I love you, I give men in return for you, peoples in exchange for your life."

The struggling feathered bodies went cold and still.

Beneath her other palm, Loreno sat up gasping, tearing from her touch.

They stared at each other. Seberina at a loss to explain that really, truly, she *wasn't* a witch like they said. Better to say nothing.

Loreno moved first, catching her face in his hands. He kissed her. His breath was warm and strangely sweet, his hands gentle.

Seberina clenched her fingers, rosary peas digging into her palm. She tucked them behind her, not daring to reach for him with hands that had so recently moved a death.

Then a gasp shattered the still night air. She flinched. Loreno's mother, Doña Yumul, and her maidservant were at the aviary door.

"Like I said, Doña," the maid reported, glaring at Seberina.

The Doña all but gnashed her teeth, crying, "Walang hiya ka!" over Seberina's shamelessness and the impropriety. "Filthy Jezebel, corrupting my baby boy. I'll have you and your whole family run out of the province for this."

The haranguing continued as Loreno and Seberina were hauled to Don Yumul's study.

"Quiet. What is the meaning of this?" The Don's voice was the low rumble of the cane crusher. It silenced even the Doña.

Seberina kept her hands fisted, her eyes on the blood-red carpet her bare dusty toes sank into. She'd removed her sandals at the door but no one had offered her house slippers.

Did roadside vegetable hawkers about to be shipped to God knows where *get* house slippers? Probably not.

She waited for Loreno to speak, but the silence was thick as molasses.

"We can pay her to leave," the Doña proposed, no longer shrill, now sweetly wheedling.

Seberina almost looked up, prepared to express that for silver they'd never see her face again. For gold, she'd leave the country. But from the corner of her eye she caught sight of Loreno's face. She bit her tongue.

"Loreno Jose Maria Yumul, how long has this been going on?" the Don rumbled.

Seberina wanted to shout that nothing was going on! Loreno was just a silly boy fixated on her rosaries, addle-headed with poison.

But Loreno said nothing, and she didn't dare speak. Not when all they needed to make her disappear was declare her a witch, a jungle mangkukulam, just like her lola.

The Don sighed. "Well, no son of mine will shirk their responsibility. We've another engagement in the family. I will speak to her uncle in the morning."

Seberina felt the trap close, tight as a snare for jungle birds.

* * *

The wedding was three weeks later. It was barely enough time to read the banns. Her tito hadn't even protested the speed! She wished her lola were still alive. She would've stopped this madness.

Ill luck just kept stacking upon ill luck. Seberina should've had a year to break the engagement, since the third Yumul son had married in spring, but the Don was of a mind for quickness, not given to the superstition brothers shouldn't marry in the same year.

It was a silly superstition. Seberina tried not to let it cloud her mind; her groom was smiling at her from the altar, as golden as ever. Though her tito, in his well-darned Sunday best was practically jogging down the aisle in his haste to give her away. She hoped he'd negotiated a hefty dowry to compensate for the years she'd been in his care.

Then the illusion shattered. Loreno's eldest brother, Dulesimo, 'dropped' the ring, sending it spinning away with a flick of his thumb. While her tito scrambled under the pews after it, Seberina heard her new mother-in-law say, "It's a shame, the whiteness of the dress is quite spoilt by the bride's peasant-brown skin."

Seberina resisted the urge to hide her morena-brown hands behind the bouquet. Last night she'd gone to her lola's garden, deep in the jungle, lush and overgrown. She'd gathered pink rosary pea flowers, green taro spikes, and purple ginger blooms. It was a peasant's bouquet, maybe even a witch's bouquet.

She'd heard for years, "You'd be almost as pretty as your mother, if you weren't so brown. She had many suitors, you know." Seberina would not flinch now.

She looked between the sneering Doña, the stern-faced Don, her silent groom, and her desperate tito. She resigned herself to her fate. There would be no last-minute objection, no escape from the cage. At least she would never hawk vegetables choking on roadside dust ever again. The wedding mass itself was a blur. The gold ring, heavy and cold as a shackle.

Seberina didn't jolt back into her body until Loreno was carrying her up from the carriage, his odd gait jostling her as he took the stairs, one, two – skip – avoiding every third stair.

"We've been granted the turret suite. It's private. A gift for our marriage," he said. "But the third stairs squeak, best avoid them. We used to play up here till one of my sisters fell – that's when Ate Salvacion became bedbound. No one's used the turret since."

It was the most he'd said to her since that terrible night in the aviary. Though it was also the first time they'd been alone. At his words, she imagined she could feel the energy of that old wound and something darker. It lingered like a chill in the air, as the tower turned its focus on her, the newest Yumul. She shuddered.

Seberina closed her eyes and counted as he went, oro, plata, mata – gold, silver, death – up thirty-three steps. But what was a little more ill luck? She was already well and truly trapped.

Loreno set her upon an elegantly carved four-poster Calabasa bed.

He was on one knee before her, but Seberina didn't meet his gaze, picking at the lace of her ill-fitting, borrowed wedding gown. She was angry. With one word he could have freed them from this trap. He'd said nothing, the coward. And she couldn't object. She'd be a pariah. He'd have been another frivolous young man. Riches forgave many sins.

"Please, Seberina, we are married. Won't you look at me?" That golden sweetness was back. She tried to ignore how it gilded her name. He came from a family of sweet-talkers. She was from a family of cane workers. She knew how much blood and sweat made the crushers turn.

He held out a glittering silver tambourine rosary. "Here, like you said, something more durable than seeds, to pair with your golden wedding band. After all, mahal ko, even if it was more rushed than we might've liked… you said you loved me. And you know how I have loved you."

Seberina almost hissed, furious at how he'd twisted her words. But then, better a devout fool in love above her station, than a witch.

"Keep it for yourself," Seberina demurred. "Rosary peas are enough for me."

She wasn't about to complete the old superstition any faster. She'd put something terrible in motion transferring death out of Loreno, she'd not continue to court it. If she had gold and silver… next came death.

* * *

Still, Loreno was a patient, gentle boy, even if he was easily cowed when it came to his family. His smiles and efforts to regain her good graces were the only sweetness in Seberina's life those first six months of marriage.

Her new family disdained her as much as the tower stair hated. When the Doña and her sisters-in-law weren't ordering her about – "Since your dark face looks so much like a servant's!" – her brothers-in-law made comments about her age, older than all their wives, even Dulesimo's. How she'd no hope of giving the Don grandchildren. It explained the Don's quickness, five weddings and still none.

She could've avoided her 'family' on the vast Yumul estate, but the servants ensured she knew no peace. Her food was served almost inedible, adobo so salty and sour it made her tongue raw, fruits near turned, sweetness half-fermented. Her laundry was returned moldy and stinking, buttons missing, hems torn. Seberina repaired them herself, stealing candles from the main house, since her lamps were always dry. The servants rarely climbed to refill them.

The Don didn't interfere. She was an object lesson, and a gamble. And her husband was often away, another organized slight. Loreno was off overseeing the sugar-mill, or gone to Manila meeting buyers.

He would return with extravagant gifts of fine silk clothes and baubles the servants broke during their rare cleanings. But he never gave her silver or gold again.

She softened, to the way he let her eat off his plate, even at formal dinners, putting aside the choicest morsels for her. And even to his sweet touches in the dark. She strung new rosary peas together for his every trip, though they rarely broke when he traveled.

Then she began to grow big with child. When the Doña noticed, her food worsened. She cracked a tooth on a rock left in her rice, and chewed cloves to numb the pain. Her lamps were filled with lard instead of kerosene, the smoke and stench worsening her morning sickness.

She hated. Her new family, the smoky, unlucky tower rooms, the man who claimed to love her. If Loreno truly loved her, he wouldn't let her suffer like this.

* * *

She was six months pregnant and suffering dizzy spells the first time she failed to avoid the third stair. She'd barely touched the tread when her rosary exploded off her, crimson and black peas scattering as if they hadn't been individually knotted in place. A thorn through her heart, like a dozen staring eyes boring into her back.

Seberina clutched the banister, awaiting the worst. No prayers for protection came to mind, so instead she whispered, "Tabi tabi po."

The ill-will coiling about her ankle loosened slightly.

A scream and a crash echoed from below; from above Loreno cried, “Seberina?!”

The weight of the tower’s attention kept her rooted. She listened to his odd gait, skipping steps even as he rushed down.

“Are you okay? Why did you scream?” His face was drawn with fear.

Seberina pointed downward. It was like fighting free of jungle lianas, the kind with clinging thorns.

Loreno lifted her off the third stair. Finally, she could breathe.

They found Doña Yumul’s maidservant had fallen and struck her head. She wasn’t the same when she woke, and was sent away to recover with family.

Suddenly Seberina’s food was as good as Loreno’s. Oil for the lamps was brought to the foot of the stair, coconut and kerosene, never lard. Seberina didn’t mind cleaning and carrying her laundry down. No one but Loreno would attempt the stairs. But her sheets came back smelling of sunshine and her silks didn’t need repair.

She felt big as a carabao, and slower, but Seberina made the trek up to her lola’s garden for new rosary peas and to leave offerings in thanks for her protection. The priest had refused holy ground to a known witch. Seberina spent hours in the deep, welcoming green of the jungle, trimming back her grave, and weaving garlands of flowers. She had no fear of the jungle at night.

"I will name her Banta… Bantog if he is a boy," she promised, hoping her lola's strength would protect her child from the Yumul curse. Before she left, she took seeds and cuttings.

She planted half the rosary peas and cuttings in the hacienda's gardens. Like her lola, she buried calamansi skins and dried fish with the seeds. She strung the remaining peas into a new rosary for herself, sealing the knots with copal resin.

Seberina ate better, smiled more, grew bigger with child. Loreno was overjoyed at her improvement. Seberina tended her garden and tried not to dwell on how the focus of the tower stair was shifting, watching her like a dog awaiting scraps every time she took the stair.

She'd not slip again. She wasn't a witch. She would not deal with curses.

* * *

"Hay naku, he's darker than his mother! Little brother, you've been so often away, are you sure this one's yours?" Dulesimo's crass exclamation shattered the solemn air of the christening. The priest stopped in the middle of the reading, eyes darting between Loreno, the godparents, Dulesimo and his wife, and Don Yumul.

Seberina did not blink. She did not look at her weak-willed husband.

"Father, the blessing for my son, Bantog Loreno Consorcio Yumul?"

Silence.

Seberina picked up where he'd stopped; she'd baptize her son herself if she had to. "—Because of the grumbling of the sons of Israel and because they put the Lord to the test—"

The priest blanched, "—Saying, 'Is the Lord with us, or not?'" He went into the gospel reading twice as fast.

* * *

At the feast afterwards, she heard the whispers, saw the looks. When Don Yumul declined to hold the baby…

Seberina had to protect her son.

Mounting the stairs, after she'd settled the baby in the nursery, Seberina took three third steps. The darkness howled.

She did not weep when word came the next day that Dulesimo had fallen from his horse on the way to the mill with Loreno and broken his neck. She just strung new rosary peas for her son and husband to wear to the wake. She traded the usual crosses of polished coconut husk for mother-of-pearl.

She did not flinch when Doña Yumul wailed on the sixth and final night of the wake that it should've been Loreno who fell, before she collapsed weeping upon the coffin.

But she asked the cook to save her the blood from a white chicken butchered to feed their guests.

That night while Loreno and their son slept, Seberina smeared a drop of chicken blood on the underside of each third step.

She prayed as she climbed, "Truly, I say to you, there are some standing here who will not taste death until they see the Son of Man coming in his kingdom." She impressed all the love and ferocity she bore in her heart for her son into the endless hunger of the stairs. *Taste this little death and be sated.*

Bantog would walk soon. She had to protect her son.

On the top and final stair, Seberina stepped onto the tread and wrote Doña Yumul's name across the step. The blood soaked into the dark wood and vanished, as if lapped by hungry tongues.

In the morning Doña Yumul and her eldest son were both interred in the Yumul family crypt.

The priest said, "She'd died of a broken heart. A mother's love is a great and terrible thing."

* * *

But still the hunger of the tower stair was not satisfied.

"So many wakes. So many burials." Don Yumul's once powerful grinding voice quavered with more than age.

Dengue fever had spread like wildfire through the hacienda. He'd never fully recovered.

How the stairs had clamored for blood. Only Seberina, untouched by sickness, had spent hours simmering protective herbs, caring for the sick, praying to see her son and husband through each night. One by one Seberina's sisters-in-law had returned to their families, desperate to escape the curse chasing the Yumul family. Until Seberina alone remained to manage the hacienda. She might've moved her family out of the tower, but better to keep a hungry wolf where she could see it.

"I once had six sons, now only two," Don Yumul lamented, his lawyer and the witnesses shuffling in discomfort at so great a man, brought so low.

His remaining sons had been sent on business this week. The Don didn't wish to disclose this change to his will.

"We could have managed that bad business deal with the Chinese. And even when the red rot came and decimated the cane but then…" The old man shook his head.

Then came the Declaration of Independence in Cavite, and war.

It took every wit, wile, and scrap of witchcraft Seberina had to see her little family through the war. Bantog turned six, three days before the Americans declared the war over. All that blood, and they had only traded one colonial master for another. And Don Yumul, who'd backed the independence movement, was much the poorer in wealth and sons.

"These eyes are failing me, Seberina, would you read?" The Don beckoned.

"I, Conrado Jose Estelo Yumul, declare this to be my final will and testament – I bequeath all my personal properties, residences, and estates as such: one-quarter to each of my two sons, should they survive me, and the remainder to my grandson Bantog Loreno Consorcio Yumul, under the guardianship of his mother, Seberina Yumul, until he should come of age."

His hands shook as he signed. The witnesses stared at her. Seberina stared back.

When the business was concluded, Don Yumul was exhausted. Seberina helped him to his room. As they reached the door, he laid a frail hand over hers.

"I admit I hoped bringing you into the family might fix things. Now I see the curse will not rest until the Yumul line is dead. I hope your son at least might escape it."

"He will."

Don Yumul patted her hand. "You are a good mother, a good wife to Loreno. For that I thank you."

* * *

That night Seberina sat alone at the top of the tower. A teacup of carabao milk warmed over a lamp. Seberina reached into her bead bag and placed three un-drilled, un-broken rosary peas into the cup. A poison could be a medicine too, and tonight she must see to the root of the curse wrapped around her son's bloodline. She must see clearly to cut true. She let her potion simmer, until the clock struck midnight.

"He saw a man blind from birth. And his disciples asked him, 'Rabbi, who sinned, this man or his parents?'" She drank the milk, holding the seeds under her tongue.

She lay down, and asked the tower stair which loomed hungry and waiting, "Who sinned, this man or his parents?"

The past rolled in like a summer storm. She dreamt of the hacienda thirty-some years ago when every acre grew thick with sugarcane.

* * *

When the current Don Yumul had been a young man he'd fallen in love with a woman selling vegetables and herbs by the roadside. A beautiful woman, golden cheeked, with sharp eyes and black hair that had a hint of blueness like moonlight.

In Seberina's own memories, her mother, Laraya, never smiled so brightly. She'd died young, of a broken heart, Lola Banta had said.

The young Don had courted Laraya with silver and gold and sweet words, but Laraya chose another.

The Don lost to one of his own cane workers, a man with strong, deep-brown peasant's hands, like Seberina's. A man the Don envied, more each day, as he saw his beloved move into the workers' huts, when he'd offered her a mansion. But the hard labor and poor conditions couldn't dim Laraya's golden beauty or joy in love.

The Don had never lost before.

He spread a rumor among the overseers that Laraya's husband was organizing the workers to strike. He only thought to run him off the hacienda. If Laraya stayed, he'd win her in time. If she left, he wouldn't be tormented by her presence.

But Laraya's husband hadn't been run off. He was beaten bloody, left among the cane, his wounds gone foul before Laraya found him.

Widowed and newly pregnant, Laraya couldn't bear to burden her family. So when Don Yumul graciously offered her lodging in the unused tower rooms, Laraya accepted.

The Don's charity soured when Laraya's gratitude did not mean she'd stoop so low as to be his mistress.

The tower rooms became her prison. Only, the Don had forgotten why it was said Laraya's skin was gold and her hair spun from moonlight. She was the daughter of a powerful witch. And on the fateful day he attempted to turn Lola Banta away, she had cursed him and his whole house for his greed and his sin, before whisking her grieving daughter, and newborn Seberina, into the hills.

Her lola's prayer for the Don rang in her ears, chasing her into waking.

"Curses shall come upon you and overtake you:
Cursed shall you be in the city, and in the field.
Cursed shall be your issue, and the fruit of your ground.
Cursed shall you be when you come in, and cursed shall you be when you go out.
You shall become an object of horror, a proverb, and a byword among all the people."

* * *

She woke in her husband's arms.

Loreno held her, weeping, "Not you, mahal ko. I cannot bear that this damned curse should take you before me. Let it be on my head, as it should've been from the start."

Her body was still heavy with the past. Bowed over her, Loreno's face twisted with grief, as it had in agony in the aviary, so many years ago.

He'd loved her then, as he loved her now. He'd been as ensnared in the curse from the beginning as she had, only she'd not known it.

"Seberina? You weren't breathing! Don't move, I'll call the doctor."

"Hush, I don't need a doctor. Come with me. It's long since time we ended this." The words came slowly, as she swam back into her body, and Loreno hung on every one.

She led him to the stair.

"That which was from the beginning,

which we have heard,

which we have seen with our eyes,

which we looked upon and have touched with our hands," Severina swore to the tower stair and her lola's curse that she knew it, down to its roots.

They took every stair hand-in-hand. The seeds of their rosaries snapped free, falling down before them like tears.

"Where you go I will go, and where you lodge I
will lodge;
your people shall be my people,
and your God my God."

She squeezed Loreno's hand, vowing to the curse she hadn't been carried up and trapped against her will, that she had chosen this man and this house.

When they reached the final thirty-third stair, Seberina emptied out her beading bag, a mound of crimson and black, an offering of gratitude for protection and revenge.

"I am not my mother. I am not my grandmother, but I am of their line, and I will say *'It is finished.'*"

Together, she and Loreno tore out the bottom step.

In the morning, it was discovered Don Yumul had passed in his sleep.

After the burial, Loreno's brother confided he wanted nothing of this cursed estate, and would take his inheritance in silver and go abroad, leaving to Loreno and Seberina the house, the land, and warehouses of golden sugar.

The Witch of Withered Hill

David Barnett

I SAW A YOUNG WOMAN today, wearing a T-shirt that bore on the front the words: *We are the granddaughters of the witches they couldn't burn*. I mean, I appreciate the sentiment, of course I do. But there was no shame in getting caught, and burned (or more likely, round these parts, hanged). How could there be? It's not as if we thought we were doing anything wrong in the first place. We didn't hide or skulk or think to protect ourselves against our own communities, because one moment they were coming to us for charms to fall in love and potions to make them rich and advice on just about everything, and the next they were whispering in keen ears to have us taken away.

Some of us weren't burned, or hanged. Some of us lived to ripe old ages. Some of us… for some of us, there were other fates in store. Not pleasant ones. I'm talking about myself, of course. But what could I have expected, really, when they called me the Witch of Withered Hill?

I'll tell you all about Withered Hill in a moment. First, I expect you want to know how I'm talking to you on the one hand about my sisters being hanged long ago, and young women in T-shirts today, all at the same time. Am I immortal? Well, yes and no. Am I dead? Sort of. Am I a ghost? Not in the way you might think, but perhaps.

I am in the black eyes of a toad, crouched on a lily pad, just before it leaps. I am in a droplet of water hanging from a leaf in the bright morning, just before it falls. I am in a cloud of midges frantically weaving invisible shapes in the sunset, seconds before they disperse, gone before they accumulate together again. I am in the twitching ears of the hare, the budding acorn of the oak, the stubborn weed in the crack of a pavement, the high-pitched twittering of a swift returning to its summer home in the eaves of a groaning old house.

I once peered from the yellow eyes of a black cat on the lap of a girl who read in an old book – old by her standards, not by mine – a story called 'The April Witch', by a writer called Ray Bradbury, and I thought, yes, he has it right. He must have known witches, or been one himself. He nailed it, that way we hop and skip and jump from living thing to living thing, hitching a ride, sometimes a passive passenger, sometimes taking the reins, though only for a short while, because that's exhausting. Yes, Bradbury had it right, mostly. I never knew a witch who could do that in life, though doubtless there were some. But in death? Yes, in death, we travel.

Almost four centuries I have travelled.

I am so very, very tired.

I suppose I should tell you of my extraordinary life, and my unusual death, and the strange, hidden place that is Withered Hill, and I shall. But first I must watch my show. It's a frippery of a thing, a colourful, discordant confection, young people acting as though they are on a stage, but playing themselves. Seeking love, or sex at least, on an island, a sun-drenched island. I have seen such places, on my travels. I roamed far and wide in death much more than I did in life. I have waited impatiently in the minds of dull-witted, lowing cattle in the holds of ships bound for far-off lands, I have looked from windows through the eyes of children as planes broke through the clouds into the unsullied brilliant blue above, I once lurked within a pot-plant held on the lap of an aged woman as a train steamed across a continent.

But I always come back. Always come home. And now I must away, to watch my show, from the rheumy eyes of a dog that half-slumbers before an open fire, as its young owners crow and caw at the shenanigans on the screen. But more, anon, I promise.

* * *

I was born on the day they hanged ten women and men, nine on the moors above Lancaster, one in York. All had been found guilty, after a trial at Lancaster, of witchcraft. I daresay you know the case I'm talking about. A bad omen, or an auspicious sign, depending on how you look at it. My father believed the former, my mother was convinced it was the latter. But then, she was a witch herself. My father, a carpenter, knew of her lineage, but thought that he could make her a better person. Thought he could cure her. Sometimes through what he believed was love, sometimes through the sharp, red anger of his fists.

He went missing when I was one year old. My mother told anyone who asked that he had gone off to be with another woman three villages away. The truth was, he mouldered beneath the apple tree near our home, feeding its roots with his blood and mulch, his head stoved in with his own hammer and his heart pierced with his own chisel, after breaking my mother's jaw with a drunken punch.

We lived on a place they called Withered Hill. Not *in* Withered Hill, but on the slopes of the hill itself. Let me tell you about Withered Hill.

It sits in Lancashire, in what is still rolling, untouched countryside today. They call neighbouring Yorkshire God's Own Country, and let them, for Lancashire is the Devil's, where women die of love and coin is freely spent on drink and joy, and they have the best tunes. A hill, then, ringed at its crest with an impenetrable, thick woodland. When I was born nobody ventured through those woods, nobody dared. At the centre was a wide, fertile plateau, though only the deer and the rabbits and the birds saw it. A funny name for such an untouched paradise, Withered Hill. I've heard tell it came later, when men did settle there and others were jealous of the bounty they reaped, though afeared of why they reaped it. But it was known to some as Withered Hill, even when I was a child, and nobody trod on its top, and I think because of my mother and her forebears.

A story told in the villages nearby was that a man approached the stone house where my grandmother lived, when my mother was a tiny babe, and asked for a boon. He had a problem. His wife was very demanding in what you might call the bedroom department, but he had also recently taken up with a farmer's daughter, who expected him to devote his favours towards her. The poor man was exhausted, and finding it hard to… well, not finding it hard at all, as a matter of fact. So he visited my grandmother, and asked for some potion or root that might restore his vitality. After listening to his sorry tale with a sympathetic ear, my grandmother took her mortar and pestle and concocted for him a salve, with instructions for him to rub it on his underperforming member nightly and abstain from any contact with either his wife or his mistress for a week. After that, she promised, things would be different. The man took away the ointment and dutifully applied it as instructed. A week later, things were certainly different, as my grandmother had pledged. The man's dick shrivelled and shrank and fell off, and after that, when word got out, they began to mutter about the witch on Withered Hill.

I don't know about you, but I find that hilarious.

It must have been when I was a girl, twelve or thirteen, that the lure of Withered Hill began to prove too much for the men in the surrounding villages. It started with a little hunting and foraging, a brave soul venturing into the thick trees and coming back with a brace of partridge, a sack of apples, a young deer. And once those outside tasted that bounty… why, they thought that they should have more. The lone poachers became hunting parties, became expeditions, going deeper into the woods, emerging into the wide, broad clearing. It was a paradise, a Shangri-La, a slice of heaven right here on earth. Fecund, fertile, teeming with life and the sweetest of fruits, the most flavoursome of meats. Slowly, over the next couple of years, they became bolder, and some decided the land within the woods that encircled Withered Hill would be a mighty fine place to set up a village.

And that, my friend, was the start of all the trouble.

* * *

Let me tell you about magic.

Forget all that you've been told about cauldrons and broomsticks and pointy hats. If witches could fly, then there would not have been nine corpses rotting on gibbets on the moors at Lancaster and one in York while I suckled at my mother's breast. They would simply have gone, taking to the thunderous skies with a cackle.

Magic is not spells and incantations and the crack of lightning. Magic is subtle and feminine. Magic is intuition and knowledge. Most of all, magic is the earth. That is why, when witches die, they go back to it. Travelling its highways and byways, for as long as they wish. I told you I had travelled for many centuries. Some do longer, some not so long. I told you, too, that I was tired. That is because we never sleep when we travel. To sleep is to sink into the loam of whatever living thing you're in, to stay there forever, to become part of it, to infuse its being with your own. I've never felt ready for that, not really. For that letting go, for that becoming part of everything. Not until…

Well. So when we die, witches go back to the earth and all the things in it. Back to the planet. Another aside; I have grown to like music over my many years roaming the earth, and once spent an agreeable weekend squatting in a cow while a music festival took place in the next field. There was a band on called Back to the Planet. That girl who sang with them was a witch, if ever I saw one.

Anyway, I am wandering again. We go back to the earth because the earth has served us. It has given us our magic. Now, I never really knew whether witches are born to this, or it's something one can learn. I was taught, at my mother's knee, but then I was my mother's daughter, and she her mother's daughter, and so on. I was taught about the herbs and the trees and the insects and the birds and the animals, how a little of one and a little of another, mixed together just so at the right time of day or night, with the right belief and the right frame of mind, could work wonders. Real wonders.

Because that is what this earth is. Wonders. Wonders, wonders, all around. Rainbows and waterfalls. The cry of a newborn. Flowers, bees, the majestic silhouette of a stag in the dawn mist. Birds. Birds! Birds fly through the skies! Men invented science and biology and physics and chemistry to try to make the wonders of the earth seem commonplace. And it worked. Birds fly over your head all the time. They fly! Look up. Look up now. See them flying. Is that not magic?

My mother died when she was barely thirty-two and I was just fifteen. After the witch trials, things had changed. Nobody came to see my mother as a matter of course. They feared her, because that was what they had been taught to do by men. Fear women who they in turn feared had too much power. It took many years, until not long after my mother died, for people to begin to visit again in secret, in the dead of night, seeking help.

And because I was my mother's daughter, I was able to offer it.

It was my turn to be the Witch of Withered Hill. And by then, Withered Hill had become a village, though nobody who was not from there went within a mile or more. It was shunned, and maligned, and easily ignored because those that lived there kept themselves to themselves, and those that didn't had no appetite to visit. When they visited me, in the dead of night, for potions and salves, they cast fearful glances to the dark mass of trees at the top of my hill, wondering aloud how I could bear to live near such a cursed place.

Because, by that time, people had begun to talk in whispers about Owd Hob.

And, I suppose, so should we.

* * *

To be a witch is to be in touch with the earth, and all the things in it and on it. But there are things that are of the earth, mostly unknown to man these days. It wasn't always like that. Once, humanity was in touch with these presences, understood them, feared them and sometimes worshipped them. They called them gods, or demons.

What they are is spirits; spirits of place. They infuse the land, they inhabit the rocks and the streams and the trees. And one such spirit resides on Withered Hill.

At some point, before my time, somebody gave it a name. Owd Hob. And belief shaped the spirit, this Owd Hob. Gave it characteristics and form. Gave *him* characteristics and form. Because Owd Hob was considered male, that was what he became. Men map their gods in the same way they map their land. They build on the spirits in the same way they build on the earth. What was once wild fields and hills becomes roads and houses. The land is given shape that is pleasing to men, and so it is with their gods.

Those who had made their home on Withered Hill began to harvest the bounty of Owd Hob. He made the land fertile, the crops healthy, the livestock fat. He rewarded those who had been bold enough to enter his domain, because it reminded him of times long gone, when men worshipped him, treated him with respect. It pleased him. But there had to be a price.

The story – which they still tell in Withered Hill today, at their many festivals – goes like this: Before men came properly to Withered Hill, before it was a village at all, the area was dotted with farms. One year, the harvest had been poor, and the farmers worried they had not enough to eat themselves, let alone sell. On this particular day, a farmer and his daughter had been selling their meagre wares at market and were walking back to their farm, skirting Withered Hill as instinct told them. It was getting dark, and they hurried on, but it was too late. They had come to the attention of Owd Hob.

The old stories describe him as looking like a man, but not quite. Pale as the moon, thin as bones, wrapped in a ragged cloak, grotesque and elongated and smelling of the earth and stagnant ponds.

The farmer shrinks back, shielding his daughter. "Begone, boggart!" he bravely yet tremulously demands.

"No mere boggart, farmer. I am of the land, and the land is of me. I am Owd Hob."

"Well, the land has not been very good to us this year," says the farmer stoutly.

"Perhaps I can help," says Owd Hob slyly. "But you will have to do something for me."

"I am just a poor farmer and I do not even have a good harvest!" declares the man. "What would you have? My last turnip?"

Owd Hob says, "I would have a wife." He peers around the farmer. "Your daughter is a pretty one. Let me take her as my wife and I will promise you a bountiful harvest."

Needless to say, the daughter is not happy about this at all, and to his credit, neither is the farmer. Owd Hob gives them an ultimatum. Bring him a bride by sunset the following day, and all the crops around Withered Hill will thrive. Bring him nothing, and the farmers will all starve.

All night the farmer wrestles with his dilemma. He loves his daughter very much, but if the crops continue to fail then it will be a disaster. But then he has an idea. Owd Hob said he wanted a wife, not necessarily the farmer's daughter. And in this inn at a village some miles away, there was a girl who was known to be a thief, a liar and a cheat.

So the farmer heads off the next day and basically kidnaps this woman, and drags her to Withered Hill as the sun begins to set. Nobody will miss her, he thinks. In fact, he will be doing the village a favour, ridding them of a woman like that.

The farmer stands with the girl, who is bound by ropes and gagged with a rag, and Owd Hob appears once more.

"I have brought you a wife as you asked, Owd Hob," he says.

"She will do very well, farmer."

"And you promise our crops will thrive this year?"

"They will!" says Owd Hob, taking the struggling, crying girl by the arm.

"And next year they will thrive also?"

"They will!" agrees Owd Hob. And then he begins to sink into the land, as though it is water, taking the girl with him, who loosens her gag and finally begins to scream, just as the soil closes above her head. Owd Hob is gone. The girl is gone. And on the breeze, Owd Hob's final words. "Provided I get another wife!"

Well, you can see the problem with this, can't you? All this happened just before my mother died, and I was blooming into my womanhood and witch-hood. And let me tell you, I was not happy. At all.

Just as men had mapped their own dull imaginations onto Owd Hob, given him the form of a bogeyman, so had they mapped onto him their own base desires. The spirit of place who haunted Withered Hill since before men even walked the earth had never demanded such a price before. This is what men do. They think if there is a price worth paying, then it should be a price they themselves would want to demand. So, the spirit of Withered Hill was given a name, then a form, then desires. He needed none of it, nor asked for any of it, but there we were. And, almost four centuries later, here we are.

It's still happening. To this very day. The denizens of Withered Hill go out into the world, and every year they bring Owd Hob a wife. A woman, who is considered to be lacking in moral fibre, to have lived an unworthy life. A woman who will not be missed, whose absence will make the world a better place.

The absolute fucking cheek of it.

As the years passed, and I settled into my life as the Witch of Withered Hill, I began to receive visits from people living in the surrounding villages, asking for my help. Girls were going missing, perhaps one a year. The magistrates weren't inclined to do much about it, for most of these girls were considered fallen women, or thieves, or unsavoury characters. It took me a while to add it all up, and realise what was going on. That they were being taken to Withered Hill. Right under my nose.

Well. Not on my watch, I thought. Obviously, I didn't think those exact words in 1658, but you get the gist. Who was making judgement on these women, deciding they were morally wanting, and would make suitable wives for Owd Hob? Who had the nerve? I admit, part of me wanted to tell those villagers I wouldn't help them, because what had they done when men came for the witches? Some of them might have even whispered in the authorities' ears, pointed fingers, made accusations. And it was only a handful of families who came to me, wondering what had happened to their daughters. Poor families, with nothing to pay me. But if I didn't help, where would it end? What happened when the fallen women ran out? Who would those in Withered Hill take next?

First they came for the witches, and you did nothing, because you weren't a witch. Then they came for the fallen women, and you did nothing, because you weren't a fallen woman. You get my drift. But I couldn't do nothing, so I did something.

And this is how I died.

* * *

The men of Withered Hill had begun to roam far and wide over the Lancashire countryside, taking their victims from farther afield. It was said that Owd Hob himself appeared to the women, and marked them. I was dubious of this tale, because the spirits of place are, well, just that. They tend not to wander, once anchored to a location. But perhaps he could send out his essence, travelling in a similar way to how witches travel once dead. It at least gave me something to focus on, because a human touched by a spirit like Owd Hob would flare like a beacon, to those who could see.

And, one spring day, that beacon flared. I found her, a wretched lass earning coin by lying with men, living in a shack on the outskirts of a village some ten or so miles distant from Withered Hill. I tried to warn her, at first, but she took no heed. I was a dried-up old crone of almost fifty years, and renowned as a witch to boot. The vendetta against my kind had subsided somewhat, but they would still be executing witches for many years to come in England.

So I turned to my craft. I kept a watchful eye on the girl, and when the men from Withered Hill began to move, I followed. And when they took her, gagging her with a foul rag and throwing her in the back of a cart, I climbed in with her, unseen.

It was a good job neither the girl nor the men could see me, thanks to my glamour. I was quite a sight to behold. Naked and wild-eyed, slathered from head to toe in cuckoos' blood. You know how many cuckoos one must catch to obtain enough blood to cover a woman's body? Never let anyone say I'm not committed to my cause. But it had to be cuckoos. They lay their eggs in other birds' nests, you see.

As the cart wound its way to Withered Hill, I quietly untied the knots of rope binding the half-conscious girl. Then, as the cart slowed to negotiate a ford on the river, I pushed her off the back of it. The men heard a commotion and looked around, but all they saw was me, lying with my eyes closed on the planks, not a crone covered in bird blood, but wearing the face and body of the girl they had kidnapped.

They had built tracks through the trees at this point, and as the cart rumbled under the green canopy into Withered Hill, my stomach tightened. I could feel the power of the place, feel the presence of Owd Hob. It terrified me. I wanted to leap from the cart and run, back to my little stone house on the slopes of the hill. I almost did; the girl was safe, my job was nominally done. But I had to see. I had to see Owd Hob.

I was kept in a wooden cage, at the edge of the woods, and all manner of hullabaloo occurred. Withered Hill seemed, on outward appearances, to be a village like any other. There were shops and houses and dirt roads, and a large town square. There were farms that were on the edge of the village, and had begun to spread out beyond the thick woodland. The people seemed like normal people, if perhaps a little more well-fed and healthy-looking than most in this area. It was only when night began to fall that they showed their true colours.

A festival sprang up, a revelry commenced. There was a bonfire, and drinking, and fornicating in the trees. I waited patiently in my wooden cell, until the crowd quieted and something began to happen. I could feel it in the soles of my bare feet. A thrumming in the ground, as though a drum-beat marking time. The villagers formed a half-circle around my cage, and in the centre the earth began to shift and move, like the tides of the sea. Then the ground broke, as though the shoots of a plant were growing through. But not a plant. Him. Owd Hob.

The villagers fell reverently to their knees, and I have to admit he was quite a sight to behold. Tall and twisted, rangy and grotesque, his flesh white as snow, his eyes bulging, his nose hooked. He was a thing formed of bone and earth and stone, a body created as he rose from his domain beneath the land, plucking the building blocks of his physical form from the strata of earth and soil. Owd Hob was of the land, and he was the land.

His back to me, lit by the bonfires, he addressed the villagers, with vocal cords formed from vines and roots. His voice was green and earthy. "Withered Hill," he rasped. "You have brought me a wife. For that I thank thee, and promise a year of bountiful crops and livestock."

Well, as they say these days, the crowd went wild. Throwing their tankards in the air, howling and singing, grabbing each other and dancing. My cage was thrown open and rough hands grabbed me, dragging me out by the arms, pushing me down on to my knees in front of Owd Hob, who looked at me with his firefly eyes.

"A pretty one," he said. But did something flicker in those eyes? A moment of doubt? Did he sense that I was not all I appeared? He seemed to shake his head, as though casting aside his misgivings. He laid out a bony hand in front of my downturned face. "Take my hand, lass. Let us away to my chamber. For this be our wedding night."

"W-What will happen?" I said in a small voice, barely audible over the singing of the villagers, my hand hovering above his.

"Thou shall become one with the earth, deep below, and I shall have my pleasure with you, and then eat you." He bared his teeth, all mismatched stones, at me. "Thou might find it pleasurable, too. Even when I consume thee."

"Or," I said, finally meeting his terrible eyes, "thou could go fuck thyself."

Then I put my hand in his. I wasn't *quite* naked, you see. I was wearing gloves, stitched together from the shed skins of salamanders. And when I touched Owd Hob, he burned.

He tried to drag his hand away from mine, but I had him tight. Flames flickered along his bony forearm, his eyes blazed. The fire danced along his limbs, consuming his head, giving him a fiery halo. Then I dropped my disguise, and his tormented eyes widened. The villagers cried out, then fell silent, and backed slowly away. They knew me, at last, for who I was. The cuckoo's egg in the nest. The Witch of Withered Hill.

I might have survived, then, but for an element I had not taken into account. The trees rustled and shook, as though feeling Owd Hob's pain. And then *they* poured from the trees. I suppose you might call them goblins or boggarts, sprites. Lesser spirits, I do not know if they had been created by Owd Hob to serve him, before the appearance of men, or he had drawn them to him from other places. But here they were, and they fell upon me, all teeth and claws.

I had denied Owd Hob his sacrifice, I had injured him grievously, and he began to sink back into the earth, howling and shrieking. I do not know how long he nursed his wounds, but as his army ripped me apart, I at least felt the satisfaction that Withered Hill would not get its harvest this year.

I watched my body breathe its last from the eyes of an owl, high in a rowan tree. Then I took to the wing, and commenced my travelling. I always wondered, later, whether what occurred that night gave Owd Hob, or the villagers, the idea for what came next. The fact that I was a cuckoo, a double, a doppelgänger. But that is a story which is not mine to tell, and you can read of that elsewhere.

* * *

It's a good tale, isn't it? And most of it is true. I curled in the head of a man and took the reins of his mind and body, and tip-tapped it out on the keyboard of his laptop, and watched from the dry fronds of a dying plant on his desk that he rarely watered as he read it back in astonishment, no memory of laying down the words. Just as I read it now, from behind your eyes, in the pages of this book. I like being in your head; it is full of interesting things and fabulous thoughts, and your heart seems bright and good.

I may, at last, just rest in you, if that would be all right. For a while. Perhaps for longer. Maybe forever, for I am so very tired of travelling, and I would welcome the darkness of eternal sleep, now my story is told. Don't mind me, you'll barely know I'm here, save for the occasional moment of unexpected magic that comes into your life. Look up, and see the birds flying, and wonder. Be the witch they cannot burn, yet know in your heart that they'll try. But I will be with you. Yes, I think I'll stay. And sleep. Just be sure, while I do, to keep far away from Withered Hill.

Catharsis

Aveline Fletcher

A SUDDEN FLUTTERING of birds caught Circe's attention, and she peered out her window to watch them fly into the air.

"She'll be here soon," she said to herself, leaning back on her heels.

She sprinkled more coriander and mint into her meal over the hearth, gave it another stir, and tapped the excess from the spoon before resting it nearby. Then, the enchantress strode outside into the noon sun, facing the direction the flock of birds had flown, and waited.

She watched as a dark spot detached itself from the sun and resolved into a wondrously golden chariot as it got closer to her island. Two drakones pulled it across the sky, their burnished bronze scales and wings gleaming in the daylight. The figure within the chariot remained backlit from the sun, their features unrecognizable as they descended towards the ground.

The drakones and chariot came to a thunderous landing a few feet from Circe, spraying dirt in every direction.

Without waiting for the driver, Circe approached the beasts and put a hand on each of their snouts. They panted in exertion; though divine, they still tired as both gods and mortals did and would need rest.

The reins around the drakones went slack as the driver dismounted from the chariot, and Circe turned her attention to her niece.

In many ways, Medea contrasted Circe, who was shorter than her niece, tanned from days in the sun, and had a more athletic figure from living on her own in Aeaea, while Medea had always been a tall, willowy, statuesque woman.

Circe tended towards bright, airy colors of dress – indeed, in this moment she wore a practical peplos the color of coral – while Medea preferred jewel tones and darker colors, as evidenced by her burgundy chiton and black silk cloak that hung from her shoulders.

Circe: barefoot and auburn hair worn loose and free.

Medea: sandaled and black hair pinned up and contained in a hairnet.

Circe could go on, for they even differed in magical practice – she an enchantress, Medea a sorceress – but this was neither the time nor the place, and she had sized up her niece long enough.

She waited for Medea to speak, meeting guarded, narrow green eyes with her perceptive golden gaze, yet Medea's pale face remained impassive as she stared at the older woman.

"Aunt Circe," Medea finally greeted her with a deep feminine voice, offering a respectful bow. "You were expecting me."

"Selene granted me a vision of your visit, during the night of the full moon," Circe said coolly.

It had not been the vision she had sought, and in frustration, she had spat out the moonstone in her mouth when she had not seen the sea-faring man she had hoped for. Still, it would've been foolish to reject the knowledge granted in that vision, and so Circe had prepared to receive her niece accordingly.

"Welcome back to Aeaea," she said more warmly, slipping the bridles off the drakones.

She pushed them hard. She was fleeing something.

"Your beasts need food and rest," Circe said. "They may have their fill of the boars and sleep where they choose.

In the meantime, come – I was just about to sit and have a meal myself. Let us eat, and then you can tell me what brings you here to my island."

Circe led Medea into her home, where she served her guest lentil soup with leeks, coriander, and mint, alongside bread and smaller plates filled with olives, cheese, figs, nuts, and salted fish. They ate their meal in silence, though Circe watched her niece with a critical eye. The way Medea picked at and nibbled her food… Circe knew the other woman was likely as hungry as the drakones outside, but something had stolen her appetite. Combined with the silence…

This is a serious visit.

Still, although her curiosity tempted her otherwise, Circe remained silent as well. Medea would voice the reason for her visit soon enough.

She didn't have to wait for very long. Sick of staring at food she didn't intend to eat, Medea set aside her bowl of soup and leaned forward, resting her arms on her knees and clasping her thin fingers together.

"I've come here to request ritual cleansing from you again," Medea said to her.

"Who did you kill this time?" said Circe dryly, as she bit into a fig drizzled with honey.

Medea's mouth pressed into a thin, unamused line, and she did not respond.

Oh, a very serious visit indeed!

"What do you need cleansing for?" Circe asked next, dropping all pretense of play.

Still no response.

"Is this something you can't say, or won't say?"

Nothing.

Now it was Circe's turn to get annoyed. She tossed aside the remnants of her fig and leaned in close to her niece.

"You know as well as I do, that I can't help you unless you tell me what you need to be cleansed of," she said in a low voice.

Medea's hands reached out and seized Circe's in a death-grip. The carefully guarded expression on her face slipped, allowing Circe a glimpse at barely hidden desperation behind her niece's green eyes.

"Please," she whispered. "I don't know what else to do."

Circe held Medea's gaze, taking in a deep breath and exhaling the air through her nose. Then she nodded, squeezing Medea's hands and giving them a reassuring pat before pulling them away.

"Very well," she said. "A simple cleansing bath, then. Tonight. Selene's gaze will be closed to us, but something tells me that Hekate will be a more appropriate patroness for this ritual."

Circe rose to her feet. "You will gather the components while I prepare the ritual site."

Medea stared at her aunt with mouth agape.

"Aunt Circe, it has been… I do not know if I remember the craft anymore. Living in Corinth has—"

"Nonsense," Circe interrupted. She strode across the room to where she kept her broom. "Go out and gather the necessary herbs and minerals for the ritual. And if you ever feel lost, let your intention guide you. Your mind may be confused, but your heart knows what it needs."

* * *

The night of the new moon had finally fallen.

A salt-laden wind stirred Circe's hair, carrying the sound of crashing ocean waves. The skirt of her ethereal, translucent blue peplos swirled around her, hanging from a single pinned shoulder, and she tightened her grip around her long, thin wand.

Starlight alone illuminated the beach she had prepared for tonight, having swept a smooth area in the sand with her broom earlier. Within the site, a basin filled with freshwater gathered by Medea stood next to a simple stone altar, upon which lay bowls containing the herbal and mineral components her niece had also collected, an empty clay pitcher, and a small knife. A couple of feet away, in the center of the swept sand, a sitz tub sat alone on a pile of bay logs mixed with dried wormwood.

"Watch over and aid us tonight, Hekate Apotropaia," Circe said in brief prayer.

She turned to face Medea, still enrobed in her burgundy chiton, arms wrapped around herself. Gone was her hairnet, lost while gathering components on the island, her smooth black hair as loose and vulnerable to the wind as Circe's thick auburn tresses, and she had abandoned her sandals as they stood on the sandy beach.

Her time spent gathering materials had done her good, as Circe had surmised, but it remained clear that something still plagued her niece.

"Let us begin," she said to Medea.

A pause. Then Medea's brow hardened as she lowered her arms to her sides and began to remove the pins from her chiton. The fabric fell away from her person with each removal, until the entire dress sank to the ground with the undoing of the last pin. Medea stood there for a moment, naked in the night air, long black hair moving in the wind, before she stepped out of her chiton and strode past her aunt, green gaze focused entirely on the tub.

Circe hid a smile and followed her niece.

She stepped around the altar, and let the wand slide in her grip until it made contact with the sand. She waited until Medea climbed into the tub and sat comfortably inside, before she began to take measured steps around her, dragging her wand in the sand behind her.

"I now declare this space for our craft," Circe pronounced as she walked. "I, Circe, daughter of Perse, shall ritually cleanse my niece Medea, daughter of Idyia, as she has beseeched."

Medea remained silent, staring straight ahead at the ocean's crashing waves, jaw set with continued resolve.

Circe halted when she'd completed a full revolution around Medea, her wand simultaneously completing a full circle in the sand. Leaning the wand against the altar, she took a bowl of herbs and a bowl of crystals, before sprinkling blueish evergreen leaves and placing transparent crystals inside the circle in the sand she had just made.

"Rue leaves and quartz crystal shall consecrate this circle," Circe said. "Let this space be cleansed and primed for the magic that we shall enact tonight."

Once again, she completed a full revolution around her niece. Now back at the altar, she picked up a second set of bowls, this time placing dark, glassy rocks and bluish-purple petals on the outside of the circle.

"Obsidian shards and aconite petals shall protect this circle. Let no harm enter or befall us within."

A third revolution, completed.

Now Circe remained at the altar, taking the large bowl containing the bath salts and placing it in the center. With the salts, she mixed two other powdered minerals, before adding a variety of aromatic leaves and several white flowers to the mixture. Setting that aside, she then mashed purple-black berries in their own bowl with a pestle.

Grasping the pitcher by its handle, Circe dipped it into the basin of freshwater next to the altar, turned around, and approached Medea.

"Let the water from the springs of Aeaea cleanse your body," she intoned.

She tilted the pitcher and poured the water over Medea.

Her niece inhaled a sharp gasp as the freezing cold water cascaded down her head and over her body, hands gripping the sides of the tub, water streaming through her black hair.

Circe turned away and retrieved another pitcher full of water, now mixing in the herbal bath salts she had prepared. Again, she poured it over her niece.

"Let salt, limestone, and selenite – chamomile, lavender, rosemary, sage, and thyme – restore your mind."

Medea gasped again, her breath now short and choppy.

A third pitcher of water. The mashed berries and white flowers went into the vase next, the water tinged with purple as Circe doused Medea a final time.

"Let the flowers and berries of the elder purify your soul."

Now Medea's body shook, her eyes squeezed shut as she endured the cold of the water mixed with the chill of the night air.

Circe returned the vase to the altar, replacing it with flint and iron in her hands. She crouched down next to the prepared bonfire and struck the two rocks together, until one of the sparks alighted on the kindling and produced a small flame. She tended to it until the crackling fire grew, and stood up, staring down at the shivering Medea.

"It isn't working," Medea hissed through gritted teeth. "I still feel—"

"What?" Circe pressed. "What is it that you feel, Medea?"

Medea shook her head and did not respond, but Circe could sense the dismay, the fury, the heartbreak; she refused to speak about what ailed her, but her stiff body and white knuckles betrayed her.

"Let the fire warm the water with wood from the earth. Breathe in the air infused with our decoction and our intentions."

Circe finished speaking and remained there, waiting for the steam to rise, watching Medea all the while. Though Medea did not release her death-grip from the sides of the tub, nor did she open her eyes, the rest of her body relaxed as the water heated up and she breathed in the warm, moist air. And while that was a good sign…

Circe had seen enough – and a warm scented bath was not going to cure Medea of her troubles. She needed something more potent than an all-purpose cleansing ritual.

She turned away once more, her footsteps suddenly leaden as she returned to the altar. Carefully, she placed the flint and iron back on the altar and grasped the knife she had used to prepare the herbs.

Circe closed her eyes, taking a deep breath as she girded herself for what was to come.

She turned back towards the bonfire, towards the tub, towards Medea, and strode with purpose to the center of the circle. Medea had opened her eyes, but they remained half-lidded, until she spotted the knife.

Green eyes suddenly snapped wide open with animal fear.

As Circe reached out towards her niece, Medea threw herself against the tub and sent it and herself careening away from the enchantress. Water spilled out onto the flames of the bonfire, purging their brightness and causing thick black smoke to billow from its remnants.

It choked out the starlight above and immersed Circe and Medea in darkness.

* * *

"*What have you done?*" Medea shrieked from the dark.

The smoke thinned just enough for Circe to spot Medea's form standing on the beach, now caked with sand, partially crouched as if anticipating an attack from her. However, this also meant that Medea could see her now, too.

"*Stay away! I will kill you before you even lay a finger on me!*"

"Dearest niece, I have no intention of ending your life," Circe assured her. She tossed aside the knife, and it thumped onto the sand. "The ritual wasn't working, and so I sought to increase its potency with a little bit of your blood. Although, it seems you did my work for me. Then again, darkness and shadows have always been your purview."

Slowly, Circe stepped around the smoking bonfire and overturned sitz bath and approached Medea, the way one might approach a cornered animal. She reached out and laid a hand on Medea's shoulder, who jerked her head towards her aunt, staring at her with wild green eyes. Fear had left, but in its absence, her face contorted with rage.

"*You ruined it!*" she screamed, and slapped Circe's hand away.

"I have not ruined anything, Medea," Circe said to her, voice going icy at the accusation. "You cannot place blame on me when you have not told me what you need. Even so, your actions have spoken for you."

She folded her hands together in front of her, and began to pace around Medea.

"You fled Corinth, alone, on Helios's own chariot. Your desperation caused you to seek me out and ask for cleansing, but your guilt or shame held your tongue as to what you wanted to be cleansed *of*. When I sent you out to gather components, you did so, using your head to gather herbs and minerals that you believed would help with a simple cleansing ritual, but your heart influenced you more than you realized. And your choices were telling, niece."

The rage melted away from Medea as she listened to Circe's words, and now she stared out into nothing. Circe leaned in close.

"Have you forgotten that aconite, elder, wormwood, and obsidian also have strong associations with death?" she asked, her voice barely above a whisper.

Shock played out on Medea's features, especially when she turned to look at Circe.

Circe leaned back, somehow managing to stare down at her niece despite being shorter than her.

"You are grieving. And you feel guilt. And you cannot heal and be cleansed until you admit and accept what you have done. Did Jason finally betray you as I warned, and you took your revenge against him? I would not blame you if you'd killed him."

As soon as the shock came, it was quickly overtaken by a shadow crossing over Medea's face.

"Jason yet lives." She forced out her response.

"Oh? How very surprising."

"There are fates worse than death. And I left him with exactly what he deserved: nothing."

"Ah, but you speak with pain in your voice. Do you still truly love the betrayer?"

"He *left* me!" The words ripped themselves from Medea's throat, and the shadows thickened in response to her primal fury. "At Corinth, he pursued the king's daughter, and neither king, nor daughter, nor Jason himself seemed to think that him being married already was a problem!"

She scoffed, shaking her head. Medea's next words dripped with disdain as much as anger. "Of course it wasn't a problem. Why would it be? Even when I tried to conform to their ways, who was I to them, but a foreign, barbarian *witch*!"

Circe remained silent as Medea raged, the smoke dancing between them. Medea's bitterness returned.

"Who were our sons to them, but half-breeds at best. The king was going to exile us after Jason married the princess. Nowhere would they be accepted and welcome. Maybe if I took them home to Colchis, where I at least had some power and sway, but that's not an option anymore. So yes, I exacted my revenge. I killed Jason's beloved princess by desecrating Helios's golden robe with poison, and in so doing killed the king as well when he tried to save his poor, helpless daughter."

"You arrived alone to my isle, did you not?" Circe said.

Medea did not respond.

"Those two drakones wouldn't happen to be two transformed little boys, now would they?"

Medea began to shake, but not from the cold. She collapsed to her knees on the sandy beach, curling in on herself as she hid her face with her hands, shoulders shaking from barely contained sobs.

Circe watched for a moment, remaining very still. Then, she approached Medea and knelt next to her.

"What happened to them, child?"

Medea shook her head, unable to speak.

Gently, Circe reached forward and took Medea's hands in her own, pulling them away from the woman's tear-stained face. Now she allowed her compassion to shine through.

"You came to Aeaea seeking my help to cleanse you, Medea. This is how it's done for your specific ailment. But you must tell me. You must speak it. You cannot let the wound fester and grow infected."

She squeezed her niece's hands.

"Let me help you."

Medea took in a rattling breath or two, and gave a slow, shaky nod. The tears continued to flow as she spoke, her voice raspy and raw from the sobs and the smoke.

"I could not leave the boys with Jason. I could not leave them in Corinth. I could not take them anywhere, not with me. Given my murder of the king and the princess, the people of Corinth would exact their revenge on me through my boys. They would be taken and tortured, or killed slowly, and they would suffer."

She shook her head violently, and another sob escaped from her throat.

"I could not let that happen, not to them. Jason forced us into this position. I thought of ending their lives with a knife, to make it quick, but even my black heart screamed at me and held me hostage from taking this action. And so I gave them a potion. They died in their sleep, painless, like drifting off into a dream."

Medea released her aunt's hands to wipe away her tears, before clasping them once again.

"That Jason is left with nothing is a cold comfort compared to the pain and loss I feel for my children. For they were mine, too. I took them with me; their bodies lie in the chariot, and I intend to bury them in a suitable place."

"What were their names?" Circe asked.

Medea hesitated, then said, "Mermerus and Pheres."

"Medea, you did the very best you could in your position in a society like that," Circe said to her. "You were forced to make not one but many impossible choices you should never have needed to make. You gave Mermerus and Pheres mercy. They might not have known that when alive, but their souls know it now. And the gods know this too. For why would Helios come to your aid with his chariot?"

She swept a hand through the smoke towards where she surmised the chariot would be.

"Why would Nemesis compel you? Why would you bear the full wrath of Hera? The gods saw Jason for what he was, and their wills were aligned with yours in exacting justice and retribution. You have their approval, and your soul has and always will be clean of these actions."

"Then why does it still hurt?"

"I told you: you are grieving. As any good mother should."

Medea threw her arms around Circe. Circe froze, not expecting the move at all, but accepted and returned the embrace, holding her niece close.

"It has made me not want to touch the craft ever again, Circe," Medea admitted next to her aunt's ear. "I killed my boys with it. And yet, Aegeus, King of Athens, has offered me sanctuary in his kingdom, if I use the very magic I was so reviled for in Corinth to help him conceive a child. I'm damned if I do, and damned if I don't, and I'm not sure what to do or who I am anymore."

Circe pulled out of the embrace.

"I once thought that people like us have no place in society," she said. "That our place was to remain alone and free in the wilderness, its companion and guardian. In some ways, I still believe that, but only for myself, for I came to realize how limited such a sweeping view was."

She reached her hands out and cradled Medea's face, smiling softly.

"You are who you have always been. These events have irrevocably changed you, yes, but that does not mean you must give up who you are. Corinth has made you believe that you are a monster, meant to always be a rejected or persecuted outsider of society, unless you renounce your ways and conform. Don't listen to such things – their opinions are fickle and meaningless and motivated by a desire for control and a fear of the unknown. I have seen you thrive in society where I would not, and I admire your bravery to walk among those people as you are, so do not falter now and believe their lies. But take my words as you will, Medea, for only you can define yourself, and only you can decide where your place is. So, what will it be?"

Circe removed her hands from Medea's face, and waited for an answer.

"I am Medea." She matched Circe's soft tone in her response. "Princess of Colchis, and…"

Medea faltered, a pensive frown gracing her face. A period of silence passed between the two women. Then, she curled her hands into fists, as determination set upon her brow like a crown.

"And sorceress of Hekate." Medea's voice grew stronger and richer with each spoken word. "I will settle for nothing less than that, even as I continue to live among people who seek to tear me down. I will not live in fear nor diminish myself for Aegeus or for Athens. And in time, they will know my strength, and the strength of all of us who command the craft."

With Medea's words, the smoke finally cleared, and starlight returned to Aeaea.

Remembrance

Helen Grant

I WASHED UP over a thousand dishes that shift. Jay, the owner, was too cheap to hire two people. He was impatient, too, tapping his foot while he waited for me to finish so he could lock up.

"Night, Ellie," he said.

My name isn't Ellie, but that was fine; I didn't want to be remembered.

I stopped off at a supermarket, keeping my head down, taking care to use the self-service till. Then I walked back to the place that wasn't really home, lugging a bag full of marked-down food. There was no lift, so I trudged up four flights of stairs, thinking for the umpteenth time how apt it was that the walls were painted the colour of crap. And there she was, leaning against the doorframe, as I'd known she would be, one day soon.

I refused to catch her eye. Instead, I fished in my pocket for the keys, and went to unlock the door, thinking that I could just slip inside and shut her out.

"Eris," she said.

I fumbled the keys, and then I dropped them.

She went to pick them up at the same moment I did, and suddenly I was aware of how close she was. I could see that mass of auburn hair at the corner of my field of vision. As usual she was dressed in sober colours, with that flash of white at the throat, but she couldn't stop her hair from blazing out; it was magnificent, like fire. And so I looked. Of course I did.

I've always thought her eyes are like amber: they are that glorious luminescent golden-brown colour, and when I look at her, there I am, suspended in each of them forever, like an insect. I stood up again hastily, but it was no good.

When the door was closed, and we were standing in the scruffy, narrow hallway, I said: "What do you want, Gabi?"

"Nobody calls me that but you," she said quietly. Then she sighed. "We need help. I wouldn't have come if it wasn't serious."

"We?"

"The town."

"Oh, the town." I leaned back against the wall, folding my arms. "That would be the town I left because they were calling me a witch."

"Eris—"

"Well, that wasn't the only reason, was it?" There's an edge to my voice. "Has anything changed?"

There was a long silence.

"Something *has* changed, I suppose," she said at last.

For a moment I thought – well, never mind what I thought. She held out her left hand, and I saw that there was a solitaire diamond sparkling on the ring finger.

"I see," I said. "I should tell you to get lost."

But I didn't. At any rate, it had resolved things, one way or another. I listened to what she had to say, then I asked for half an hour to pack and message Jay with some plausible lie.

This thing, this witchery or second sight or whatever it is, began when I was in my teens. Back then, I just blurted it all out, whatever I saw. I mean, you wouldn't let someone walk into a building if you knew there was going to be a gas explosion, or set off on a journey that would end with tangled metal and blue lights, would you? You'd try to save them. But here's the thing: people weren't grateful.

They were weird, or even hostile about it. They'd want to know why the hell I'd said whatever I'd said about something horrible in their future. Often, of course, that thing would actually happen. Other times, I guess they avoided it because of whatever I'd told them. But they didn't see it that way. They said I'd cursed them. *Witch*, they called me, with fear in their eyes.

I moved on so many times I can hardly remember where I came from. Always small rural communities, because the only thing that gives me any peace is the wild land, where the milestones of the future are storms and floods and fallen trees. The only place I stayed longer than a year was the small town we were heading for now, and that was because of Gabi. She actually tried to understand, offering sympathy instead of hate. But eventually something came up that I couldn't ignore, and I tried to warn people. Then it was *witch, witch* again, and even Gabi couldn't talk them down.

So I went to the city, where I was anonymous, and I took care not to get close to anyone again. That worked, in a soulless sort of way. If I spaced out sometimes, or rambled to myself, Jay would just tell me to stop dreaming or he'd dock my pay. Jay's going to live to be very, very old. There's no justice, really.

There have been no trains to the town for sixty years. We drove for hours in the battered little car that was all a church salary could afford, through darkness that was first punctuated by glittering lights, and later by nothing at all. Gabi kept her eyes on the road. I looked out of the window into nothingness most of the time. Now and again I glanced at her profile, softly underlit by the dashboard lights, but her left hand with the diamond on it gripping the wheel was a talisman between us.

"Tell me about the body they found," I said.

I heard her let out a long breath. "A farmer found it. He was digging a drainage ditch or something. That bit of land hadn't been touched for years. There wasn't much left of her; they couldn't even be sure of the cause of death."

"So why are you so certain it was murder?"

"Because she was under a load of stones and branches. If she'd gone for a country walk and, I don't know, had an aneurysm or something, she couldn't have burrowed down under all that." Gabi paused. "Anyway, I knew her, a little. She wasn't the sort of girl to take long country hikes. When she disappeared everyone thought she'd left for the city… like you did."

"And nobody followed up, tried to check she was okay?" I couldn't keep the bitterness out of my voice.

"Of course they… Eris, you know I—"

"Sure, Gabi. We don't need to do this now. Or maybe not ever. Tell me about the other ones."

"Always the same story," she said. "All of them went out after dark and never came back. One was the girl they found. The other three… no sign. None of them were carrying more than a little backpack when they left. If you were running off to the big city, you'd take more than that, wouldn't you?"

"And the police are all over this, presumably?"

"Yes… and no." She sighed. "Like I said, there's no cause of death for the one they found. It was probably murder, but it could be a case of unauthorised burial."

"That's usually murder, though, isn't it?"

She nodded. "The other ones… Well, there are tens of thousands of people reported missing every year. And it's a small town. If teenagers go missing, there's a good chance they've headed for the city lights. You don't jump straight to thinking: serial killer."

"But you did, right?"

"Not just me. People are afraid. Everybody is watching everybody else. Parents don't want their teens going out after dark and of course the more they try to stop them, the more determined they get."

I thought about this. "You know there's no guarantee I'll see anything?"

"Yes. I was just hoping you'd try."

"I can't even try, not really. Mostly it just happens, or it doesn't. If I could do it whenever I felt like it, maybe I *would* be a witch. And don't tell me it's God's gift or something," I added quickly. "It's a bloody curse. Why else would I be earning a pittance washing dishes?"

I slumped back in my seat and for a long while after that there was silence. I had a bad feeling, but then, I nearly always do.

We got to the manse in the early hours of the morning. It was a large, ugly building set back from the road in an unkempt garden. It smelled like a church hall, and the décor wasn't much better – scuffed furniture not old enough to be antique, and flaking paintwork. For a moment I was surprised Gabi's intended wasn't there to greet us, but of course he wouldn't have been there at that time of night; ministers of the church aren't supposed to have lovers.

The guest bedroom wasn't too bad. The whole house was horribly draughty, but Gabi had put a little portable heater in the room, and with the curtains drawn it warmed up to a tolerable temperature. After she had closed the door, and I'd heard her footsteps receding up the landing, I sat for a while on the bed, hugging myself. I had a feeling it was going to happen, the way I've heard people prone to migraines can sense one coming on, even if there's no actual pain. Maybe it was the dislocation I'd undergone that day, or maybe it was the emotional upheaval, or maybe it was just a random thing. It always starts in a soft, indistinct sort of way, like mist swirling slowly around me, and gradually, gradually it crystallises into a solid sensation of being at the hub of something. And then it seems as though some vast and mighty wheel ponderously turns one hundred and eighty degrees on its axis. I am still where I was in the present moment, but instead of looking behind me down the long corridor of years, I remember *forwards.* There is still a sense of the past, in the way that a regular person would see the future: as a dim set of milestones, things that might or might not be. What I will one day know, and see, however, is there in my mind, and as with all memories, the closest and most significant parts are the clearest.

I guess it's obvious now why I wash dishes for a living. If I started on something more complex – I don't know, dispensing medicine or playing concert piano – and this thing happened, I'd lose track completely. Hell, I don't even drive because of it.

Anyway, I was right: it happened. First that slow, disorienting, nauseating swing, and then that other perspective sliding into view, like a rolling landscape stretching into the distance. The far horizon is the end of my life, and beyond it is only black water. Lethe.

Look back on life and you remember the big things: first day at school, losing your virginity. It's the same with the future: some things are so huge you can't take your eyes off them. Something was dragging my attention to it like an evil lodestone. A funeral.

"No," I groaned, shaking my head uselessly.

Gabi's funeral. Glimpses of a coffin being carried into the parish church, seen from a corner at the back of the building. Pews filled with people I didn't know, mostly dressed in black, a few of the younger ones in brighter colours. A dark-haired man at the front, his face stony, waiting like a bridegroom. Whispers. Sidelong, resentful glances at me.

Some things can be altered. Some things are truly curses.

Nearer to now were other events, as grim as tombstones. A newspaper headline: *Body Found in Demolished Hotel.* Gabi leaning towards me over the kitchen table, her face a mask of horror, telling me that another girl had disappeared.

And tomorrow morning, Gabi, smiling, with the dark-haired man I had seen at her funeral.

"This is Adam."

Knowing what sorrow lay ahead of us.

Then the vertiginous shift began again, and when it was over I found myself sitting there with tears running down my face.

I slept badly that night, tormented by the question of what I should tell Gabi, and I was still no nearer an answer in the morning. When I heard her moving about I went downstairs, and just before I opened the kitchen door I felt an impulse to tell her everything, whatever the consequences. But she was not alone.

"Good morning, Eris!" she said. "This is—"

"Adam," I said.

Surprise registered on her face for an instant. Then I suppose she thought she must have told me his name the night before. Her expression cleared.

"Yes," she said.

"Hello," said Adam, and held out a hand. That felt a little formal, but I took it anyway. He had a firm handshake, and

I wondered if he gripped hard on purpose, to show what a strong, sincere guy he was. Then I reminded myself that I was probably going to struggle to love anyone Gabi was engaged to, and I should make an attempt to be civilised, at least.

"Hi," I said. I looked Adam up and down. He was very good-looking, all strong jaw and cheekbones and thick hair tamed into a suave cut. Dressed well, too. He and Gabi would make a stunning couple. I felt, if possible, even more sour than I had before, but I bit it back. "It's nice to meet you," I lied.

"Same," he said. Adam paused. Then he said, "Gabriella says you… see things."

"Yes," I said. We looked at each other. I saw him open his mouth, and for a moment I thought he was going to make one of those stupid quips people think are so cute. *I hope you won't see anything about me.* But if he was, he changed his mind.

"I should go," Adam said, and when he went to kiss Gabi goodbye I turned away.

I didn't tell her. I said to myself that when it happened again, the remembering forwards, I'd try to recall what she was going to die of. Otherwise, what would be the point? Without knowing specifically, a person could go mad trying to avoid every possible hazard. No; let her enjoy her time with Adam, for now.

I did tell her about the missing girl, and the body that would be found in the hotel.

"What was the girl's name?" she wanted to know.

"Holly. Holly McEwan, or McHugh, maybe."

She looked troubled. It wasn't enough; we both knew that. As for the body in the hotel, Gabi said there were currently three disused hotels in the town, all of them shut up tight with boards nailed over the windows, all of them liable to future demolition. After pushing breakfast around our plates, we walked around the town, our breath drifting like smoke on the cold air, and checked them all over as best we could. So far as we could tell, none of them had been broken into. Not yet, anyway.

At least four people greeted Gabi by name. All of them eyed me with distrust, and they weren't the only ones. Heads half-turned as we went past, as though there were some disagreeable odour on the air. It was very plain that people had *not* forgotten my time here, and with very little encouragement they'd be surrounding the manse with pitchforks and flaming torches, or whatever the modern equivalent was.

Burn the witch. Oh yes.

"I wonder," said Gabi uneasily, "whether I did the right thing, asking you to come."

I didn't say anything to that. I was wondering the same thing too, though neither of us suggested that I should leave. Gabi, I suppose, was thinking of the missing girls; I was thinking of that funeral, and whether I could prevent it.

In the town square we passed a noticeboard with a faded poster on it: HAVE YOU SEEN SHONA? it read, under a grainy photograph of a teenage girl. I stopped for a moment to look at it, and was very aware of the gaze of the ne'er-do-wells and loafers hanging about the place. It was difficult not to be infected with suspicion. The tall, skinny man with grey-tinged skin and greasy hair – was he the one? Or the beefy guy with the insolent expression and his hands shoved deep in his pockets – what about him? I reminded myself that I had to *see*. I know all too well that you can't judge by appearances.

When we got back to the manse, I excused myself and went upstairs, where I stayed for most of the day. I heard the doorbell sound on three different occasions, and once I heard raised voices downstairs, but I stayed where I was: curled up on the bed, willing it to happen again.

Of course it didn't. Hoping, trying, *longing* for it to happen – none of that works. The longest I've ever gone without it happening was about six weeks and I was praying it wouldn't be that long this time, because by then the town would probably be too hot to hold me.

Not long after the sun had gone down, Adam came over; I knew Gabi had a visitor because I heard the front door close, and a little later I heard his voice briefly because he raised it.

What was that about? I wondered. There was no telling; he lowered it again and all I could detect was the faintest murmur. The disquieting thought crossed my mind that perhaps he had heard something from the busybodies who'd been eyeing me when I walked around the town, but then I told myself off. *Not everything is about you.*

It was though, inevitably.

When Gabi called me down for dinner, her intended had gone, and she looked unhappy.

"Adam wants me to go, doesn't he?" I said. She was actually wringing her hands, I saw.

"He's worried," she said. "Someone in the town has been telling him… well, I don't need to repeat it."

"Worried about me, or worried about you?" I said. "I don't think they'll burn *you* at the stake," I added bitterly.

She wasn't listening. "It was wrong of me to ask you to come, and expose you to all this again."

"Well, I'm here," I pointed out. "And Gabi – we *know* at least one more girl is going to disappear. Let's at least wait until I've seen something more."

And until I figure out what's going to happen to you.

Gabi still wasn't listening. "Eris, the police have picked someone up," she said.

"What?" I said. "Who?"

"Sean McLaren. It's in the paper; Adam told me."

I knew who she meant, instantly. You don't live in a small town for any length of time without getting to know this stuff. Sean was a loner. He lived in a scruffy bungalow whose front garden was constantly full of broken furniture and car parts. He also owned a large and evil-looking dog that was the terror of the local postmen. If you'd had to finger anyone as the local killer, it would probably have been Sean.

"Are they holding him?" I asked.

"I don't know," she admitted.

"Well, maybe it's him and maybe it isn't," I said. "If they've got the right person, nobody else will disappear. If not… maybe I can still help."

Gabi looked unhappy, but she acquiesced at that. We ate dinner in silence, both of us lost in our own thoughts.

Three days later, and thirty-six hours after Sean had been released under investigation, a girl called Holly McGowan vanished. Four days later, Gabi, Adam and I had a row.

I didn't even know Adam was in the manse. I walked into the kitchen to get a glass of water, just in time to hear him tell Gabi in an elevated whisper that she really, really needed to get rid of me, right now.

"It's not up to you," I said.

"Really," he said flatly.

"Eris—" began Gabi, but she didn't get any further.

"I'm her fiancé—"

"You're not her boss, though," I snapped, folding my arms. "She asked me here to help."

"Help? How are you helping? Half the town is talking about you being here. No, strike that. The *entire* town is talking about it."

"Adam—" Gabi tried.

"Let them," I said.

"Let them? You're dragging her reputation through the mud. Don't you realise how serious that is, for someone in her position?"

"I can't help it if they're a bunch of small-minded—" I controlled myself with an effort. "Look, has she told you what I can do?"

"She's told me what you *say* you can do."

"Well, I *can*. The girl who's missing, Holly McGowan – I *saw* that. Tell him, Gabi. Four, maybe five days ago."

Both of us stared at Gabi. She looked utterly miserable. "Yes, she did."

"Damn right I did. And when it happens again, I'm going to try to see who's doing this – who's taking these girls. *Then* I'll go."

I turned on my heel and stalked out of the room, but not so quickly that I didn't hear Adam saying: "What is she? A *witch*?"

I had barely made it back to my room when I felt it happening again: the vague drifting sensation, like smoke trailing on the breeze, gradually solidifying into the turning of a gigantic wheel. I closed the bedroom door and leaned on it, breathing hard. Some moments of sliding and nausea, and then the world seemed to tremble and settle, and I found myself looking down the barrel of tomorrow.

The baleful gravity of the funeral dragged at me. I strained to see, to *remember* what Gabi had died of, but found nothing. Like Holly McGowan, she had stepped outside of her life; by the time she was found, there was no way of knowing. Tragedy, anger and blame hung over it all like storm clouds, but there were no answers.

My beautiful Gabi; my bright, flame-haired love. I wondered if I would ever know how it had happened, however long I lived.

And then I saw that I *did* know.

Far, far in the distance, almost at the edge of the black water that was the end of my life, there was a memory. Between here and there lay years of life: many different places, events, faces; even a few lovers, though no love like Gabi. At the end of it all I would be old, tired, even more cynical than I was now. In spite of all of that, I would still carry a faint, guttering torch for her; I would still have enough interest in the topic to notice the news headlines. *Deathbed Confession. Vicar Among Victims.* And in the byline, the killer's name: Adam Fairfax.

I slid down the door and slumped on the floorboards, my head in my hands.

Adam.

It wasn't Sean at all. Adam was the killer, and he was going to get away with it, not just now but for *decades.* I doubted the final confession would be prompted by guilt. He would probably just want everyone to know how very, very clever he'd been.

And he was going to kill Gabi.

Time turned slowly back again, and as it settled into place I heard the front door close, a little more soundly than usual. Adam had left.

I admit it; I followed my first impulse instead of thinking it through. I ran downstairs, burst into the kitchen and said, "Gabi, you've got to listen to me. It's Adam."

She turned to me with a bewildered look on her face, and I was so afraid for her that it all came pouring out in an incoherent flood, how he had killed them all and he was going to kill her too, and we had to go now, go somewhere safe—

I saw her expression turn from confusion to understanding and then to disbelief, and then it hardened into anger. Gabi hardly ever showed true anger; it was all tamped down under strata of duty and responsibility. Now it erupted with magmatic force.

"How *dare* you?" she screamed. "How *dare* you say that?"

She was so furious that I took a step back in spite of myself.

"Gabi…" I faltered.

"Don't call me that! Adam was right. I shouldn't have asked you here. And now I want you out. Gone. I want you to pack and leave – right now."

"No – listen—"

She actually put her hands over her ears. "No. I'm not listening to your lies. Get out of the house, you, you—"

And then she said it, and I knew it was all over, because Gabi *never* swore.

"You fucking *witch*."

I crept back upstairs and started packing, stringing it out in the hope that Gabi would calm down and change her mind. But when I finally opened the door and went out onto the landing, I could hear her downstairs on her phone, telling Adam what I'd said. She was still incandescent with rage, otherwise perhaps she might have thought better of that.

When she heard the stairs creaking she glanced up, held the phone to her chest for a moment and pointed at the door.

"Gabi, please..."

She shook her head, implacable. After I had stepped outside, I heard the key turn in the lock and a rattle as she slid the chain across.

It was getting dark, and it was very cold. I walked to the bus stop, shivering, and found that there were no more buses until morning. The town was long past its heyday; there was only one hotel still operating, so I went into the bar and asked about rooms. The young barman served me a soft drink quite happily, but when the manageress came out to see about the room, her face went from friendly to stony in an instant.

"There are no rooms vacant," she said.

At that moment, incredibly, I felt that sensation once more, the beginnings of the shift happening. It rarely, if ever, happened again so soon. Already there was that nauseating sense of *turning.*

Probably I looked a little drunk.

"You need to leave," said the manageress sternly, fists on her hips.

"Can I just use the ladies'?" I begged.

"Very well. But if you're not out in two minutes, I'm coming in to turn you out myself."

I staggered into a cubicle and sat down on the closed seat. And I remembered *forwards.*

Gabi's funeral was still there, a hideous milestone in the future landscape. Adam was still going to kill her.

It didn't matter that I'd warned her. Or perhaps it was going to happen whether I'd done that or not.

But something else was there, something I had never experienced before. Things can and do change, but this time I *saw* it happening. I looked to the far horizon and saw that the dark water was no longer a distant border. It was sweeping towards me like a tide, obliterating everything in its path. Death was coming for me, and it was being decided at that very moment. Closer it swept, and closer, until I was standing on the very brink of it, and there was a brief memory of a dark road, and lights—

I guess the manageress forgot her two-minute warning, or else she was distracted by other guests coming in, because when I staggered out of the ladies' fifteen minutes later, she was nowhere to be seen. I felt sick and unsteady on my feet, but not completely out of it; I still managed to leave via the hotel kitchen and pocket something on the way.

It was fully dark when I passed the sign marking the edge of the town. The nearest railway station was seventeen miles away; the nearest proper town the same. Between here and there were a couple of hamlets but otherwise miles of undulating, unlit country roads.

So here I am, walking briskly in the moonlight with my backpack bouncing against my shoulders. If I keep walking for another five hours or so, I'll get to the station. But I don't think that will happen.

I think that sometime soon, a pair of headlights will appear in the distance behind me. I'll probably climb onto the grass verge, because it would be easy to be run over by accident, wouldn't it? And I think that as the car approaches the lights will wash over me, and I'll be clearly visible, standing there with my hand in my pocket.

The car will slow, and stop, and the window will slide down.

"Oh, it's you," he'll say, or something along those lines. "No hard feelings, eh? Do you want a lift to the station?"

Just the same as with all those other girls. And like them, I'll say, "Oh, thanks," and open the passenger door with my left hand, because the right one will still be tight around the knife with its long, serrated blade.

And after that… well, if I'm quicker, justice will be done, but nobody will know it. Gabi will live, but she will never forgive me, and I'll have to thank my lucky stars I don't live in an earlier age when they burned murdering witches like me alive.

Maybe though, he'll be quicker. He's had the practice, after all. Then I'll be gone and he'll murder his way through the decades with every appearance of innocence.

That grim black tide I saw rolling towards me doesn't bode well. Not everything can be changed, however hard you try.

Wish me luck.

A Woman Grown

Lisa L. Hannett

SNARES ARE SIMPLER set-ups than cage traps, but it only takes one neck-kill for Payton to toss those crude nooses in the fireplace. No need to garrotte whatever critter's dumb and hungry enough to slink into Heddy's yard, she thinks. The stray cats and raccoons. Squirrels and skunks. The raucous, murdering crows. Seems unfair, somehow, snuffing the poor, greedy things without even offering a mouthful of bait. Just letting them run along well-trodden paths, into the wire loops she's rigged on nearby dowels; whisker-thin tricks that tighten and tighten, snagging the leap right out of their limbs, blacking legs with cut circulation. It's too cruel, she thinks, hobbling them like that. Leaving them to die with their bellies still grumbling. Blocking the blood's natural flow.

But *borrowing* some critters for a spell? Keeping them whole and hale until she's snicked what little she needs? A little catch, clip, release?

No harm in that.

At least in the cage, they get a good hunk of meat to stave off the terror.

On the back stoop, Payton snatches her apron off a rail-spike nailed beside the screen door, and ties it around her waist. The dirt-stained calico clunks against her knees, iron and steel weighting its front pocket. Howls become barks in the distance. Feral frustration.

"Hold your horses," she sing-songs. "I'm coming."

Leaning into autumn's bite, she hitches up her faded black skirt and thunks barefoot down to the garden. Dead leaves shush underfoot until she reaches tangles of fat orange pumpkins, late-season cabbage, turnips and rutabagas planted in ragged rows. Soft-stepping now, she avoids good growth while plotting the straightest route across the yard. Patting stalks out of her way. Pinching caterpillars between callused fingers. Merely delaying the inevitable. Any eve now, she thinks, the village lads will come stomping through here, armed with cudgels and companionship and All Hallows courage, daring each other to smash the heddle-witch's gourds. At least, that's the yarn Heddy spun her once. A rare tale to treasure.

Everyone's affeared of old Heddy, but won't muster a whimper for you.

Payton snorts. Glances over at the path running alongside her property, a generations-long groove worn in the dirt between the schoolhouse and society. It's a good hour yet until the bell rings and the bravest kid shortcuts it through the woods, daring to sprint past this old place in broad daylight. For now, she's on her own.

Sharp yips scold her onwards. The rattle of galvanised wire.

"Coming," she huffs, cursing herself for breaking routine. How foolish proud she'd been yesterday, lugging the trap all that way out to the gully beneath the train tracks, just to camouflage it among the brambles and blackberries bristling there. A ripe spot, sure. Certain to bag her some variety, something wilder and stronger than the grackles and hares so common close to the house. Today, though, a backdoor bunny doesn't sound half bad. Payton's stout legs wobble as Heddy's acreage rolls like a treadmill underfoot. Pushing hard, she trudges around vegetables and vines, aims for the lawn going to seed out back, the littered slope, the brushwood where yesterday's arrogance is causing today's pain. For hours and *hours*, she makes no headway.

Except, when her cold toes finally strike the metal box, the sun is the same small bleach stain on the sky's wide grey blanket. The weatherboard cottage is now a dollhouse far behind her. The footpath is still empty.

In the leaf-shadowed cage, low growls cough into barks.

Snap out of it.

Fierce little vixen, Payton thinks with a grin and a fog-clearing shake of her head. Crouching, she takes in the trickster's gut-smeared muzzle, her wily gaze, her milk-heavy teats.

What a prize.

"Steady now, mama." Restraint rasps the edges off Payton's voice. She's careful now. Controlled. Calm. "There, there."

With one hand, she eases hound-nail clippers out of her apron pocket. The other flips her long braid out of fangs' way then slowly unhooks the trap's latch and slides its rear panel up. Takes some wrangling to separate claw from critter, but Payton's no scrawny girl anymore, no weak little waif without a skerrick of power to her name; she's a woman grown. The fox barely gets a nip in before she hugs it tight, jams its head up under her pit and hogties its dainty paws with her fist. She feels stronger with every click and snick of the halfmoon blades. Stronger even than Heddy. Once, twice, three times she snips before the snarling thing writhes free and sprints for the dense scrub. Thorn-studded creepers scrape and clatter as it scrambles for the hidden tunnel it once travelled. Branches bend and braid together.

The vixen hollers.

"Not my fault you're stuck," Payton says, thumbing the small bounty of claws in her palm as the creature stumbles, gets back onto her dainty black feet, trots a few paces, stumbles again. It yowls at the overgrown hedge. At her.

You got to find your own way, girl.

After collecting the empty cage, Payton follows the angry fox back to the garden. Three clippings is good, she tells herself, turning its nails this way and that. Three tiny horns of plenty. The tips could be sharper, sure. The cuts a bit smoother. Still, three is fine. Three will do.

The ground is firm now, hurrying Payton close to the cottage where she tilled a fresh plot for this planting. Setting the trap aside, she straddles the length of rich brown soil. Hikes up her heavy skirts. Squats.

Wind shears through the yard, thin as sticks skittering across roof tiles.

What you want is a spare set of hands.

"All right," Payton says, delving three knuckle-deep holes in the dirt. One by one, she drops the shards in. Leans close.

Horks great gobbets into the hollows. Three is enough, she thinks, patting them down. While her spit seeps in, Payton takes a deep breath. Conjures up a threadbare series of overheard rhymes. Ragged soundscapes that pull at something deep in her gut, something modern phrases can't contain, something primal, immortal, maternal. Rhythms she *feels* more than understands.

Old Heddy's witchwords.

Now hers.

Working quickly – there's the bell! – Payton fossicks under her skirt, digs the moon-rag out of her bloomers. Voice low, she chants while she squeezes the sodden cloth, wringing a first-day-flow's worth of blood onto the seeds. That's plenty, she thinks, jamming it back into her drawers before her lips shape the spell and her hands knead the earth and her heart pounds a prayer to any goddess who'll listen.

Let them live.

Let them thrive.

On all fours, she sings and sobs into the soil.

"Are you okay?"

"Oh!" Slowly, Payton sits back on her haunches – best not startle the child – and cuffs the snot from her face while she side-eyes the girl on the footpath. Twelve or thirteen at a guess. Scab-kneed. Scuff-shoed. Freckled. Tousled. Pinafore and cardigan are both secondhand, but the care buckling her dark brow is brand new. A concern so honest and pure, it practically hurts.

"Yeah," Payton says, flushed from hairline to collar. "All good."

By her feet, the dirt trembles. Quakes. *Roils*. Anthills erupt above the quickening claws, the mounds soon bulging big as goose eggs. Apples. Sourdough loaves.

"Thank you," she says to the air. Gaze fixed on the swelling ground.

The girl stretches on tiptoe, but can't see past Payton's bulk to her low workings. "You're sure?"

Nod nod.

Gravel crunches. The girl scoots right before one, two, *three* little heads crown in the garden. Payton claps, eyes brimming – until the ears crop up. Neither pointed nor round, they're soggy flaps of skin that slap against sunken yellow skulls. Necks like warmed tallow glob into pond-scummed torsos. Toothful gobs haw like concertinas.

Shoulders sagging, she nudges a couple of the flesh sacks out of the soil, more cartilage than bone, more sideshow hit than domestic pet. With a sigh, she plops them face-up in the dirt. Mucus-hued marbles roll in their sockets: lidless, sightless, senseless. About as playful as a pair of trash bags. The third – wizened as a walnut – *almost* passes as a blue tabby. At least it's got four legs and a tail. Patchy pelt. Amber eyes.

Its meow is almost sweet.

Won't last more than a day, Payton thinks. Taking the ball-peen hammer from her apron pocket, she mops the wet from her eyes. Turns her head. Flails at the two maggot-kits, pulping them into a porridge. "Sorry," she whispers, scooping the slop straight into the cage trap. Scavengers will choke down any old crap, she thinks, raw or rotten. Long as she sets something up, they'll sniff it out and pig it right in.

This last one, though…

Payton hefts the beast in her palm. Takes its measure.

Swaddles it tight in her skirts.

* * *

Bit off more than you can chew, Pane.

Payton shakes her head, mood darker than the splotches mucking up her front. She swished the worst chunks off at the pump, but this mess wants vinegar and salt and a soul-deep scrubbing. Upending another steaming pot into the basin below the cottage's only clear window, already half-filled with cold water she pailed in from outside, Payton turns the spell over in her mind. Did she forget a phrase? She strips to her undershirt and bloomers, stuffs a new rag in the gusset, and plunges the rest of Heddy's filthed hand-me-downs into the wash. Did she mix up the melody? Garble the lines? Again, she shakes her head, but more slowly this time. Doubt whispers in Old Heddy's voice.

Should've listened—

"I did," she says, a thunk from above cutting her off.

Should've listened.

Nostrils flared, Payton expels a hard breath. Flicks pinkish suds from her hands. Leaves the clothes to soak.

Old Heddy's cottage is squat, square, and almost entirely kitchen. Soot-stained beams hang low over a central worktable, dangling a hooded oil lamp that brains Payton whenever she stretches the kinks from her back. A hatch in one corner leads to the root cellar, a cobwebbed ladder climbs to Heddy's attic, and Payton's narrow cot *just* fits between the sink-stand and back door. From floor to ceiling, sturdy timber shelves line the left and front walls, their dark lengths stretching unbroken across casements and formal entrance, only stopping at the stone chimney breast. Sufficiently wide to hang three iron pots at once, the fireplace crackles day and night. Now Payton shrugs on a wool shift, then hoists a copper kettle up off the hearth and clunks it onto the worktable. Muttering, she starts in on tonight's supper, filling out the bone broth with carrots, spuds, bitter greens. Adds a splash of cider. A pummel of pepper. Same way Heddy did it.

Exactly the same.

So how come the spell keeps a-spoiling?

"I swear I remember every word, but—"

Little Pane, Heddy teased once, and the nickname stuck. *Transparent as glass. Think I can't see the very warp and weft of your thoughts? Your whims weaving this way and that?*

Payton knows this isn't true.

It can't be.

Listen.

Go back to basics. Blood, soil, nails—

"I *know*."

What you want is a spare set of hands.

She slouches on a stool, letting things simmer. On the table, carrot-tops and potato peels moulder beside half a dozen earthenware crocks holding crumbs of Heddy's old potting mix. Jugs of milk sour near bottles of pure full-moon water. Marrowless bones jut from enamel cups.

Hair and fur eddy in the gaps between plates. Hieroglyphic recipes scrawled with the heddle-witch's notes lie like placemats beneath carving platters and scalpels, ink puddled on watermarked parchment. Try as she might, Payton can't make head nor tails of such writings, so as always, she studies the specimens cluttering the shelves, preserved in bell jars and oversized cloches, stuffed and displayed on lacquered stumps. Humble wrens regrown as clever ravens. Field mice replanted into golden-eyed lynx. Cats turned coyotes. Farm hounds, wolves. Proud creatures, one and all; hunters and gatherers, each bigger and bolder than the last. Decades of success, the best ones bespelled long before Payton came along, the boast of Heddy's collection. The cruel beauties looming over Payton's ugly failures.

There, between the broad-winged bats and black falcons, lies her own botched basset hound. And over there? A snake-tailed guinea pig. A litter of headless hares. A flock of featherless, faceless canaries. So many mouthless un-kittens.

And *there*, backlit by a shelved-in window's grey light, her most precious parings of all. Five tiny, see-through bods. Flesh paler than raw dough and twice as pliable. Arm and leg nubbins curled in like cashews. Bulbous heads, too heavy for pinkie-thin necks, flopped into the hollow curves of their chests. Her own handful of disappointments.

For three cycles, she's practised and practised, and kept these near-misses – in baskets, fishbowls, mason jars; some brined, some left bare – their awful chests fluttering, blank eyeballs staring, skeletons rubbery and crooked. Wretched, wilful things. None fully dead yet. None really alive.

"What more can I do?"

She deflates forward, elbows sinking to knees, with a gut-deep sigh. Lightning bugs flicker around the stool's rungs, her hairy legs, ruddy feet. Darkness edges in.

"What am I missing?"

No matter how closely she follows Heddy's lead, they just come out *wrong*.

You're not listening.

She closes her eyes. "You're not helping."

Listen.

Outside, the pump's handle squeaks. Stops. Squeaks. Water spatters the ground near the drive. A small voice coos.

Payton holds her breath to hear better.

Squeak.

Her spine straightens. That was fast, she thinks with a smile. Above the mantel, the cuckoo's barely beaking five o'clock. Scarcely time for a trek into town and back, especially for one with such spindly legs, and it's not a trip many'd make this late in the day. Payton thought it'd take until morning, at least, when the girl was heading back to school…

Stupid whim.

Kids suck the life right out of you.

The stool screeches as she pushes back from the table. One, two, three stoneware dishes clunk down near the table's edge. *Just look at you, Pane.* Hot soup slops into each. Spoons clatter. She'll carry Heddy's bowl up later, but first—

You grew so goddamned fast.

—she creeps over to the door. Rests her hand on the knob. Waits for the:

Knock knock.

Deep breath. Exhale.

Heart pounding, Payton cracks it open. "Yes?"

On the stoop, the girl holds out a dripping, shivering mass of skin and cat whiskers and foxtail. Still in school clothes, she's drenched from the knee socks down. A pack of boarding-house biscuits is wedged in her cardigan pocket. A gift pilfered from the warden's understocked cupboard.

She's alone then, Payton thinks.

Alone or unwanted.

"Is that for me?" she asks, pointing at the monogrammed package. Smiles as the soft-hearted girl soldiers on.

"I tried to give it a drink." Her dimpled chin quivers, throat tight with tears. "I think it's sick? Did I—"

"Not at all," Payton says, elbowing the door wide and propping it open with her hip. Gentle as can be, she reaches out. Cups the girl's wet hands. Supports her shaky grip on the bait.

"It's all right," she says. "None of this is your doing."

* * *

Magpies aren't known for their dawnsong, but this one's summoning the sun in a raucous red fit of warbling. Sleep still crusting her eyes, Payton's out in the garden again, ankle-deep in morning dew, her bed-fuzzed braid stuffed in a baker boy cap, a patchwork blanket cloaked around her thin nightdress. Arms crossed, she stares down at the devil-throated bird cocking its smug head inside the cage trap. Chortling up at her.

"That's enough out of you."

It's second nature now, the trapping and trimming. While Payton goes through the motions – mesh door up, wings pinned under pit, dagger-beak clamped in one hand, lizardish toes pinched between fingers, talons snicked – she flushes, thinking about the girl. How she gave Payton her name in that lazy drawl. *Norah*. And the care she took with that little wrongkin. And the way she tried not to goggle at its siblings when Payton invited her in. And how flighty she got then, inside the warm, shelf-full cottage, dim with lantern and fireglow. Soon as she spotted the bowls of soup, the girl said, *Looks like you're expecting company*. Plunking the biscuits on the table – the cheer-up snack Norah stole, just for *her* – she said, *I should go*.

"Off with you, then," Payton says, pocketing eight black seeds as the magpie half-flies and half-hops along the pumpkin patch, weaker for overnighting in jail. At the end of the row, its gimlet eyes lock onto something nestled among the beanstalks. Its mocking song sharpens into a carrion caw as it launches into the air, then dives blade-first into the greenery.

"Go on, now." Payton jogs after it, shooing and shouting. "Get!"

Clawless and cranky, the bird swoops until Payton catches up, then flaps a few metres away with a crawful of ginger bristles.

The vixen is sprawled on her side in the dirt, russet fur garish in the first blush of morning. Far as Payton can tell, the animal is no worse off than yesterday – no visible wounds, despite the magpie's avid stabbing, no broken bones nor sockets out of joint – and yet, she's just *lying* there. Breathing shallow but steady. Tongue lolling. Skyward eye unblinking. Just glowering up at her and gruffing. Stiff with fury at this rotten turn of fate.

Pane in my backside, you are.

Payton shakes her head. This isn't *her* fault. The fox should've made it. The trap was harmless, the clipping a cinch. She barked and ran off, right? She *survived*.

She should've survived.

Yeah, and the seeds, the spell – the whole shebang – should've sprouted little sweet-peas for Payton to play with and pamper and parent.

Something's off.

Something in this soil's not right, she thinks, draping her quilt over the miserable creature and its accusing glare before trudging back to the house. The magic isn't the problem; it's the materials. Down in the root cellar, she raids Heddy's dwindling hoard of blood and bone. Carries a cup of it up to the worktable. Fertilises a new pot of dark loam. Wheezing, she coughs up a lungful. Spits. Swipes a finger along her hatline and mixes in the salt-sweat. Her moon-cloth is drier than yesterday, but she coaxes out a red drizzle. Last, she pops in a kernel. Just one.

Stirring, she sings.

What you need is—

"Shut up," Payton says, the spell's ninth refrain uttered and her energy spent. Resting her damp cheek on the gritty tabletop, she blinks at the botcheries lining the walls. Quietly sniffling, she waits and wishes for – *a spare set of hands* – a win.

What you need—

"Hush!"

Something shifts in the pot. A tinkling like sand falling in an hourglass, softening as the pile grows. Payton sits up. Hands balled against her chest as a downy grey head slowly emerges. It's got blinkers big as pennies, firmly wrinkled shut. Hooked sliver of a beak. Wings snug against a potato-sized body. Feathers wispy as dandelion clocks. Puffing itself clean, the owlet kicks its twiggy feet. Hisses like a cobra.

That's good, Payton thinks, heart hitching. That's normal. Owls don't hoot right away. They *hiss*.

"Hello," she whispers. "You're here."

Carefully cradling the heavy pot, Payton takes the sprout outside for a better look. You're so beautiful, she thinks, grinning like a jack as the last dregs of sunrise dredge his plumage in gold. "You're perfect," she clucks, spinning like a girl. Startling him awake.

Opening those eyes.

* * *

"Did he make it?"

Payton sees Norah over there near the water pump, right where she'd set the unfox sprout yesterday. She hears the girl's question. Her shoes scuffing the kit's dried goop-stain into the footpath. Bookbag on one shoulder. Ponytail drooping. Pockets empty.

Doesn't matter.

"Miss Payton?"

What. Her gaze sludges back down to the thing aspirating like a bellows in her lap. *You*. Fluffing and preening. Its face-holes clustered with sea anemones. Thrashing, peach-tentacle eyes. *Need is*— Who knows how long she's been sitting here. An hour now? Maybe two? Time enough to numb her rump on the porch step, anyway, and for the day's first freight train to shriek past, scaring flocks of cornfield crows. Scattering them like maple keys on the wind.

Still, she's got nothing.

No one.

Maybe this is it, Payton thinks.

Maybe she just can't do this.

Not on her own.

"Miss?"

At last, she looks up. Squints.

Focuses.

—a spare set of hands.

"The kitten. Is he okay?"

"What?" Payton says, shaking off her gloom as the trigger plate of a plan clicks in place.

Steady now.

Almost there.

You've been so patient.

When Norah hups her backpack and half-turns to go, Payton lets herself imagine, just for a second, what it would be like, always having someone to talk to, someone who asked smart or secret or silly questions – *is that moon full or is a slice still missing, do you really want children, is that poor kitten of yours okay*? – the kinds of things friends and kin natter about. Someone to share meals with, real hearty feasts, not soup and mash and invalid gruel, but cornbread, roast game, and a big pumpkin pie like the one Heddy baked that time, just that once, *before*. Two cycles ago, give or take. Two months of solitude. Just her and the gourds. The growings.

Now, though.

"Oh sure," Payton says before Norah skedaddles. Tempering her tone – *steady, steady* – she calls her over. "Got him right here. Wanna see?"

"Yeah, I'd love a peek."

While Norah drops her bag and skip-hops across the crabgrass, Payton bunches her nightie around the owlet. A hot coal of certainty blazes in her belly as she starts gnawing her fingernails. Scissoring the pointer off with her teeth. She tongues the jagged piece until the girl is parked right in front of her, craning to see the muffled thing on her lap, then takes her best shot.

"Ugh!" Norah glances down at the grimy nail snagged on her sweater. "What'd you do that for?"

"Sorry, pet," Payton says lightly, dabbing spit off her chin. "Forgot myself there. Not used to having company."

All this time, she thinks, I've stupidly done all the planting. Same as before.

"It's okay," Norah eventually says, sneering as she goes to brush it off.

Same way I always did for Heddy.

She tilts her head at the owlet's flowerpot. Its blood-damp dirt.

"Toss it in this pot here, would you? Not on the ground? And, maybe, tamp it in a bit? Until it's hidden?"

Brows furrow. Disgust turns to wariness. Still, the girl hasn't bolted.

"Why?"

"Call me superstitious," Payton says, forcing a chuckle. "Don't want to leave bits of myself just lying around. Think you can give me a hand?"

In the attic, the heddle-witch moans.

"Okay," Norah says, the word stretching thin as her trust, and plucks the nail off her sleeve. Flicks it like snot. Pat-pats it into the ready soil. Palms the grime off on her dress.

"Listen," she says, already retreating—

Finally.

"—I gotta go."

"All good," Payton says, relief runnelling her cheeks as the girl hightails it. Across the grass. Down the footpath. Gone.

Finally.

Facing the pot, Payton sinks straight into the spell. Heddy's strongest scratchings shush from her cracked lips, their familiar rounds and rhymes repeated nine by nine times. A cyclical, sacred monotony.

This will work, she thinks, wringing her dreams into this song, this seed, this scion.

Upstairs, old Heddy roars.

Finally.

Soon depleted, Payton falls silent. Fireflies swarm in her vision, flaring and fading around the rattling pot. Chimes jingle in her ears as the first fractures appear in its fired clay. Crisp air chuffs in and out, her mouth and the cracks now gaping, spilling joy. Payton's pulse races as shards scatter in a shower of soil. Life stirs. Stretches. Screams. *Finally*. Before long, mandrake-wails calm to a newborn's milk-mewling. Onion-paper skin pudges and pinkens around belly and bottom and button nose. Rootlets flesh into fingers. Toes.

Finally.

Look at you.

Payton's mind tells her to scoop the child into her arms, to cuddle and kiss and pinch every perfect bit of it, but her body has other ideas. She slumps against the porch rail, limbs heavier than hearthstones. *Just look at you*. It takes her a month to blink. Another to breathe in. Another to exhale. Now the baby plumps itself upright. Stands. Now it toddles around. *How'd you get so strong, so quick?* Payton slides down the back steps. Her tired head lolls against sanded timber. Her heartbeat stutters. *Slow down, pet.* Years trickle and blub and rush away.

Now her sprout's a lean girl. Now she's looming above her. *How'd you get so tall?* Now she's got her moon bloods and hopes of her own. *Slow down. I need time to teach you—*

Now she's a woman grown.

The Stone Boat

Melissa Bobe

Lupe

"IT'S GETTING AWAY FROM ME," she muttered, eyes flickering across screens as her fingers tapped determinedly at clicking keys.

"How?" he demanded. "I thought you had it locked in."

"I don't know; it's different."

"How could it be different? Didn't you write the original code?"

"What do you want me to tell you?" she returned through gritted teeth. "It's changed."

"Listen, we didn't hire you to—"

Lupe tore off the headset. "That's enough of that." She narrowed her focus, magic guiding her hands as they carefully navigated the keys. "Now: where are you trying to go?"

The Nairn wasn't supposed to behave like this. She'd created it with a set homing protocol and it always came back to her, but Lupe had been calling it for days. It almost hurt to be avoided like this, especially now that it was within her sights.

When Lupe had set out to code a magic-tracker into existence, she'd avoided NetWork recruiters, though they'd been courting her for years. NetWork wanted beasts, basically rabid dogs that would tear a magical entity to pieces before its code could even be analyzed.

Lupe didn't want that, which was why she'd made the Nairn. Rogue magic might always be hunted, but plenty of people could see the value in studying and even taming such magic. As long as she could maintain the life she'd built on the edge of the city, casting across the interwebs as she pleased, Lupe was happy to take jobs from companies that appreciated the nuanced strength and skill of a creation like the Nairn. Of course, the asshole she'd been on the line with only knew that the Nairn had found a valuable piece of rogue magic on the interwebs and his bosses wanted it. But she had bigger problems now.

"Come on, baby," Lupe murmured, flexing her powers towards the Nairn. It was on edge, its movements quick and reckless. "Come back to me, now."

Using her left hand on the piano keyboard beside her, she began playing the Nairn's favorite tune while maintaining her line on it with the standard keyboard. Lupe had plenty of methods by which to bring a program home, but music was her preference.

At the sound, the Nairn froze. Lupe advanced, knowing she had a tiny window in which to bring it home.

Then, suddenly, they were no longer alone.

On one of her screens, the image of a placid lake overtook what had previously been rows of code making up Lupe's personal rooms, her interwebs home.

"What the…?"

Lupe typed furiously, but there was no way of pushing it out. The front-most room had been breached, and a sudden electrical zap came from her main keyboard, burning her hand.

"Ow!" she yelped, pressing the wound to her mouth. Her eyes remained on the lake.

A boat appeared, coming forward through mist that rolled out over the water. As Lupe looked on, she saw the boat was crudely cut from stone; it floated, empty, slow and sinister.

Suddenly, the tune she'd been playing sounded from within the rooms, but it no longer came from Lupe. An unknown entity had come forward; Lupe couldn't quite make sense of it, but it was playing her music, mimicking her presence, copying her personal codes.

"Shit," she breathed.

The Nairn turned towards the entity, and Lupe brought her good hand back to the keyboard but found her hardware unresponsive. She pulled out another headset, one on a network for emergencies.

"Call SWitch and say everything we feared with the Nairn... well, this is worse!"

Suddenly, she smelled salt air, heard the crashing of waves all around her.

"What..." Lupe backed away from her console as the image of the boat slid onto the next screen and the next. The music grew louder, and then her feet were in water up to her ankles, thick fog rising all around. "This isn't possible!"

Every firewall she'd put in place kept programs from manifesting in the tangible world. There was no way to breach her rooms; the only people who knew how would never dare to, in part because they were friends and in part because Lupe could do the same to them.

She raised her uninjured hand to trace protective spells in the air. Her console glowed behind a wall of fog, keyboards and screens fading from sight.

The hull of a stone boat became visible, drifting towards her.

SWitch

I got the message on the train, of course – can't even take a short ride across the city uninterrupted.

Sighing, I pulled out my portable spellbook, flipped it open and started typing. Some people moved away, which I had gotten used to since I'd started casting in public. I liked it better that way; now there were enough free seats for me to put my feet up. My boots had really been starting to kill.

I know what you're thinking. What kind of a witch works out in the open? I should be holed up somewhere: a remote cabin, right? Or, since I'm more of an urban type, an abandoned building. I should probably be anti-social, too. I mean, I don't love parties, but you're thinking socially awkward – afraid of people, even. Oh, and I should be negligent of my personal hygiene.

What can I say? I smell great, my clothes are always on point, and once you get me started, I'm actually a decent talker.

But when I went to find Lupe, I couldn't. Well, it's not that I *couldn't*; I can do pretty much whatever I want. The problem was, there was nothing to find. All her rooms were uncharacteristically quiet.

If I'd been irritated by the interruption of what had otherwise been a relaxing day, I was now actively pissed. First, Lupe gets an automabot to give me a message she should've delivered herself. Don't get me wrong, I'm not biased against bots or anything. I just would've preferred to have heard from her directly. Sure, I'm not always available, but she could've *tried*.

"Although I'm beginning to wonder whether she could," I murmured, then contacted the automabot again.

"Hello, SWitch," it replied. "How can I be of assistance?"

"When you relayed Lupe's message to me: how did she sound?"

"I am not entirely sure I understand the question," the bot replied hesitantly.

"Did she sound hurt? Or threatened?"

"This is difficult for me to assess," the bot answered. "I believe the human emotion infusing her vocal patterns was closest to fear."

"Thanks."

"Happy to be of help."

I didn't like it. Lupe doesn't scare easily, and her rooms were never empty. She'd brought up our concerns about the Nairn, that it might be manipulated by NetWork or something like that. Magical folk on the interwebs dreaded entities like the Nairn, but Lupe always made sure her creations did no harm. It was why I'd been willing to help her streamline things whenever she brought a program to life.

Suddenly, in the middle of the train, I felt a strong breeze. I glanced up, but we were still moving and the doors hadn't opened. I looked around, assessing whether there was magic nearby, whispering a spell to check my surroundings.

The breeze hadn't come from anyone in my vicinity. And it had a taste: salt? I glanced at the narrow panel windows of the car. We were dead in the city's center, nowhere near the coast.

Lupe's rooms remained empty. Something was definitely wrong, and I knew I was the most likely witch to figure out what. But I'd need help.

Edynn

"What do you mean you can't find her? I'm looking at her now."

I heard SWitch hesitate, and SWitch never hesitates, so I triple-checked. But there was Lupe, in her central room.

"Then where the hell's the Nairn?"

That, I couldn't answer. "Maybe out hunting?"

"I don't like it." I could practically see the frown on SWitch's face, though it had been years since we'd encountered one another in the tangible realm. "Lupe's dramatic, but she doesn't send messages unless something's wrong. And the Nairn—"

"I mean, you don't think it's already... *out*, do you?"

"Are you asking if I think our little baby's not lost in the forest anymore, Edynn?"

I sighed, leaning into the smell of lilac blooming at my back. "I'm asking whether it's time I leave the mountains."

"You'd ditch your little garden and come back to earth?" SWitch laughed. "Now I've heard everything."

My 'little garden' was the vibrant home I'd created for myself. I'd met Lupe and SWitch when I'd first started playing with magic on the interwebs, learning to hack and listen along the networks. But I've always been a gardener. I love the two intricate worlds in which I live: the bustling, ever-changing realm of the interwebs, and the garden around my small cottage, complete with every plant I can cultivate and the purest air a witch could breathe.

"If the Nairn is loose in the world, we'll have problems," I said. "Magic-tracking on the interwebs is one thing, but if it follows its programming in the tangible realm and Lupe isn't there to guide it…"

"We'll be outing a lot of magical folks," SWitch finished for me. "And if NetWork catches on, it's all over. They'll have a Lupe prototype to reverse-engineer right there."

"You talk about the Nairn like it can't feel."

"And you're the only witch I know who lives in a garden but sheds tears for automabots and manifested programs."

I had said it before and knew I'd need to many more times before anyone understood – not that anyone was likely to. "My two worlds are not diametrically opposed. They're more akin than you know."

"If you say so."

"My magic does." I threw some light at one of my roses, which was looking wilted. "Anyway, why are you so concerned for Lupe?"

"Try to contact her."

I did, first in the central room and then on her emergency line. In both locations, I got her standard at-rest message, which would normally make me think she was blowing me off, except for everything with the Nairn. Besides, Lupe wasn't one to blow friends off; that was more of a SWitch thing to do.

"Nothing, right?"

"Let me try one more thing." I turned to my cauldron, filled to the brim with rich, dark soil, and thrust my arms in until they were immersed above my elbows. I cast a complex locator spell, connecting through root and vine, feeling every breeze on every leaf in the garden and then beyond, every movement within and above the earth.

What no one gets about plants is that they have their own interwebs.

Several minutes later, I came out of the spell. Withdrawing my arms, I said shakily, "Okay, SWitch. I'm not going to pretend I ever like it when you're right, but this time, I'm really not happy about it."

"She's missing?"

"According to what I've just seen – or wasn't able to see – there's no trace of Lupe on this earth."

"And aside from that bullshit at-rest message, there's no sign of her on the interwebs either. Tell me how that's possible, Edynn."

"If she were dead, I would know," I said. "Her body would've been visible. So, if she's not on the interwebs and she's not in the tangible world…"

"Where the hell else is there?"

SWitch

It had been years, but Edynn looked the same.

"I'd offer to bring you back to my place, but I get the sense you already have a plan."

"I think I know who we can consult," she said, not meeting my gaze, "but you aren't going to like it."

"Why not?" I asked, not liking that she'd said I wouldn't like it.

"Well, I know you don't love the games..."

I didn't try to stop my groan; no sense holding back how I really felt. "The Tafl Twins? *Really*?"

"They know everything there is to know about world structure," she reminded me.

"But they're insufferable."

Edynn gave me a sidelong glance. "Are you annoyed because they're very young or because they're very good?"

"I mean, I had the decency to wait until adulthood to get as good as I am," I reasoned. "And I can keep my eyes on the person I'm speaking to without having to distract myself with checkers."

"I think their games are a bit more advanced than that."

"I don't think they're old enough to know the meaning of the word 'advanced'."

We grabbed a southbound train to the arts hub of the city, where the twins liked to hang around.

"We should learn their names if we're going to ask favors," Edynn murmured, eyeing my spellbook.

I snorted. "Get your own damned book."

She rolled her eyes and started to say something back, but our train suddenly screeched to a halt. An announcement to stay calm sounded over the crappy speakers, but I'd already sensed something nearby.

"You still know how to cast outside that thing?" Edynn tapped my spellbook.

"Do *you* know how to cast when there aren't any daisies around?"

We joined hands and extended our magic together, seeking the source of the trouble. And just like that, I felt a presence I'd never experienced outside the interwebs.

"Well, you weren't wrong about the Nairn," I muttered. "It's on a scent, too – ran straight across the tracks. That's why we stopped."

"It's hurt?" she asked.

I shook my head. "Lupe built it nimble enough not to collide with a moving train, but it was probably a near miss. It's close, though, and more than a little freaked out." I continued searching, feeling the path of distress the Nairn had left in its wake. "Lupe's the one who really knows her pets, but if I'm sensing things correctly, it's not just hunting; something is hunting it."

"Once we're out of here, I'll let the plants know."

I looked at her skeptically. "What's that going to do, keep your daisies from getting stomped on?"

"They'll watch for what's hunting the Nairn and report back if they notice anything."

"How? We have no way of knowing where the Nairn's headed."

Edynn gave a wry smile. "Plants have their own networks. We don't need to know where it's going – as long as it's out and about in the tangible world, my daisies can send news."

Even I had to admit that was pretty amazing, though I didn't out loud. The train started up, and we were once more headed for the arts district.

Edynn

It was impossible to convince SWitch to be nice, but I was hoping the twins wouldn't notice.

When we approached, a small crowd was observing them. This wasn't unusual, from what I knew of the brothers. Their games were infamous, and many who gathered in the arts district to watch street performers regarded this as much a creative show as anything else they'd come to see.

The board on which they played shone through the downtown haze, luminescent inlay making the pieces on the surface seem like so many shadows dancing at the whim of either boy, one with a burgundy cloak wrapped around him, the other wearing a sleeveless tunic from which slender arms emerged. They were identical, it was said; upon closer inspection, I could see it was true.

"My brother is approached by a witch," the cloaked one said, eyes unreadable beneath the hood on his head.

"And so is brother mine," replied the other, a smirk visible on his face.

SWitch gave a look of disgust, so I quickly spoke first. "We were hoping you might offer some wisdom."

The one with the cloak said, as he shifted a piece on the board, "Ask your questions, earth witch. We have all day, but you don't."

"Our friend is missing," SWitch chimed in, hands on hips. "There's no trace of her on the interwebs, Edynn here says she's not on this earth, and we've run out of places to look."

The twin in the sleeveless shirt seemed surprised, though he and his brother never glanced up from their game. "There are always more places to look."

"What you need is the place your friend is most likely to be," his brother added.

"Would you happen to know where that is?" I kept my voice patient, though I was starting to understand all of SWitch's protests.

"Your friend," the one with arms visible spoke again, "is responsible for the magic-tracking creature that's been loosed in the city?"

SWitch and I shared an uncomfortable gaze. I was sure we were both wondering whether the twins would hold a magic-tracker against us. They weren't exactly non-magical themselves.

"You needn't worry about retaliation from us," the one in the cloak murmured. "We're known to all and don't fear any who might seek out rogue magic."

"Though roguish we may sometimes be," his brother said with a chuckle. "But the scent your friend's creation caught came from a very distinct location, neither of this world nor the interwebs."

"Then where the hell does it come from?" SWitch had gone from obviously irritated to borderline hostile. I couldn't say I was far behind.

"There is a world that exists below," the one in the cloak went on. "Its inhabitants are both like and unlike those of this world, but they covet what they do not have."

"Lupe? They covet Lupe?" SWitch looked ready to smash the gameboard to pieces.

"They covet," said the brother with no sleeves, "the ability to create, for nothing in that world can make something new. All they have is what they take from others."

"And how do we get to this world?" I asked coolly, despite the slow crumbs of information dropping between each move of their game.

"You don't," the cloaked twin told me. "It will come to you."

"When?" SWitch's arms were now waving wildly. "Where?"

The brothers fell silent for a long moment, both staring intently at the board. Whatever had happened in their game was obviously of significant interest, onlookers murmuring audibly. We waited, and for a helpless second, I thought this might be all the aid we would receive.

"Find the last place it breached this world," the cloaked twin finally advised. "The walls between will be thinner there, and you may even find a tether by which your friend has kept hold of where she belongs."

"Lupe's console," SWitch murmured.

We left the twins to their game. I could only hope Lupe hadn't moved since we'd last visited.

SWitch

It turned out Lupe had kept her same old haunts in the tangible world. By the time we got there, my spellbook was indicating she was also active on the interwebs, spending time in her rooms.

"There's no way," I told Edynn. "She'd never just sit around if she knew the Nairn had manifested."

Edynn nodded silently, using her hands to cast a protective shield around us as we approached the entrance to Lupe's place. With neither of us buying the digital line of bullshit, we had to be careful because whoever was using Lupe's rooms clearly thought they were putting on a good show. Sometimes I wonder why no one knows a talented witch when they see one – or two, in our case.

Once inside, which took some doing because we had to override Lupe's security protocols, we found the place empty. There was, though, a certain aroma I'd caught earlier that day in the middle of that crowded train.

"Do you smell the ocean?" Edynn whispered.

Before I could reply, Lupe's screens displayed a greeting.

Hello. What are you doing in my home?

Edynn and I shared a knowing glance: impostor.

"Hey, Lupe," I said, not bothering to touch the keyboard. "It's been a long time."

Yes. Is everything all right?

"Why wouldn't it be?" Edynn asked.

You're in my home.

"We were supposed to meet, remember?" I said, ready to test this witch or whatever it was impersonating my old friend. "You're late."

Of course. I suppose as there's no record of us planning to meet, I must have forgotten. How silly of me.

I didn't look at Edynn then, because it was letting us know: I've been watching you, too.

"I don't know what to tell you, Lupe," I said. "Where are you? We'll come to you."

I had to leave, but I'll be back soon.

"We can wait." Edynn was testing it, too.

You shouldn't. I'll find you.

With that, the impostor left the rooms, heading out into the interwebs.

"We can go back to your place now," Edynn told me, saying nothing about the impostor since we both knew

Lupe's place was compromised and every word we spoke could put us in danger. "I'm sure she can find us there."

We both stood waiting, and suddenly, there was a glitch on the screens. I could sense an attempt to gain access to the rooms, one that ultimately failed. Then, drifting across the central screen, came four words:

TWO GONE

ONE LEFT

A moment later, they flickered and vanished.

"I think Lupe was hoping to have us decorate a little here first," I said, struggling to keep my tone neutral because, let's be real, that isn't a thing I do. "Are your daisies ready?"

A broad grin split Edynn's face. "Oh, they've been dying to pop up all day."

Edynn

I used more plant magic than I probably ever have at one time, but I knew just as SWitch did that the entity impersonating our friend had to be as good as we were to make off with a powerful witch after breaching both her interwebs rooms and her home in the tangible realm.

Once a magic-infused wall of vines surrounded us, SWitch asked, "You're sure nothing can hear us through this?"

I pointed to the bluebells. "They'll let us know if any presence comes close enough to listen in, whether via the interwebs or the front door."

"What do you think that message meant? Aside from the fact that it was Lupe, the *real* Lupe."

"The number of times she's tried to get through, maybe?"

"It would make sense," SWitch murmured. "She'll get locked out for good with a third attempt, I guess."

We were silent for a moment. Witchcraft is all well and good, but sometimes, you need to think on a problem. Staring at my plants, I sprouted an idea.

"Can you call the Nairn to you?"

"In this world?" SWitch frowned. "I'm not sure."

I crossed my arms. "Is the great SWitch admitting defeat?"

"Whoa, there – I said I wasn't sure. Let's not get carried away. Why do you want to call it?"

"If its presence in the tangible realm is linked to Lupe's abduction, then maybe bringing it back to the scene of the crime will help us recover her, too."

SWitch's eyes widened, a light I'd been hoping to ignite filling them. "You mean the link Lupe's holding on to – what those two gamer nerds were talking about."

"Wouldn't it make sense that it was the Nairn?"

"Oh, I have a much better idea than anything those twins could turn us towards," SWitch said. "But it'll mean baiting two pretty pissed off parties at the same time."

I thought about this. "We don't have reinforcements."

"Nope."

"And I don't even have my tools to work with, beyond the plants. My console and cauldron are back home."

"Also true, although I've got my spellbook."

"And if this doesn't work, we could end up trapped with Lupe, or worse."

"Yup."

"All right," I sighed. "It doesn't seem like we have much choice."

"I knew it was good that I called you," SWitch said, setting down the spellbook and preparing for the most dangerous plan either of us had ever hatched.

SWitch

There are a lot of good things about being me. One such thing is that, when I need to (and sometimes when I don't), I really know how to piss people off.

Once Edynn had coaxed her plants into a snare, I started running my mouth.

"Hey, Lupe! Lupe!" I shouted at the screens, typing into the keyboard so my words would immediately broadcast on the interwebs even as I stood there screaming. "Are we going to have to wait for your ass all day?"

It took several moments, but finally, new messages appeared.

I thought I told you I would find you.

"Yeah, well, here's the thing: I don't buy your bullshit."

A long pause after that. I knew it was going through everything it could find on my relationship with Lupe, trying to understand what might make me speak to a friend like that.

I don't know what you mean.

"Of course you don't," I replied. "You're not Lupe."

Another pause, and then, *I'm Lupe, SWitch. I know you and Edynn well. Why would you say such a thing?*

"Because I don't believe you're my friend," I went on. "And neither does Edynn. We know Lupe. Just because you can mimic her code doesn't make you her."

That's not true. Stop saying it.

"Why don't you make me?" I returned petulantly. "Prove you're Lupe, if I'm wrong. Where's my friend? Where is she?"

And, as we had known it would, the entity found itself with no choice but to leave the interwebs. The form it took was identical to Lupe's; I had a hell of a time not backing down as it emerged from the screen and stepped forward wearing my friend's face.

"Here I am, SWitch," it said with Lupe's voice.

"No," I told it, backing away from the console and hoping it would follow. "You're not her."

A presence not far from Lupe's home, and Edynn stepping silently towards the console, her plants rendering her unnoticeable as she moved; I had to keep going.

"If you were Lupe," I went on, "you would've greeted us the way you do whenever we meet in person."

The impostor frowned, now sensing there were many things it could not glean since I'd separated it from the interwebs. Its eyes fell hungrily on the spellbook in my hands, and I almost laughed aloud at how well the trap was working.

"And how would I greet you in person?" Its voice had fallen away to a crackling rasp that made the hair at the base of my neck stand on edge.

Or was it a familiar presence just outside that was giving me chills?

"Well, for one thing," I said, seeing Edynn shoot me a nod, then turning to open the door, "Lupe would greet the dog first."

In bounded the Nairn, exactly the huge, fire-eyed fluff monster Lupe had programmed it to be. It was magnificent, poised at eye-level with all of us on its four nimble legs, tail swishing in the air behind it, blazing fur standing on end as it stared down the impostor and growled its fear and frustration.

The entity that was not Lupe looked stricken, its mask faltering. I realized what it was, and called, "Are you two ready to banish a shapeshifter, or am I going to have to finish this gig myself?"

Behind the impostor, Edynn was gripping Lupe – the real Lupe – by her hands, chanting spell after spell to recover our friend. I could see Lupe struggling, and a world I did not know, which had somehow split a rift across the one I did, was close on her heels. There was a thick chain of sorts wrapped around her waist, flickering with code and magic I'd never before seen.

"You will not take her back," the shifter snarled. "We will have you all!"

The Nairn decided it'd had enough and did exactly what I'd hoped one of Lupe's pets might in such a situation: it dove for its mistress, landing next to her in one graceful leap, and sank its glittering teeth into the chain that held her, tearing the oppressive links to shreds.

The moment she was free, Lupe came forward with all the strength of a witch enraged, raising her hands with a vicious spell aimed right at the shifter. Immediately, Edynn and I drew mirror spells of our own, ready to banish this monster from the face of every realm we knew. The Nairn yipped and huffed in eager anticipation, ready to be rid of the thing that had taken its Lupe and frightened it into the tangible world.

But as we took aim, our spell did not reach the failed impostor. It deflected our magic, and with one last snarl over its shoulder, used the console to dive back into the interwebs, racing from Lupe's rooms before we could trap it there.

"Dammit!" I swore.

Edynn looked up in distress. "Now what do we do?"

Lupe suddenly started laughing, and the Nairn nuzzled her face, demanding cuddles, of all things.

"This is why I don't understand dog people." I shook my head.

"Hey, can't I be happy to be home? I was in a pretty scary place for a while there."

“We heard,” Edynn said sympathetically.

“Who from?”

“Two brothers with a taste for board games.”

“The Tafl Twins?” Now Lupe laughed harder. “It’s a cold day in hell when SWitch will visit those two!”

“It was,” I replied. “Aren’t you worried the shifter will come back?”

“It did threaten us,” Edynn said, frowning.

Lupe shrugged. “Well, the Nairn has the scent. And it’s eager to go home, aren’t you, baby?” She continued doting on the creature, which even I had to admit she’d coded to be pretty cute. “We’ll find it eventually. It can’t hide forever; it’s not like the interwebs are infinite.”

“That’s true,” Edynn remarked. “And it’s been nice to be around old friends again. I wouldn’t mind staying, if one of you could put me up while we get the job done.”

“Well, I guess that really just depends on one thing,” I said. “Do you prefer a home with or without pets?”

Kittycat

Amanda Mason

"THERE'S ANOTHER ONE," said Edie.

Kit shoved the last of the binbags into the back of the car and slammed the door shut before turning to look. A little way down the lane stood a woman. Tall and athletic, she wore jeans and a waterproof jacket and her scarf was a slash of red at her throat. She looked perfectly at ease, staring at them, the quizzical tilt of her head suggesting something like amusement.

And after all these years, Kit still felt a sharp jolt of panic.

"Listen, do me a favour, will you?" she said. "Just nip inside and put the kettle on."

"Why? Is this one actually going to come in?" Edie was sixteen, too old now to be bossed about as if she was a kid, but she still sounded a little unnerved beneath the bravado.

"You never know. Maybe."

"Yeah. Right."

Green Howe Cottage was the only house on a narrow stretch of road which led to nowhere in particular. In the usual run of things there were no passers-by; no cars, no hikers, no delivery vans looking for a shortcut, no one. But today, Kit and Edie had barely got started before the first of them arrived. Mrs. Smailes, grey and elderly, and walking with a stick these days, had appeared at the corner of the lane.

Coming out of the house and recognising her, Kit had raised a hand in greeting, but she hadn't been too surprised by the lack of response. The old lady hadn't stayed long, just long enough to be sure.

The rest of the day had been punctuated by similar encounters. Familiar figures, all of them seemingly content to keep their distance; silent, still and purposeful.

"These people," said Edie as Bill Walker, who used to run the Post Office, took his turn. "These people need to get a life."

This woman was bolder than the rest and she had ventured a little closer. She didn't move, she didn't call out; she simply stood by the hedge, waiting patiently as the sun began to sink behind the moors and the late afternoon shadows began to lengthen.

"Mum?"

"Please. Go inside, would you?"

* * *

She held her ground as Kit approached.

"Kittycat. I heard you were back."

"Hello, Claire."

She hadn't changed at all. She was a little thinner, perhaps, and someone was making a better job of bleaching her hair these days, but Kit could still see the girl she had been and wondered briefly if the same could be said of her.

"You're selling up, then?"

And of course she knew, the whole village must know by now, although Simpsons were yet to put up a sign.

"That's right. We're just here to clear a few things out."

They had thought it a good idea for Kit to bring Edie up to Yorkshire, to allow Peter a bit of headspace and some time to work out a plan of action.

"That's a pity. It's a nice little house."

"I suppose so."

The cottage was small and damp. The front garden was a scrubby patch of lawn, and the whole of the property was enclosed within a crumbling dry-stone wall.

"It needs a bit of work."

"Oh, people don't mind that, do they?" said Claire.

"No. No, they don't."

"It's the way things are these days, isn't it? Half the houses in the village are holiday lets now. Young people go away, for uni or college or whatever, and they don't come back. No one comes back. It's a shame. Still, I suppose it brings in the tourists. I was sorry," Claire added, "to hear about your mum."

She didn't sound sorry.

"Thank you."

"It was very sudden, wasn't it?"

"Heart attack."

Kit's mother had lain undiscovered for several days, not in the house, thank God, but in the back garden in the shade of the apple tree; a detail Kit was determined to keep from her daughter.

"Just the two of you, is it?"

"Yes. Peter has a work thing he can't get out of."

Claire smiled. "Men. They're never around when you really need them, are they?" Her expression was guileless, but Kit had the feeling she knew more than she was letting on. "Solicitor, isn't he?"

"Accountant."

"That's it. Lowell and Lowell. You took his name."

"I did." Anything to get away from being Kit Thorpe.

"And that's your girl. Edith." Claire nodded towards the house, where Edie hovered anxiously by the doorstep, phone in hand. "Are you here for long?"

"No," said Kit, despising the conciliatory tone she could hear creeping into her voice. "A couple of days, no more than that."

"Oh, that's a shame," said Claire. "When you've come all this way. I thought we might catch up. Sophie's still here. You remember Sophie, don't you?"

"Sure."

The two of them had been friends right through school, thick as thieves. Wherever Claire Miller had led, Sophie Jacobs had followed.

Claire shivered. "It's getting late," she said, "I'd best get on. I'll tell Sophie you're back. They took on the pub when she married Mick Morris. You should call in and say hello." She smiled. "It'll be a laugh."

* * *

"What was all that about?"

"Oh, the usual," Kit said, as she walked back to the

house. "Sorry for your loss and all that. Come on, we've done enough for one day, I'm hungry."

Edie turned then caught her breath. "Ow," she said. "Ouch." Her jumper was tangled up in the bare briars that surrounded the front door. She tugged gingerly at one of the stems, but only succeeded in pulling the threads of her sweater. "I can't..." She tried again, grasping the briar more firmly. "I can't do it... What's that?" She twisted away from the door, looking towards the road, ensnaring herself even further. "Can you hear... I think something's hurt."

"I can't hear anything. Hold still." Kit picked delicately at the wool, slowly pulling it free from the thorns. "OK. Let me see your hand."

It wasn't a cut, as such, more a series of punctures; lacerations running across Edie's palm, bright spots of blood blooming.

"We should put something on this."

"Mum. It's literally a scratch." Edie frowned, glancing again towards the lane. "Are you sure you didn't—"

"I mean it." There was a risk of infection, wasn't there? With this sort of thing, it needed cleaning properly at the very least.

* * *

Kit looked around the kitchen as Edie stood at the sink, washing her hands. They had cleared her mother's bedroom, and most of upstairs, but they hadn't even started in here and the day was almost done.

The house resisting all change right up until the end.

A couple of days, no more than that. She had been disappointed when she'd tried booking rooms at the pub. But now she thought about it, maybe the woman on the phone had been Sophie. She had sounded vaguely familiar, smug and not sorry at all when she said they were fully booked, even though Kit had used her married name, even though it was still only March. It was better, perhaps, to stay out of everyone's way, or at least keep to the house.

"There," said Edie, drying her hands on a tea towel. "Good as new."

"Even so, we should keep an eye on it. Get some antiseptic ointment."

"Wouldn't Gran have something?"

It was odd to hear Edie call her that, their relationship having been conducted entirely by post, supplemented with the occasional call on the landline. They had been closer than she thought, Kit realised with a little pulse of shock; close, despite her best efforts.

"I don't think so, sweetheart."

But Edie was already opening the pantry door.

* * *

It was a long, narrow room, its ceiling a little lower than the kitchen. Her mother had always insisted that it was the oldest part of the house, possibly the remains of a much older building altogether. It was dark, with only a single small window at the far end, cracked and moss-stained.

Edie flicked the switch and the bare lightbulb flickered into life.

Most of the shelves were empty and covered with a thick layer of dust; her mother had long since given up buying in bulk from the nearest wholefood shop. But the upper shelves were exactly as she remembered. Row upon row of glass bottles and jars, meticulously labelled and dated.

Edie picked up a small brown bottle, which might originally have held cough mixture.

"Don't," said Kit.

You weren't supposed to touch, that had been drilled into her when she was a child. Her mother's remedies weren't to be messed with. Then, as she grew older, she had wanted nothing to do with them.

"It's OK." Edie shook the bottle gently; something viscous swirled, smearing the brown glass. The ink on the label was faded. "For pregnancy," she read aloud, before putting it carefully back in its place.

The light from the window dimmed briefly, as if someone had passed close by the house; and Kit thought she could hear something padding softly across the kitchen floor, mewling, hungry.

"Right," she said, briskly. "Can we agree to leave all this stuff alone, please?" And, turning, her foot caught something metallic, sending it clattering across the flagstones.

Edie bent to retrieve it. It was a shallow dish, embossed with stylised kittens and still encrusted with hardened scraps of something meaty and unpleasant. "I didn't know she had a cat," she said.

"She didn't, not really. She used to take in strays, occasionally."

There had been a succession of them when Kit was a girl. Sickly and flea-ridden and battle-scarred cats, thin and feral. All of them devoted to her mother, and prone to lashing out viciously at everyone else.

Wrinkling her nose, Edie put the dish on one of the lower shelves. "Hang on," she said. "There's..." She reached to the back of the shelf then straightened. "Look."

It was a book, its soft leather covers worn and mildewed. Someone had wedged a stick of chalk inside as a makeshift bookmark.

They took it to the kitchen table, and Edie opened it. "It's a bible," she said. "I didn't think Gran was religious."

"She wasn't," said Kit. "Not in that way."

The paper was stained and crumpled. There was a list of names on the title page, in hands which varied from an elegant copperplate to a familiar no-nonsense Biro.

"They're all women, look," said Edie. The older names each had a pair of dates dutifully recorded next to them. Towards the bottom of the page there was Kit's mother's name, Lilian Margaret Thorpe, there was her own name, her maiden name, Katherine Mary Thorpe, then – and it chilled her to see it – there was Edie's name. Or rather a version of it.

Edith Abigail Thorpe.

"The female line only," said Edie, softly. "No husbands or fathers." She looked up at her mother. "I quite like it: Edith Thorpe. I might change it when—"

"You'll do no such thing." Kit spoke more harshly than she'd intended.

"It was a *joke*, Mum." Shaking her head, Edie slid the chalk free, then flicked through the delicate onion-skin pages. It was apparent that the bible had been used as a journal over the years, and any blank space or pages had been used for notes; they were filled with words, phrases, odd little diagrams, circles and arrows and disjointed stick figures. The end papers were dense with lists and instructions, ingredients and methods: a sure way to bring on a woman's courses, to promote sleep, to ensure a safe labour.

Her mother had sat at the same table, turning the pages of the book with the same reverential air.

"This is knowledge, Kit. This is... power."

"Can I write Gran's date in?"

"No."

Absolutely not.

"Someone should, don't you think?"

It was all Kit could do not to snatch the bible away and tear it into shreds; to set a match to it and watch it burn.

"I'll do it later, sweetheart. Just... not right now."

Breathless suddenly, she stood and opened the door. The garden had a lonely and untended air about it; she had the sense that it must have got too much for her mother long before her death. The vegetable patches, once so orderly, had been colonised by weeds, the herbs planted among them were wild and overgrown, and nettles had sprung up around the dry-stone wall, which was badly in need of repair.

Beyond the garden the woods loomed, and beyond the woods, a patchwork of damp green fields swept up to the moors, barely visible now in the fast-fading light. One of the fields was a green burial site these days and that was where her mother lay. Buried with no service in accordance with her wishes; no mourners, no flowers, nothing. A wicker coffin lowered into the ground, earth tumbled on top of it.

The smell of it all, the house, the damp grass, the promise of rain sweeping along the valley was so chokingly familiar she thought she might cry.

And there on the doorstep was a cheap white carrier bag.

Something rustled through the undergrowth, a rat, maybe, shuddering through the clumps of nettles, and in the distance, down by the beck, she thought she could hear children laughing.

Kit took the bag to the kitchen counter and unpacked it. Tea, a loaf of cheap white sliced bread, butter, half a litre of long-life milk, a lump of cheese, half a dozen eggs, and a couple of jars of home-made jam. *Gooseberry* read one label, *Raspberry* the other. At the bottom of the bag was a tin of cat food.

"Wow." Edie picked up one of the jars and unscrewed it.

"Don't," said Kit, sharply.

Edie hesitated. "Why? You don't think there's anything wrong with it, do you?"

"No. I just didn't expect..." Her heart was pounding. It was as if the years had rolled back, as if nothing had changed.

They had once brought a bag of shopping just like this, but instead of leaving it by the door, they had gathered up the nerve to knock; Claire and Sophie. They had spun her a line about wanting to be friends. And back then, Kit had been naive enough to believe them.

"Come on, Kittycat. We'll go down the woods, it'll be a laugh."

"Look, we never – we weren't very well liked when I was growing up here."

"Because you were, like... poor?"

"No. Not exactly. You've seen the garden, the pantry. She was eccentric, your gran, she sort of set herself up as a healer."

Edie nodded, and Kit had the sense this part of the story wasn't new to her daughter. "So, she helped people, yeah?"

The thick, dark mixture. For pregnancy.

"Sometimes."

"Cool."

"No it wasn't, Edie. It really was not."

They had come back to the village when Kit was seven years old. Her grandmother had died, and her own mother, a sensible woman, at that point in time, a single mum, a staff nurse in a busy hospital, had come back to the village to sort out the house and to sell up.

But it had never happened. An unexpected holiday had been extended into a longer absence, until one day, her mother marched her into the village school and into Miss Harte's infant class. They had come home for good.

Kit had never been certain what had driven her mother away in the first place – a boy, perhaps, or a need to get out and see the world – and she had never fully understood what had persuaded her to stay.

It wasn't as if they were ever made welcome, not really.

"People are old-fashioned here," Kit said, "and, you know, it was just me and my mum."

Edie laughed. "You make it sound Victorian. It was what, the 1980s?"

"Everywhere else, perhaps. But here… hippie was still an insult, and a single mother… It wasn't ideal, OK? People used to leave her stuff, gifts. We'd find them by the kitchen door. Food, you know – like this." She gestured towards the shopping on the counter. "But it wasn't out of gratitude, or kindness. People would come to her for help; but they didn't like her."

"Why not?"

"Because when people want your help, they tell you things, and when you know things about people, they resent you."

And there was something else too.

"I think they were afraid of her."

There was a long silence. "Is that why you want to sell up?" said Edie. "Like, bad memories?"

"I want to sell up because we can't possibly keep the house on, love."

"But when you and Dad— You're not going to stay with the firm, are you? You can't carry on working with him."

"You let me worry about that. But I'm not—"

There was a sharp crack as something struck the kitchen window, and for a moment, neither Kit nor Edie moved. Then Edie darted to the open door. "Who's there?"

Kit followed her outside.

The next stone fell short, landing harmlessly among the weeds.

It was almost fully dark, the figures that were clustered by the gap in the wall, in the corner where the apple tree grew, were little more than shadows.

"Who's there?" Edie shouted. "Show yourselves."

There was another shower of stones. Then a brief silence which was broken by a soft insistent mewling.

"Edie, please. They'll get fed up, they'll go away. Come inside." Kit raised her voice. "You need to go home now. Go home and leave us alone."

The shadows seemed to shift and ripple, and for a moment she thought she had scared them off, but as her eyes grew accustomed to the dark, the group seemed to become more determined, more solid.

They had followed the path down to the beck, they had kicked off their shoes, and paddled in the icy shallows.

"I said, go home."

Then Sophie had stumbled and, clutching at Kit, she had knocked her to her hands and knees.

There were maybe a dozen people: Mrs. Smailes and Mr. Walker among them. Claire too.

She was still trying to catch her breath after the freezing shock of it, and the explosion of laughter echoing down the valley and then—

"You've had your fun. One night, that's all, and then we'll be on our way."

Claire, always fast and strong and good at games, had jumped on top of her, winding her.

"Our cat had kittens and my dad drowned them."

"I'm calling the police," said Edie, pulling her phone out of her pocket.

"You do that, sweetheart." Claire's voice drifted coolly through the garden. "We'll be long gone by the time they get here. If they bother to come at all."

A knee in her back, hands pushing her face into the water.

"It's OK," said Kit, laying a hand on Edie's arm. "They won't come in. Not after dark. Come on, sweetheart. Come back inside."

"Oh, Kittycat, that's not right, is it?" Claire scrambled over the wall. "Because there's nothing to stop us, is there? Not anymore." She jumped down, landing lightly, then turned to address the shadowy figures behind her, stretching her arms wide. "See? What did I tell you?"

They won't come in, her mother had always promised her, scrawling the chalk marks, the very worst of her eccentricities, on the door. "*Wards, see? Powerful magic and better than any lock*." Every evening as night fell, her mother labouring at the front door and the kitchen door; muttering under her breath, keeping them both safe.

Kit could almost hear the rush of water, her skin prickling and puckering and needled.

"There's nothing to keep us out now, is there?" said Claire. "All her old magic is gone, and what are you going to do, Kittycat? Eh? How are you going to stop us?"

"I— I—" She didn't know what to do. She should have realised, when they turned up in the lane, all of them watching and waiting. She hadn't thought they would come back. She hadn't thought they would try to get in.

Claire was walking slowly towards the house, laughing at her as if it was some sort of joke. "Come on, then. Show us what you've got."

It can't have been more than a few seconds, not really, a few brief moments of panic as she struggled, fumbling desperately at the rocks underneath her. Then she had— she had—

Pushed.

"Stop!" Her voice loud, clear, determined.

And it had worked.

Claire hesitated and for a moment all was still.

The pressure had vanished and she had reared up on her knees, gasping for air.

Then the silence was broken by a soft mewling.

"What's this? What have we got here?" Claire bent down, crooning softly, then made a sudden grab, catching the cat by the scruff of its neck. She stood, holding it at arm's length as it shrieked and thrashed wildly. "Got yourself a pet, have you?"

"Let it go!" Edie was outraged. "Mum! We have to do something—"

But Kit ignored her, dragging her back inside the house, throwing open the kitchen drawers, frantic.

"Kit?" Claire called out. "What are you up to in there? Don't you want to watch?"

"Our cat had kittens—"

"She's hurting it," said Edie, agonised.

Kit snatched up a knife. It wasn't a silver blade but it was sharp and she hoped it would do. Her mother had told her once, when she was showing her the book – back when she thought her daughter might follow in her footsteps – that words and marks and rituals were all very well, but they counted for nothing without instinct, without intention, without will.

You have to want it, you have to *push*.

The bible still lay on the table, the stick of chalk next to it. She grabbed them both, slipping the knife into her back pocket.

"You stay here, love," she said. "No matter what, you stay inside."

Claire was waiting for her in the garden, illuminated by the kitchen lights, but the others still huddled in the dark, too old or too afraid to breach the wall themselves.

Squatting, Kit took the chalk and swiftly drew the symbol she remembered so well on the doorstep: a crescent moon above a jagged stick woman. Then she stood and turned to face them all, holding the bible to her chest, like a shield.

"What's all this, Kit?" said Claire. "Have you finally found a backbone?"

She was holding the cat by the throat, and its struggles were slowing, the fight slowly ebbing out of it. Edie forced her way past her mother, hurling herself at Claire.

"No!" Kit cried out.

"Silly little—" Claire dropped the cat and pushed Edie to the ground, kicking out and catching her in the ribs.

"I said no!" And acting on instinct, nothing more, Kit dropped the chalk and the bible. Pulling the knife from her pocket, she raised her left hand, slicing it open in one deliberate movement, from below her ring finger to the base of her thumb.

Then falling to her knees, she slammed her hand down onto the step, sealing the ward.

There was a moment of total silence, as a shudder seemed to move through the garden and the distant spectators. "Now, get out," Kit said, clambering slowly to her feet. "Get out and *stay* out."

"Oh, you're going to need more than one of your mum's old scribbles now," said Claire.

"You killed it," said Edie, crawling towards the cat. She picked it up: it lay limp and helpless in her arms. "You—"

Claire turned, ready to kick her again and Kit stepped forward, still clutching the knife.

And she pushed.

"No!" The single word sliced through the dark.

Claire staggered as if struck, a hand to her face, and the cat shook itself free from Edie's grasp, grey and thin and cunning, streaking past Kit into the house.

"Look. Look what she did." The light from the kitchen window washed over Claire as she turned, lifting her bloodied hand from her cheek to reveal a deep cut, a sweeping curve clawed into her face, running from the corner of her eye to her chin. "Look what she did."

She sounded triumphant.

Kit raised the knife so they could all see it. "Get away from us! Go away and don't come back!"

"You heard that, did you?" said Claire. "She wants us to leave her be."

Beyond the wall, in the dark, there was a faint murmur of assent and the shadows began to shiver and retreat. And Kit understood that the next time she saw them, these people she had known for most of her life, there would be no acknowledgement of this encounter, no apology or attempt to set things right, just barely disguised distaste for her and her family.

"Edie, get up. Go back inside."

"Mum—"

"I mean it."

Edie stood and walked slowly up the path, her hands and knees stained and soiled, and when she got to the door, she took care to step over the chalk marks without smudging them.

"We'll go," said Kit, sliding the knife back into her pocket. "We'll go. We'll leave tomorrow, and we won't come back."

Claire sighed softly. "Oh, Kit. We don't want you to leave. Of course we don't." She set about cleaning up her face with her scarf, pressing it gently against the wound. "Do you know what it's like here now?" she said. "Do you have any idea at all? They come up for a weekend, or a summer. They buy up our houses, our shops and barns and outbuildings, and everything changes. We're being stifled. We're dying. No one remembers anything."

"I remember things, I remember you and Sophie. I remember this whole bloody village set against us."

"Yes, well. That's the way it is, isn't it? That's the way it's always been. That's the way it's *supposed* to be. You know that as well as I do."

"Not now," said Kit. "Not anymore."

"We've lost everything else," said Claire, sharply. "We're not losing this. You need to stay. Here. In this house."

Kit had a sudden, desperate urge to laugh. "You're mad. You don't even like me."

"Liking doesn't come into it, I don't need to like you—" Claire peeled the scarf away from her ruined face, gesturing towards the house and the bloodstained ward. "But I know what you are. I've always known."

The pressure had vanished and she had reared up on her knees, gasping for air.

And underneath the relief, the realisation of what she could do; the thrill of it.

"They need us, Mum." Edie was standing in the doorway, the grey cat, scarred and flea-bitten, was wrapping itself around her ankles, mewling softly. "That's it, isn't it? You don't like us, but—"

"Go inside."

"But Mum—"

"Go on. Find that bloody cat some food – go on."

Kit's hand hurt; it itched and burned. She slipped out of her sweater and wadded it up against the cut, flexing her fingers.

"No husband anymore," said Claire, "and no job either, once the divorce goes through. And here – you won't go without, you know. You or your girl. All you have to do is come home."

"This is not my home," said Kit. "We were only going to stay for a while, me and Mum. We were going to sell up, put a deposit on a nice modern flat. She wasn't going to end up stuck here like her mother before her, and her grandmother too. I'm not doing that. Edie isn't doing that."

She bent to pick up the bible, and felt more than a little satisfaction as Claire stepped back, fearful; more than a tiny thrill of power. Blood magic, her mother had told her, was the most powerful kind. Violence would bind a person to an act, to a place, to a promise.

And there was her blood, mingling with her mother's work after all this time.

"Fine. Send her away, keep her away, if you can. But you can't tell me you didn't feel something, Kit." Claire's smile was sour. She looked tired, old. "You can't tell me that didn't feel… *right.*"

* * *

Kit stayed in the garden for a while, watching as the moon rose and the whole valley came alive with the sounds and scents of the night, clear and sharp; listening to Edie moving around the kitchen, fussing over the stray cat, murmuring endearments.

It would be for the best, she thought, to send her away.

She could already hear herself explaining to Peter and pretending not to hear the relief in his voice; she would ring once she'd put Edie on the morning train. All she needed was a few more days to sort out the house, a week at the most.

She was holding the chalk, rubbing it back and forth between her thumb and forefinger. They wouldn't come back, she knew that much, but her mother had been so diligent; she had drawn the marks on both doors, every night, and it wouldn't do to leave the work half done.

Kit picked up the bible and went to the front of the house. Slowly, and more precisely this time, she drew the crescent moon and the broken figure in the centre of the door, as her mother had, and her mother before her, and all the women of the house had, time out of mind.

A few more days, that was all.

Then, unwrapping her hand, she pulled at the wound on her palm, re-opening it, before sealing the ward with her blood.

The Tallow Feast

Damien Kelly

YEARS AGO, a woman – reputed to be crafty – berated Alma's mother in the market square for rendering her tallow with salt and water.

Your oil will lose all goodness that way, she said, *and it will spoil.* She said it idly, half-smiling, as if sharing advice, but she meant it as an augury and a curse and every wife within hearing knew it. Because she was a witch.

"She's no witch," Alma's mother told her later. "She just fancies herself."

And as she added salt to the beef fat and water, Alma's mother educated her daughter on the realities of rendering tallow. And curses.

"You can skim the oil, without touching the water. Know your depth. Control your heat. Else you can cool and rewarm the solid tallow cake any number of times, to ensure the salt and water alike have sunk below. Take the time. Take care. Because it is a fact, daughter mine – and no witch can change this – that neither salt nor water dissolve in oil.

"So, if it's there, it's because you let it in."

Her tallow was always white as snow. Never smelly or salty. And it never spoiled.

* * *

Tonight, Alma has set her table with a supper made with time and care. And tallow.

There are crispy fried potatoes, a few fried hens, and a soup of onions and barley. She has baked bread and furnished bottles of beer. There is cheese, honey, cob nuts and hard-boiled eggs on a bed of salt.

On a second table by the door is a bowl of water and a fragrant soap; this, too, was made with Alma's own tallow. The floor is freshly washed and the fire is roaring. If any visitor can play a tune, there's a whistle on the shelf and a guitar on the wall.

Alma fills the kitchen with hospitality and lights candles all around the room. Then she opens the door.

There's a wind that would take the breath from you. The door clatters, so Alma puts a stone to it. Then she retires to her seat at the table, facing out into the night. She has a wool skirt and a jumper on, against the elements, but she's in her flat shoes rather than her boots. She doesn't intend to go out.

The fire in the hearth flattens as the air blows in, but it blazes away determinedly. The candles gutter, but they don't blow out.

Alma's mother has been dead almost a year. Peacefully and in her own time, she went with the Lord, happy and sanctified. But tonight, there are no crosses on the walls. Neither wreaths, garlands, nor iron nailed in place. Alma has removed them all. She took the bible to the chapel and left it there. She pulled up every practical plant from the little garden and burned them.

She doesn't know anything about craft; not the natural arts or the secret work of women. She thinks she's met a few more witches since the woman in the market square, but that might just be a lack of generosity on her part. Regardless, she herself has no idea how else to achieve what she wants. How to bid something welcome in any other way than this. Whoever they may be.

Because no particular power is being invited into Alma's house. But none are barred. The door is open and they can make of it what they will.

"Good evening, Alma."

"James. Good evening," she calls out to him.

James Rodgers is her neighbour and *his* almost immediate appearance is of no surprise. Never married, his parents also dead, he walks the roads like a stray goat for want of company. He's more nosy than randy, though. He smiles broadly and stoops to wave in, though the door isn't low in any way.

"This wind is fierce. Are you having a crowd in?" He's inside the front gate now, and points at the food on the table. "I haven't seen a soul on the road."

He's dressed for weather, but smartly; wool suit and an overcoat, brimmed hat and his neck tied. He's always open to invitation.

"I don't know who I'm having." Alma pours herself a glass of beer. "Maybe just yourself."

His face is a picture: his smile fixed but his brow furrowed, eyes squinting against the breeze. But the smell of the food is undeniable and the warmth of the kitchen goes round his shoulders like a friendly arm.

"Me?"

"Will you come in?" she asks him. "Can I offer you something?"

"Um—" But he's already over the threshold, hands clasped as if in supplication.

"You can wash your hands, there, before you take a plate."

He touches the soap with his index finger, but stops.

"I'm surely intruding, no? You must be expecting someone."

"I am, James. Someone or *something*. I genuinely haven't the foggiest. But you're as welcome as any."

His hand pulls back from the soap, one round indent left in it from where his finger rested. *Something?*

"I don't understand." His hands meet again, but he's wringing them now, rubbing the soap residue away. His eyes squint again, but it's not the wind.

She sighs. "It really isn't any more complicated than I've said. The door is open, the food is ready. My offer is literally on the table."

Alma herself knows how uncanny this must appear, but there's really no other way to explain. If she asks James Rodgers for what she wants, she'll get nothing more than what she asks for. And she wants more. More than James Rodgers can offer.

He seems to sense the depth he's waded into, all unwitting, and begins to back out again.

Hadn't his mother said something about old Missus Dawson and food? A warning.

"Actually, do you know? I can't stay at all. I was actually on my way to, um… But, goodnight to you, Alma."

"Goodnight so, James."

He slinks down the path, but stops at the gate.

"Are you sure I can't pull that door behind me, Alma?"

His concern is a greater kindness than he knows, but it's not what she's after.

"No, James. I want it open."

* * *

As James passes the bend and the lights from Hatton's Bar come into sight, he finally sees someone else on the road.

The woman is only half dressed, her grey blouse open at the neck and nothing on her head. Her shawl is bundled in her hand and her hair is flying.

"Hello," he says to her, and she turns briefly to acknowledge the greeting, though she doesn't return it.

Her eyes are gold.

James knows where she's going. He knows, too, that it would be both the Christian thing and his own soul's peril to try and stop her getting there.

He runs for the bar, where there might be souls braver than he.

* * *

When the woman with the gold eyes reaches the open door, Alma is putting the soup pot back on the stove to reheat.

"This isn't craft," she says, and Alma starts, almost spilling the soup.

"*God help us!*" Alma sputters, unintentionally.

The woman's voice is husky and older than her face. She laughs at Alma's outburst and it's the sound of a crow clacking.

"Indeed! Put your cross back up, stupid woman, and don't mock the likes of me again."

Alma steadies her legs by holding onto the chair.

"Will you have something to eat, miss?" she asks the woman with the gold eyes.

"None of that, Alma Dawson! I told you, there is no craft in this. Where is your dignity? This is nothing more than begging."

"It is nothing of the sort," Alma maintains, and comes round to sit again. "I'm offering hospitality. Beyond that… I don't know. I'd have to hear what else was on the table. What do you offer me?"

Gold Eyes' hand has been inside the bundled shawl until now. She draws it out with a knot of herbs and feathers between her fingers, which she raises to toss into the house. Alma really hasn't known what to expect this evening, but this at least she's prepared for.

"If that comes in here, it's mine. In my own home, I will treat it as a gift, freely given. I will claim its power, its utility and its purpose. If it enters my house, it is mine to use, though I vow not to use it against *you*. It'll harm neither of us, I promise you, if it comes inside."

The woman with the gold eyes stops, mouth bent like a taut bow, her tongue an arrowhead poised to loose. Fury makes her eyes bulge and tears bud at the corners. But the knot stays in her shaking hand.

"How *dare* you…"

"Because I know how curses like that work, miss. How the meaning is negotiated. A witch cursed my mother once, you see."

Alma holds her hand up, asking the woman with gold eyes to listen. Her tone is not imperious, however;

she speaks gently, face still. *Know your depth. Control your heat.*

"It didn't work, though, her curse – least, not how she expected it to. She fancied herself, you see, this witch. That's the phrase my mother used. Prideful. But she couldn't render tallow from wet."

Gold Eyes, pursing her lips but lowering her eyelids from their heights of indignation, puts the knot back in her shawl bundle. She sets the whole thing down on the ground and squats to sit upon it.

Alma reaches and takes a portion of chicken and a handful of potatoes from their platters, while she continues her story.

"She had done so well, convincing the rest of us she was craftier than anything, this witch started believing her own myth. So, when she couldn't make the wet rendering work as well as dry, she decided it must be because it just wasn't possible. She told my mother as much, just telling the truth as she saw it, but she was clever enough to tell it at a time and place when that truth would eventually sound like a prediction and look like a curse."

Alma rises and takes the plate to the doorway.

"Eat, please. Without obligation."

Gold Eyes accepts the plate and eats.

"My mother never made bad tallow, though. She was careful, attentive. Clever. She taught me with patience and kindness and I make grand tallow, too. My mother was a wonderful, generous woman, who would have done anything for anyone. She'd have shared her tallow with them and they'd never have had a day's trouble with it."

Alma finally sits back down at her table.

"But nobody would accept tallow from my mother. Nobody came to eat here who knew anything about her. She gave lodging to men and women hired for the seasons and they, down at the bar, would praise the great food they enjoyed in this house. But for her own people to accept her hospitality? *No, that woman's tallow is cursed.*

"That's how it began. But it grew. They went from avoiding the food she made to avoiding the house itself, until they were avoiding us both, everywhere. It didn't matter that the curse didn't do what the witch wanted it to. It still worked. But, as you would say, there wasn't any craft in it. She didn't plan it. Some power, separate to her, took the start she made and gave the curse a life of its own.

"Miss, I would like to make contact with such a power."

"Your woman was no witch, I agree," Gold Eyes says, setting her plate down inside the doorway while she stays seated without. "But you're wrong about her curse. It had no life of its own. She mightn't have had any craft, your *witch*, but she had intention. That's enough for power."

She stands.

"Intention, after all, is what has brought me to your door. I felt it from miles away. And I won't be the only one. There are powers such as you describe, only too eager to latch onto an intention like yours. You're just damned lucky I found you first."

"You weren't, as it goes."

The clacking laughter comes again and Gold Eyes lifts her bundle.

"Aye, I met your gentleman caller on the road. I think he left here unsatisfied, though, for he reeked of hunger still." The laughter leaves her gold eyes as quick as it came. "But there are things hungrier than him that would readily answer such artless intention as you have shown this night. Things that would demand more sacrifice than your fine dinner."

"I'm quite ready for sacrifice, I assure you."

"What do you know about sacrifice, stupid woman?"

"As much as you do about hunger, miss. Lick your lips."

Gold Eyes experiences a moment of confusion, but her arrowhead tongue does as it is bid. Quite suddenly, the gold eyes bulge in fresh indignation.

"You bitch!" And she backs away from the open door in horror.

"No obligation!" Alma cries out. "Peace! I beg you. I promised you, no obligation. I meant only to show you that I was serious."

"Who is this?!" Gold Eyes screams and retches on the path, as her fists go white with rage.

"My mother," Alma tells her.

Gold Eyes freezes, stares at Alma in terrified awe.

"You couldn't—"

"Rendered as sweetly as any jar of tallow made in this house. Even the undertakers avoided us, you see. So, I prepared her, laid her out. Did everything but bury her myself. And I kept that much of her, for just this purpose. Such was my intention. Such was my sacrifice. Such is my hunger."

"I should— I'll *kill you!*"

"Do worse. Introduce me, miss, to one of these hungrier things."

* * *

Gold Eyes crosses the road, walks into a field on the other side.

She tramps the grass for a moment or two until her foot finds a creeping thistle. She pushes her fingers deep and plucks the weed from the ground, leaf and root. It is the roots she wants and, ripping them free, she bends to wrap the tendrils around and between her toes. Then she digs her toes into the earth again, reburying the roots and herself with them; bound to the spot, safe from whatever blows through the house of Alma Dawson.

This far into the field, she can see the bar and the small crowd of men coming out of it. The hungry little man from the road has raised the alarm. Alma won't have long to make her bargain.

Gold Eyes has purged all she can from her stomach, but the flavour of Alma's mother's fat is still in her mouth. She, quite rightly, fears that whatever bargain the daughter might make with her mother's tallow might end up including Gold Eyes as well, however inadvertently.

That's why Gold Eyes has summoned something that won't settle for carrion.

Take the flesh of Alma Dawson, she intones, toes rooted against the wind.

Her fat is what you want.

* * *

The potatoes and chicken are cold.

Alma waits at the kitchen table. She can see the figure of Gold Eyes in the field, standing still despite the wind.

Help me, Mother, she asks in silence.

"Surely, your mother has helped enough?"

The stone stopping the door is dislodged by the shaking of the wind. It slams shut.

The woman seated opposite Alma is white as milk: hair, skin, eyes. She looks young, but smells sour. When she speaks—

"Is this your offering, Alma Dawson?"

—Alma can see she has no teeth, and as she reaches out to grab from the plate of potatoes, there are no nails on her long fingers.

"W-Wait," Alma says.

Sour Milk waits and her blind eyes narrow.

"There is a washbowl and soap over there, if you want them."

Sour Milk smiles and stands. She is dressed in white ribbons, bound and braided and so tight about her neck that she looks to be choked by them. She crosses to the bowl of water and dips her fingers in daintily. Then she reaches for the soap and mashes it in her fists. Dropping the crushed bar on the floor, she plunges her hands violently into the bowl again and scrubs at her hands until the ribbons at her wrists are hanging in sopping shreds, the bowl is empty, and the floor awash with white water.

Then the bowl falls and breaks. Alma wants to cry. Her voice breaks, too, despite her best intentions.

"Please… eat. No *ob*— no obligations."

"Oh, but I am very much interested in the obligations. You've gone to so much trouble. Intention. Sacrifice. Put your own mother on the table."

"Only her tallow. Her soul is beyond bargaining."

Sour Milk closes the space between them, white feet slapping in the foul wash water.

"*Pah!* What is a soul? We are creatures of this world; the soul is no currency to us. The cleanest tallow has more flavour than any soul."

"Then… eat."

Sour Milk puts her hand to the platter of potatoes and flips it over, its contents rolling from the table to the floor.

"Your mother's tallow is cursed. It has lost its goodness. It is spoiled."

"That's not true."

"What is it you want, Alma?"

Alma rights the upended platter.

"What would you give me for the supper I've made, lady?"

"Nothing."

With the white figure leaning over her, Alma has to bend to ease herself sideways off the chair. Sour Milk does nothing to detain her, but turns to follow her as Alma crosses to the door and opens it again.

"I am sorry to have wasted your time, then," she tells the woman in white.

But Sour Milk makes no move to leave. "Offer me something else."

"You mean offer myself."

"Yes."

"My own tallow."

"Yes. Offer me that."

"In return for what?"

"What is it you want, Alma?"

Alma lets go of the door and stoops instead to lift the pieces of her broken washbowl and the lumps of ruined soap. She takes them to the table and sets them beside the cold supper. Again, Sour Milk follows her closely.

"Will you not leave, lady? I have nothing to offer."

"You have something to offer."

"And if I offered that, what would you grant me?"

"What is it you want?"

Alma leans on the table to steady herself, her hand on the broken crockery.

"I want the curse lifted from my mother's tallow."

Sour Milk steps back, her blind eyes wide and her mouth loose. She takes a long time responding.

"Is that all?"

"It is no small thing," Alma declares, her voice straining. "So, if I offered you my own tallow, would you do that?"

"And will you render it yourself or would you let me do it?"

"Answer what I asked, please."

"Yes. If you offered me your tallow, I would end the curse."

"Good. End it, so."

Sour Milk lifts her hands, still wet from the washbowl, and cups them in front of Alma's face.

"When I have you, the fat of you, here in my hands."

The reek of her breath burns Alma's throat and she almost coughs in reply.

"Yes. End the curse, then. Please."

Sour Milk closes her round fingers into fists.

"Not until then, sweet Alma. Not until I have rendered you so."

"You have had all you're getting. Now, meet your obligation."

The white abomination opens her mouth to taunt again, but something seems to catch at her throat. It's like the ribbons around her already constricted neck pull even tighter, close to cutting the skin itself.

Her blind gaze is directed downwards, to the broken bowl, the lumpen mash of soap. White, fragrant soap.

"*No!*"

Lashing out, she grabs Alma's throat with one hand, choking her as surely as Sour Milk herself is being choked. The other hand pulls up the jumper from Alma's waist, exposing her belly. And the half-healed scars across it.

Alma forces breath out in spit-laden gasps—

"Meet… *your… obligation!*"

She is thrown backwards. The chair behind her goes flying as she hits it, but Alma stays on her feet.

White ribbons whirl around the room, smashing everything they catch upon. The guitar explodes as it hits the floor. But the ribbons at Sour Milk's throat continue to cinch, until her sole focus is on pulling them loose.

"Meet your obligation, lady," Alma shouts. "You had my tallow, offered and accepted. And you washed it away, rejected my sacrifice – you have no more claim! But your obligation remains."

"You get nothing!" Sour Milk screeches back. "It's a trick!"

"This is not a trick! This is *craft*."

Sour Milk screams like a hurricane. The wind enters the house completely, pulling the breath from Alma's lungs.

Help me, Mother, she prays again.

You let it in.

Staggering, Alma heads for the door. She can still see Gold Eyes, standing in the field. The witch is pointing down the road and Alma catches men's voices on the wind. She puts her shoulder to the door and forces it closed.

There is a pop of silence.

Sour Milk is at the centre of the silence. The stricture at her neck has eased.

"The curse I will place instead," she hisses, "will make you ache for rancid tallow."

"I have been faithful to every part of our—"

"*Fuck your faith!*" Sour Milk's toothless maw is wide and howling. "I will have your tallow. You can play tricks and call it craft, but you were told where the power lies. Intention. Sacrifice. Hunger. And none of that has changed. You have raised power this night, and I intend to make you pay the price of it."

* * *

On the road, James Rodgers has led his brave souls to Alma Dawson's gate.

None of the other men (merry as they are at the prospect of a grand story) have noticed the witch with the gold eyes in the field beside them. James is unsure what to make of that.

They're all waiting for him to bang on Alma's door. He just needs a moment for his frozen fingers to work up to it. He rubs his hands together to warm them, feeling a stickiness there that he's forgotten the source of.

* * *

A curse, Alma has learned, is wet rendered.

Salted with hunger, boiled in sacrifice. But if it is your intention to purify it, then that's where the craft comes in. You can try skimming the surface, attempting to avoid what's bubbling underneath. But more often, you have to accept that the cake still has impurities in it, melt it all down and start again, sacrificing more and more for something that, at the end, will be clean. That will not spoil.

"I have another offer," Alma tells the woman in white. "A tallow *debt*."

Sour Milk stays silent, but cups her hands as she did before. To be filled.

"There is a man outside the door, he also took tallow from me tonight. He offered nothing in return that I could accept. He has my tallow still. My hunger marks him. I would offer you his debt, to settle what remains between us."

There comes a rap on the door; short, and a little timid.

Alma gives the witch a moment to consider, then she turns to open the door.

The wind blows out this time, rather than blowing in.

James Rodgers feels it go through him like a blade and he stumbles back. One of the men coming behind him has to catch him from falling on his arse completely.

"*Woah*," the man exclaims. "Has the Devil struck already, James?"

James straightens for a moment, but he's clearly still reeling from the prospect of what he expected on the other side of the door.

"I think, begging your pardon Miss Dawson, that Rodgers here might need a seat. Can we come in?"

"Of… of course. Please."

The crowd crosses the threshold of Alma Dawson's house, probably for the first time in their lives. Whatever rumours they grew up hearing about the place, the wreckage in front of them now wasn't a part of those.

"I'm sorry," Alma begins, "the wind—"

"Not the Devil?" And they all laugh.

"Sorry?"

"James was convinced we were coming to save you from the host of Hell. Witches, Old Nick himself."

"God, no."

Someone rights a toppled chair and they settle James Rodgers in it. Then the whole assembly sets to tidying Alma's kitchen.

"Thank you," she tells them. "I'll get poor James a cup of something."

She pauses, then says, "I have a whole supper made, actually, if any of you would like something to eat?"

If they once knew a reason not to accept food in this house, they don't remember it now.

"I'll just need to fetch a clean bowl of water for your hands," Alma tells them.

"And I have more soap."

Flame Water Turns

Eugen Bacon

yellow moon still high—
she wades into black waters
its malice too big

Her face is veiled. But everyone can see the wattles on her throat. Well, you can. There she goes, black-clad through the trees. Step, step, steppity step, glide-o-glide in a dance of the woods. The stars look on with shiny eyes, winking at the dark forest and its invitation of a folktale. This is where the story begins. With a witch on a solitary dance-walk-glide that is a mistake to follow. But you do. Even when her apprentice or familiar stops, cautious, turns, and you freeze – one foot hovering above the ground. Can you hear the mopane trees? Hear how they sigh. They know what you should. Absolutely, yeah.

This is your hour of truth. That etiquette on the matter of witches says, Do not follow. That sanity insists, Go back, go back, and you might live a longer life where bigger things don't happen.

* * *

Because, you see, there is hard water and soft water. When it's soft, it rushes gently – its touch on Naledi's skin a kiss. Sometimes she hears the whisper of a name. Today, the river slurs and Naledi doesn't hear or recall the name it utters. The words in each ripple are lost in translation. She tries to swim but the water will not give. Each stroke cuts through wet ash – this is how hard the water feels.

A sable dingo gazes down at her from the branch of a tall mopane tree on the river's shores.

Now her body has forgotten the kiss of water. The art of locomotion eludes her. She tries a backstroke, but she could well be a stone. Every part of her wants to sink. Her feet are plaques. She swivels to a swimming crawl, works up the attempt of a kick, rotates from her hips along the waves for streamline, kick, kick – it's no use.

trapped in a warzone—
water hums, never neutral
her breath gone all rogue

The dingo wades in from the shore and travels the waves to find her.

once upon a time,
she tried to live with humans—
came back to bite her

Dusk. She takes a broom and walks – not rides – using it as a staff along the valley sanctuary of lava and ash, as the moon casts two shadows, one of a companion. Naledi measures each ledge and fissure with her toes, until she closes the wide chasm from her hut to fucken Woop Woop.

She reaches the end of the rocky side, emerges into a grassland that yawns into a township with a disused dam, shoplets and all. She walks over cobblestones and knocks on a gingerbread hut but it's neither gingerbread nor a hut. A clear-eyed man with dreadlocks and a magical smile opens the blackwood door, waits for her to turn to stone but she doesn't. So he leads her into a two-bed chalet that's as modern as townhouses come, with a chimney, a laundry, a kitchenette, a shower – no bathtub inside, just an abandoned one by the side of the house, and no backyard or garage either.

She picked him from tea leaves. He is low-quality fodder, but he'll do.

"I am here to be your wife," Naledi says. "And Siya will help me." She beckons her companion.

The man, whose name is Umwojo, looks at Siya's wild hair and keen eyes, all the way to the girl's hands as if they are clawed. He offers Siya, not Naledi, a hand.

Siya says to him, "I happy to catch your hand."

all Siya knows best—
the murmur of a cauldron
her broken language

The simplicity of Siya's dialect doesn't faze Umwojo, even when she says, "Let we see the abode."

"Stay and of your own free will," he says in a voice that never sounds like it comes from a man.

He reclines on a sofa, takes a stick that's a remote control and clicks on a box that's a television. He watches a game called cricket, where men with flat batons hit a ball as far as it can go in a field called an oval, and another man swings and tosses a ball at the man with the cane to make sure he can't hit it, or, if he hits it, someone in the field will catch it mid-air, then it's a 'wicket', which means that the man with the bat is out of the game. Sometimes there's a 'runout', which means batshit to Naledi.

She and Siya take to house chores. The dust on the mantel puts Siya to a coughing fit. The pile of shorts, denims and shirts in the laundry makes her yelp. She whines at the dishes, but Naledi is more measured about the tasks as she vacuums the carpet.

She makes a pot, and observes that Umwojo uses teabags, not tea leaves. She rips open three bags, stirs them with a finger into lukewarm water in a bowl. Peers to tell a new fortune as they settle.

Nothing.

She cooks him a rainbow plant stew of white beans, sweet potatoes, kale and fermented groundnuts.

she sleeps in his bed—
Siya purrs in the other room
he turns to his side

Umwojo wakes at dawn with a shriek, and looks in shock at his watch. Naledi wonders what it is about, but her new husband keeps it on to his shower and dressing, and he abandons the house.

Naledi and Siya dust, launder, dishwash, vacuum and cook. Spinach and arrowroot stew simmered in hot chilli and oil meet Umwojo on his return.

"You never cook me meat," he says.

"You're yet to kill it," says Naledi.

oh, dear gods—
past bargain and denial
grow a pair

He's no hunter. Won't even try – she'd accept half a rodent on a pole across his shoulders. Instead, he takes the local bus to a construction site in the city where he works as a labourer for thirty-six dollars an hour.

The watch still zings him at dawn and he star-jumps from the bed with a howl.

"I sleep through alarms," he says. "Can't be late for work."

One day Naledi says to him, "You don't have to do lightning on yourself with a device to push you from sleep. Just ask me to wake you."

"It's not lightning – it's a tase watch," he says in a mood, and gives a fart that smells like something has crawled up his arse and died.

He showers, dresses in denims, and departs for work.

Naledi and Siya dust, launder, dishwash, vacuum, cook. A plate of crushed eggplant and peanut stew meets Umwojo on his return.

He's not good with masking his feelings, so Siya asks him in her broken way, "How much sulking you must make for to be happy?"

He says nothing, takes to bed.

The next day, it isn't the tase watch that wakes him, but a bewildered Naledi who shakes him in the stillness of the watch.

"Stop, it's the weekend," he says.

"But the device on your hand did not spit lightning."

"The alarm watch is automated for weekdays only," he says.

He sulks around the house with big and small exhalations as if his life is an arduous place to survive. His moaning makes it uneasy for Naledi and Siya to do normal house chores. Siya can reach anything, rotate her wrists into the smallest nook and cranny, but Umwojo's proximity unsettles her. He yells when she crashes into his mindless walking, chatters when he gags, "What, no!" as she sweeps the chimney.

Siya does not chortle back at him, just puts the broom down, and asks him, "How you feel? In real."

"I'm fine, just fine," he roars.

"You're going there?" Naledi asks him quietly.

But she encourages Siya to go and sweep the cobblestones outdoors instead. "There's an army of termites that could do with a good lick," she says.

Umwojo looks confounded.

Naledi is bending for the laundry in the machine when he takes her like it is theft. It happens in a rush and from behind. He adorns his copulation with wilderness sounds. Ugghh, ugghh. Then he goes supine. She shakes him off her, washes the drool of his seed that smells like cockroach eggs.

As if with acute eyes and smell, sensing something has transpired, Siya looks at him funny when she returns, but only says, "You was angry."

He reclines on the sofa, puts his legs over the arm, watches cricket where, sometimes, an edge hit of the bat carries the ball to a 'boundary', sometimes, the ball gets caught in a wicket across the slips. Umwojo yells, "Out!", waves his fist at the telly.

peep, stalk and a rush—
take Naledi from behind
Siya out of sight

* * *

The apprentice is an industrious worker. She fetches water from the dam, even while there's an indoor tap that spurts out fluoride-tinged aqua. Still, she stabs it with her finger for tilapia. There's biodiversity of cichlids, catfish, algae, water hyacinth, lilies, kelp, reeds and harmless water snakes. But there's no tilapia. So she balances a big pot of water on her head, holds it upright as if for show, exposing a beautiful neck and the walk of a queen – the sun in gold across the plains. The apprentice walks with a certain kind of intimacy, but it's also majestic. She uses the dam water to bathe the witch. She's an unusual one, the apprentice. Sometimes, she stalls. Rubs herself very gently against the bark of a wild marula tree – regal in its lean, crowned with a perch of the noisiest hornbills. Gok rroh. She's nimble when she bounds, frogs up the bark of the tree to the freshest fruit, fangs it open. Its aroma is so floral, oh, how nutty. Just looking at that juicy texture, you can taste the citrus tartness. The marula fruit is creamy inside, you can almost touch it. The aroma reminds you of passion. Like the one the apprentice shows when she navigates to the wispiest branch, steals into a hornbill's nest, cracks into her mouth – not the yellowest yolk, but an unformed baby bird drenched in mucus. Gok rroh rroh!

she bounds across the valley—
launches herself at osprey
a beast always at heart

Siya knows what to do with the disused bathtub at the side of the house, and Naledi accepts. She steps, naked, into the heated dam water, lays her head back as Siya kneads Naledi's face, her neck, breasts, stomach… all the way to her feet… with mud. Rinses it off patiently, lingering her touch, as if it were a love song.

Naledi has no doubt Siya loves her fiercely, intensely. She'll do anything for Naledi.

Anything.

And it drives Umwojo berserk.

But there are times when Naledi thinks Umwojo looks at Siya in the strangest way. A new molten gold enters the pupils of his normally clear eyes. It's as if he's recollecting what Naledi said when she told him, *I am here to be your wife. And Siya will help me*. The gleam in Umwojo's eyes suggests his mind, if so, is not on a good sort of 'help'.

He may lust, but he's obvious in his dislike. Doesn't like it when Siya sniffs at his back and growls. His annoyance is unmasked when Siya licks the length of Naledi's arm, all the while purring a ritual cleanse. Sometimes Naledi reminds Siya that she must wear a garment.

"It no happy," says Siya.

"But it's what people do. They dress." Not stalk around in the nuddy, even when Umwojo is at work or unencumbered with the deep, deep sleep of a potion.

But Naledi's caution is needless. The man knows better than to do anything that enacts the untoward upon Siya.

Because when it comes to Siya… well, Siya.

* * *

She slips in and out unnoticed, makes herself unseen. But you see. You know how well she digs – furrows with her hands and face to haul out the moistest earthworm. Eats it alive as if it's grass. Gobbles feather grass too, sometimes. Then coughs it out with a yelp. That's it. She's a strange sort who sometimes forgets herself and turns. Not in a big way, but like this, in ways you notice. It's not a complete transfiguration, just in part. She can stand still, then rotates her neck so the back of the head is in front, then stares at nothing, all the way past you. Then her eyes glower and she springs at a mouse, a dung beetle, a lizard. Birds too, the yellow feathers of the weaver still scattered. A splash of crimson on the walkway.

* * *

Naledi is reaching for a plate in the dishwasher when suddenly he's on her, pants to his knees, thrusting like a rabbit. Ugghh, ugghh. Then he dies on her back. She shakes him off her, ignores his resuscitated self as he pulls his trousers up, and she understands that this is his way. He's no legend of a bull. Each coital encounter will be as swift as it is unremarkable.

A month goes, then another. Ugghh, ugghh. None of his seeds take.

One day, Siya chances upon him thrusting on Naledi's back. Siya throws her broom, yelps then howls, scales the distance and lunges at him. Naledi moves away from his cries as Siya bites off a chunk of his torso.

beneath the dark skies
entwined in the phantom rain—
she strokes Siya's mane

"I sorry," Siya chatters.

"Sssss. It's been a minute. No one came here to cause trouble."

"I trouble."

"He provoked the attack," Naledi says.

"Hard agree."

They stay like this in stillness, a precious moment to themselves, like how it was before Umwojo. Later, when she is calmer, Siya asks Naledi, "How you feel? In real."

"I'm feeling a lot."

"Hear you."

"I'm feeling a certain kind of way because I don't do low-quality fodder. This is a safe place. But we've stayed longer than we should."

"Hard agree."

Naledi's mission is a flop. Umwojo can't give her what she wants.

fire storm in her dreams—
a womb where nothing happens
flames rush down her throat

Naledi slips a moss stone from the cemetery into a bubbling cauldron, puts three twigs of a desiccated tree, adds five fingers of the hunched skeleton of a dead husband and a pinch of his sun-dried skin, but it's not enough.

She wears a hood and a cape, hovers on a broom and into the windless night to steal into other people's lives, where she caresses her wattled throat, and watches as a bub takes to his mother's breast. He touches her chest with his chubby hand, the widest, brownest eyes on the woman's weary face—

—yet she will draw him a bath in a basin, dip him feet first as she cradles his head, rinse his hair backward from his brow. Yet she will use a washcloth and baby shampoo, scoop water in her palm over his tiny body to keep him warm, rub him dry in the softest towel. Yet she will dress him in secondhand fades, place him half-drowsy in a cot, touch the moonlight on his face as he falls to deep sleep. Yet she will abandon his trust and

will worry a meal in the kitchenette
for a roving husband
banging for a pint
or banging a whore
in a tavern.

But *she* will breach the threshold, steal into *his* moony sleep by the window, watch him fidget

until he rolls on his side,
until he sighs and whimpers,
until he leans chubby cheeks on his palm
and calms himself.

she stands like a shade—
he twitches as she reaches
tweezers in her robe

He coos and gurgles, flutters his feet in the deepest slumber as if potioned.

she breathes—
syncopated time
fuck, who's safe

She touches his head and tugs the blackest curl to feed her dreams.

the wind turns—
listens to the pleas
burns where else

The dingo looks at them with intelligent eyes outside the window. Naledi whips her hood and takes to the broom. "Let's go," she whispers to the windless night.

The familiar waves a bushy tail, slips out of sight, then reappears, loping agile and racing after the broom all the way first to the cauldron, then step, step, steppity step, glide-o-glide in a dance of the woods, as the stars look on with shiny eyes, winking at the invitation of a folktale that ends and begins in a river.

Because there's hard water and soft water.

The moon is high. The air is alive with coming rain. Naledi wades naked into the black river.

This dusk, her body remembers the water. The art of locomotion is as easy as a wish. She sculls, arms and legs extended, swivels to her back and floats. When she swims, her body cuts smoothly through the water at the head and shoulders. Her hands catch the ripples and she flows, streamlined all the way. The river's kiss is a dance, as is the...

whisper of a name—
rushing gently on her skin
before sun is nigh

She thinks of a young woman aged beyond her years. The mother of a child whose curl is for Naledi's dreams. Batter wounds on the woman's arms and ribs, the kind of damage the fist of a man makes in places no one thinks to see. She puts her heart into a bowl with flour, water, pink salt and sacrifice. Forms and kneads the dough with callused hands that have known much labour, then rests it to first rise. Punches it down and shapes it the way she would like to shape her man but can't, or won't just yet. She lifts it from second rise, arranges it into a tin where she'll bake it golden, all the while listening for her baby's whimper. Poor woman. How she slaves for a man who'll never notice. Because… his whores? He's her mate for life. That is what he will take. Her life.

mostly on good days—
he locates a fine carcass
clad in wifely flesh

Whose story is this? Hers. Ours. For every woman who has seen domestic violence.

Naledi knows this as she slips facedown into the playful lapping.

feels the water's touch—
from the river to her chest
he coos and gurgles

* * *

Etiquette says, Do not follow. Sanity says, Go back, go back, and you might live a longer life where bigger things don't happen. This is your hour of truth. You've seen what you have seen, and you know what it does. It's transformed you to an enduring state that feels… that feels. Out of sight.

what is life is death—
wrap strong fangs on a rodent
make the most of sun

This is a story where big things happen. Would you like to become an apprentice?

* * *

A dingo has acute sight, hearing and smell. She knows, with or without her sable pelt, the uterus of a river. Siya cocks her head to its murmur, a whisper of words that say:

"Nikiwe, Nikiwe, Nikiwe..."

Are tea leaves ever wrong?

A clap of thunder. Rain spits in a fury from the skies.

Siya watches, curious, from the mudflats as Naledi scoops from the riverbed to her breast a newborn with a black, curly head. Siya wades in, silent, travels the water to find mother and child.

The Weaver

Kay Hanifen

"ELIZA COOK, Eliza Cook, she signed her name in the Devil's Book!" the children chanted as they surrounded the woman.

She ignored them, hefting her piles of weaving from her handcart into the market stall. It was far too much for one person to make, especially in a short period of time, and yet she claimed to have completed it all herself because she had no one else to help her with it.

Eliza Cook had no family to speak of. Her mother, father, and siblings had all died over the course of several winters, and she never married. She was a spinster in both senses of the word. As for friends, she tended to keep a polite distance from the rest of the community. She was never rude or insulting and went to church every Sunday, just as the Lord commanded.

If you made conversation with her, it would be a pleasant but forgettable talk. Were it not for the weaving, she would have been an unremarkable woman among unremarkable women in Greyshire.

But, somehow, without the assistance of anyone else, she sheared her sheep, dyed and spun her wool, and wove bolts of fine fabric while also maintaining her family farm. No one knew how she did it alone, but she returned to the market every week with something new for the women of the town to lust over. The rumor among the children (and some adults) was that she was a witch, and she'd made a deal with the Devil. In exchange for her soul, he would come to her home every night and do her chores for her. Though parents also wondered if this was her secret, they scolded the children who bothered her. After all, even if she wasn't a witch who would hex them for their rudeness, they didn't want her to take her business elsewhere, not when she sold the warmest and softest wool clothes of anyone nearby. Those who bought her fabric often found that their births were easier, their children were healthier, and their crops flourished. With all this in mind, they could ignore her peculiarities.

"Eliza Cook." William Alder approached with a cocky grin and leaned against her market stall, jauntily tipping his hat in mock friendliness. Years before, he had proposed to her, and she had turned him down. It wasn't out of cruelty on her part. In fact, she thought she was doing him a kindness by freeing him to find someone else, someone who actually wanted to be with him. But, though he'd married another, far more eligible woman, he only saw the rejection.

"William Alder," she replied without pausing in her task. Around them, the children continued their chant. "May I ask what brings you here?"

"Am I not allowed to visit the market?"

"I meant my stall, specifically. Is there something you would want to buy?"

He theatrically scanned the different colored bolts of fabric and felt the wool like he was an expert. "I'm merely curious. How have you been, Eliza? It must get lonely in that hovel."

She shrugged, arranging the last of the bolts to her liking. "I'm quite happy with my own company, thank you." She straightened and turned to face him. "Now, would you like to purchase some fabric? If not, I will kindly ask you to leave so that I may attend to paying customers."

His eyebrows shot up. “Do you speak like this to all your visitors?”

Eliza smiled sweetly. “No, my good sir. But I fear what the town may whisper if they saw you with me unchaperoned. And if those whispers were to get back to your gentle wife…”

“Perhaps you should worry less about the town’s whispers and more about what the children chant,” he snapped.

She turned away from him, smoothing out a bolt of wool fabric impossibly soft as silk. “Then we’re agreed. You’ll see to your business, and I’ll see to mine. Can I interest you in a green ribbon for your wife’s lovely hair?” Producing the ribbon from below her stall, she held it up for him to inspect.

With a sigh, he gave her a couple of coins and stalked off. Smiling to herself, she placed them in her purse.

Business for that day was successful, and she used the money to buy salt for preserving meat and flour for bread, along with the makings for her dinner that evening and meals the next day. Some of her customers had also paid in vegetables, spices, and preserves, further adding to the haul.

As the sun began to set, she loaded the remaining fabric and her purchased and bartered goods into her handcart, and with aching feet, began her trek home. Most women would fear the night, especially when walking home alone with a cart full of expensive goods, but not Eliza.

A few years ago, there had been a time when a highwayman roamed the roads leading to and from town, always striking on market day. He'd robbed and murdered at least ten people, creating a reign of terror the likes of which the sleepy village had never seen. But then, one day, they'd discovered his desiccated corpse suspended in the trees by a strange thread – strong and supple, and neither wool nor linen. And below that strange corpse, they found a scrap of Eliza's fabric.

As Eliza walked, footsteps seemed to follow from just off the trail. She paid them no mind. They would show themselves at home. Unfortunately, she was so used to putting the sounds from her mind that she didn't notice the second set walking behind her, just out of sight.

She reached home to find that the sheep and chickens had been fed, and the day's chores had been completed. Smiling, she unloaded her cart and poured out a bowl of milk, leaving it on the front step as a thank-you to her benefactor.

Her house was little more than a cabin. It was humble, with a fireplace, table, and bed upon the floor. The only thing an outsider would note as strange was the fact that there were, in fact, two looms and two spinning wheels, for one woman who lived alone.

Once the fire was roaring in her fireplace, she tucked into her simple meal of bread, cheese, and apple preserves. As expected, there came a series of knocks at the door; a brief but familiar pattern.

“Come in, my love,” she said, smiling to herself as her door opened, revealing the secret to her impossible weaving.

Araneus stood in the doorway, smiling as they sipped from the bowl of milk. They were tall and thin, almost twiglike in appearance, and had skin the color and texture of birchbark. Six arms protruded from their back, and their face was dotted with eight aspen eyes, each blinking of their own accord. They smiled, revealing fangs. Her spider had arrived.

Most who saw her lover would scream and flee in terror, but not Eliza. As a child, people would whisper that she was a changeling, for she was unlike the other children. She was strange and quiet, always observing without ever joining in with her peers. Her mother told her the stories of the fair folk and kept to the traditions even as the rest of the town scoffed and called her mad. But she paid her respects, and Eliza maintained the tradition after she had passed.

Then, one day, while her ailing father rested in bed, she went out searching for a lost ewe and heard a cry from the woods. Though it didn't sound like her missing animal, she followed it. The source was one of the fae, who had their ankle caught in a hunter's crude iron trap. Cold iron was one of the few things known to hurt the fair folk.

"You poor creature," Eliza tutted as she removed the iron bolt piercing their foot. She supposed she should have been afraid of the monstrous thing in front of her, but she felt only pity.

As soon as the fae was free, they ran, vanishing into the trees like they'd never existed. The next day, she found a finely woven cloak on her front step. The intricate embroidery was mesmerizing, and the cloak itself seemed to adapt to the temperature, never letting her get too hot or too cold.

She didn't see them again until after her father died, when she was struggling to maintain her farm and fend off suitors. She had always been an excellent weaver and survived off the fabric she sold at the market.

It was risky to go alone, especially with a highwayman on the prowl, but she was running low on food for herself and her animals. In the few times she had gone to the market since losing her family, she'd always had the sensation of being watched. It never felt particularly malicious, and she didn't want to risk earning its ire by calling it out.

Eliza was so used to the sensation that she didn't notice the man watching at first. In the misty evening, he stood silhouetted by moonlight. When she spotted him, she stopped short.

"I'll be taking all that, miss," the highwayman said. He tilted his head. "Now, if you're a good girl who doesn't put up a fuss, I might let you leave with your honor intact."

Her blood ran cold as she removed the pouch with shaking fingers and tossed it on the cart. "It's all I have. Just take it."

He stepped closer, just out of the shadows enough for her to finally see his face. It was scruffy and smudged with dirt. He leered at Eliza with heavy lids. "You're pretty enough. I think I would like to take just a little bit more," he slurred. Even from a distance, he reeked of alcohol.

Before he could take another step towards her, a blur lunged at him from the shadows, moving so fast that she couldn't tell what it was. A gunshot went off in the scuffle, but it didn't deter the highwayman's attacker. Between blinks, the robber was dead, and the fae she'd rescued stood over him, covering him in a strange thread.

Eliza recognized the creature, but didn't dare move, lest they set their sights on her. But then she noticed the blood sluggishly pumping down their arm. "You're hurt," she said, untying the ribbon from her hair. It had been her sister Mary's favorite until she died of a fever last spring, and Eliza wore it in her memory. She hoped the blood would come out of the fabric with a few washes.

"I am fine," they said, suspending the highwayman in the trees. Their voice was soft and susurrus, like the wind through autumn leaves.

"This will help stop the bleeding and keep it clean." She offered the ribbon to him. "As my thanks for the rescue. You may call me Eliza." It wasn't her full first or family name, so she figured that it would be safe to use. "What can I call you?"

The fae paused for a moment in thought. Then, they said, "Araneus."

"It's a pleasure to meet you, Araneus." She held up the makeshift bandage. "Please allow me to treat your wound. If you would like to come home with me, I can give you a proper meal as well."

They tied it around their arm themselves. "Our debts to one another are repaid."

"Well, perhaps," she said, rocking back and forth on her feet. "But I am rather lonely. It would be nice to have some companionship again."

Araneus stared at her as though weighing her soul against a feather. "I would be amenable to that."

Her spider had visited her every night since. For years, they had been together, enjoying each other's company in secret. Eliza would feed them, and in return, they would help take care of the farm, joining her to do the spinning and the weaving, creating and enchanting fine fabric for the town. In time, she'd learned that Araneus was the last of their kind. As humanity encroached on wilderness, the rest of the fair folk had either died off or slumbered deep below the earth, never to be woken. All but Araneus, who could not bring themselves to disappear like the rest. They were just as lonely as she was.

When William proposed to her, the wave of horror and repulsion she felt shocked her. It was then that she realized her heart belonged to another, to her secret love.

Eliza Cook did not sign her name in the Devil's Book, but she did make a deal of sorts. A lonely girl met a strange creature, and she found a way to live her life without the judgement of others.

"I will never understand why you tolerate their… disrespect," Araneus said as they worked on their weaving with Eliza. They placed their free hand on her knee. Tonight, they were spinning wool into thread with one set of hands and weaving with another while she worked her own loom, creating another bolt of soft fabric for the market, infusing her positive intentions in every row.

"It's truly not so bad as you think," she said. "I keep to myself, and aside from William, the townsfolk keep to theirs. They may not love me, but they trust that I mean no harm and look after me in turn."

"Is eating him still off the table?" they asked.

She rolled her eyes. "Yes, darling. You are not allowed to eat any members of the town unless you are defending yourself."

Araneus huffed, pouting like a child and drawing a giggle from her. "If you insist."

She took her hand from her loom for a moment to give their hand a squeeze. "I thank you for your sacrifice."

The chuckle was soft and warm, like a summer breeze. "Do you regret it?" they asked suddenly.

Eliza nearly missed a thread in surprise. "Regret what?"

"Not saying yes to marrying William Alder. He is handsome, by human standards, and wealthy. From what I understand, these are the primary factors that humans consider when choosing a mate."

She laughed out loud this time. The only reason William was so fixated on her was because she had no desire to be with him. If she had thrown herself at him like many of the girls in the town or rolled with him in a hayloft, he would have immediately lost interest. "You forget the most important factor: personality. Honestly, I've met horny, diarrhetic goats with more charm than him."

"Surely there was someone in the town who you would have consented to marry."

Eliza shook her head. "None that I can think of. Where is this coming from?"

"Fear, I suppose. And guilt. The children in town call you a witch. What if those whispers become shouts and burning stakes? I would not wish to deprive you of the life you deserve."

She stopped her weaving completely and turned towards them, tugging their hand. "Araneus, look at me."

They did, their aspen eyes unblinking as they focused on her face. They even stopped their spinning and weaving. Getting to her feet, she pressed a kiss to their rough, dry lips. "I love you. I choose you. No mortal man or woman could ever measure up. My life may be short compared to yours, but I cannot imagine it without you."

They leaned into her touch as she cradled their face in her hand. "And if you are accused of witchcraft, I will stop at nothing to protect you."

She pressed another kiss to their forehead and then stifled a yawn. "Today has been long. Come to bed with me."

"But the weaving…"

"Can wait." She tugged one of their arms. "Will you leave your love so alone and cold in bed?"

Outside, there was a small thud. Both looked up. "What was that?" Araneus asked.

"I don't know." Eliza grabbed her hunter's knife from the table and slowly crept towards the door.

Opening it, she peered out. Nothing. The night was as dark and still as a grave. "Who's there?" she called out, not afraid of any potential robbers. Araneus may get their meal after all. But there was no response. Whoever it was, they had run.

"Allow me," they said, pushing past her, kneeling on the cold earth, and digging their hands into the ground. "One set of human footsteps. Headed towards the village." Araneus turned back to her, their eyes wide with fear. "Eliza, pack your things. We must go. Now!"

This was her family's cabin. No one knew when it had been built, but generations of Cooks had lived there. It broke her heart to abandon it. But better a broken heart than burned as a heretic. So, she did as Araneus said without argument, packing provisions and clothes in her handcart. The sheep bleated as she left, giving her pause.

"The animals."

"Alder and his men will likely distribute them among the townsfolk," Araneus replied, taking the handcart. "I will check on them in three days' time. If they're still here, I'll set them loose."

Her eyes brimmed with unshed tears. "Thank you, my love."

"Where do you think you're going?" William Alder called from the trail. He was on horseback, flanked by three of his friends. All carried fire and iron. "I didn't want to believe you were the Devil's whore, Eliza, but it seems the rumors are true."

"Eliza, run," Araneus growled, dropping the cart and stepping between her and the men.

She shook her head, drawing her knife. "Not without you. As I said, I intend to spend my life by your side, no matter how short it may be."

"Get them!" William cried, spurring the horses into action. The men swiped at Araneus with their iron weapons as they passed, like knights in a joust. The ones that struck Araneus elicited a cry as the iron burned their flesh.

"Don't hold back," Eliza said. "You may devour them."

Araneus grinned before charging, unseating William and leaving him stunned on the forest floor as his ignoble steed fled the battlefield. One of his friends struck Araneus in the back, and the spider yanked him off his horse, bashing his head into the ground until it resembled a crushed watermelon. Araneus's skin sizzled with the iron blow, and they grunted before turning their attention to the last two men still on horseback. They had surrounded Araneus, and as though moving on a silent signal, they charged, wielding their iron pokers like lances. Araneus parried one, but the other came up from behind and pierced the fae's upper right shoulder. The scream was enough to shatter Eliza's heart. They fell to their knees and tried in vain to pull the iron from their shoulder.

She couldn't just stand there. She had to help. Heedless of her own safety, Eliza drew her knife and joined the fray, stabbing the one who had wounded Araneus in the thigh. The first of her family to die had been her eldest brother, in a terrible accident. His inner thigh had been pierced by an axe when he slipped and fell on the blade while chopping wood in the dead of winter. He'd bled out in minutes. Now, she prayed this man would do the same as she ripped the hunting knife from the wound. He and his horse sped off, blood trailing behind.

And then there was one. The last of William Alder's friends took a final look at the dual expressions of rage on the lovers' faces and fled. Once she was sure he was gone, she turned her attention to Araneus, dropping the knife, cupping her hand to their cheek and pressing a kiss to their lips. "Let me get this out of you," she said. "I'm sorry, my love, but it will hurt."

"Do it," they grated. She braced herself against their chest and pulled it through, tears streaming down her face as she forced herself to ignore their screams.

Once it was free, she wrapped her arms around them, holding them close. All six arms wrapped comfortingly around her. One hand gently stroked her hair.

And then there was a sharp intake of breath. Araneus twisted suddenly as though trying to shield her from something. Eliza didn't know what, though, until she felt the sharp blade protruding from their chest, the sudden gush of hot blood. Araneus went slack in her arms.

She forced herself to look up. William Alder stood over her with her hunting knife in his hand, the black blood gleaming in the moonlight.

"I look forward to watching you burn like the heretic you are," he said. Distantly, she realized that he hadn't given the ribbon to his wife, instead tying it around his own throat. A ribbon that was woven by her and Araneus's loving hands. How *dare* he? How dare the town happily buy her fabric but still call her a witch and murder the one she loved most in cold blood? The audacity of it filled her with rage.

All those years, she'd ignored their jeers, their children's chants, the way that people looked at her in church. She made them fine fabric, protective fabric that would not only ward off the elements but bad luck, too. They'd never lifted a finger to help with her farm or her sick family, and never gave her an overture of friendship outside of the occasional discount on her food, which felt more like an offering to avoid her ire than any real desire to show they cared. Araneus was the only one who had truly cared for her, truly loved her. They were her greatest joy, and instead of allowing her peace in exchange for protection, those people had murdered her lover.

Well, it was a witch they wanted. Now, a witch they would get.

Over the years, practically everyone in town had used her fabric in some capacity. It had been woven in love, imbuing it with blessings. But now, she let her rage and hatred fill her, and she turned those blessings into curses. The people of the town froze to death in their sleep or died of heatstroke. Those that hadn't were strangled by their own clothes and ribbons. None were spared her wrath.

William's smile faded as the ribbon tightened around his throat. He let loose a strangled cry, his eyes bugging out as his fingers scrabbled for purchase in the green fabric, desperately trying to pull it off. In the pale moonlight, she watched the blood vessels and capillaries burst in his eyes as his mouth opened and shut like a beached fish, trying desperately to suck in air.

Eyes rolling back in his head, his legs gave out underneath him. Still, he thrashed for several long minutes before going limp.

In that time, she never let go of Araneus, instead holding them close as their shuddering, choking breaths slowed to a stop. Then, with their arms still wrapped around her, she laid down.

When dawn approached, she extricated herself from their stiffening limbs. With a final kiss to their forehead, she began to build a pyre. By the time night returned, she had made a bed of logs and kindling and adorned it with flowers. Then, she laid Araneus out, wrapping them in the lovers' final, unfinished project, and set it all aflame. For a moment, she considered joining them on it, but that would only have been giving William Alder and his ilk what they had wanted in the first place.

So no, she would live. For Araneus's sake, she would live.

Eliza Cook never signed her name in the Devil's Book. She never rode naked on a broomstick or enticed good people to sin. But she was a witch all the same and was going to make the world regret ever calling her one.

About the Authors

Ally Wilkes's debut novel, *All the White Spaces*, was a Bram Stoker Award finalist, and her second novel, *Where the Dead Wait*, was one of *Esquire*'s best horror books of 2023. Her short fiction has been published in numerous magazines and anthologies including *Nightmare Magazine*, *Cosmic Horror Monthly*, *FOUND: an anthology of Found Footage Horror* and *Darkness Beckons*. Ally grew up in a succession of isolated – possibly haunted – country houses and boarding schools. After studying law at Oxford, she went on to spend eleven years as a criminal barrister, learning how extreme situations bring out the best (or worst) in human nature. Ally now lives in Greenwich, London, with an anatomical human skeleton, and far too many books about weird things. Whatever the time of year, she's probably thinking about Halloween. Visit allywilkes.com or @av_wilkes (Instagram) and @unheimlichmanvr.bsky.social for more.

Eliza Chan is a Scottish-born speculative fiction author living in Manchester, UK. She writes about East Asian mythology, British folklore and reclaiming the dragon lady. Her #1 *Sunday*

Times bestselling debut novel *Fathomfolk* and sequel *Tideborn* – inspired by diaspora feels – are out now. Her short fiction has featured in various magazines and anthologies including *The Secret Romantic's Book of Magic* and *The Best of British Fantasy*.

Angela 'A.G.' Slatter is the author of the gothic fantasies *All the Murmuring Bones*, *The Path of Thorns*, *The Briar Book of the Dead* and *The Crimson Road* (Titan Books). She's also the author of the Verity Fassbinder supernatural crime/urban fantasy series, as well as twelve short story collections, four novellas, two books about writing, and a Hellboy Universe collaboration with Mike Mignola, *Castle Full of Blackbirds*. She has won a World Fantasy Award, a British Fantasy Award, a Shirley Jackson Award, a Ditmar, three Australian Shadows Awards, eight Aurealis Awards and a Premier Ignotas Award. She's been a judge for the World Fantasy and the Aurealis Awards. Her work's been translated into Bulgarian, Chinese, Russian, Italian, Spanish, Dutch, Japanese, Polish, French, Turkish, Hungarian, Czechoslovakian and Romanian. angelaslatter.com

Mark Chadbourn is a *Sunday Times* bestselling author and two-time winner of the British Fantasy Award, a screenwriter and a journalist for national media.

Muriel Gray has had a forty-year career in the media. She has written three horror novels and many short stories. She is currently the joint vice chair of the board of trustees of the British Museum, and a non-executive board member of the

British Broadcasting Corporation. Despite her beginnings as an artist and punk, she has so far, quite demonstrably, failed in bringing down the establishment. Muriel can be found on X as @artybagger, and on Instagram as muriel_gray.

Buhlebethu Sukoluhle Mpofu is a medical practitioner and author with hands-on research experience, having served as co-author on two peer-reviewed publications: 'Are Cape Peninsula baboons raiding their way to obesity and type II diabetes?' (2023) and 'Advancements in Marburg (MARV) Virus Vaccine Research' (2024). Her recent book *Forgive, Love, and You: A Guide to Unburdening the Heart* was published in 2025. You can find her on X/Twitter @shortbread00.

Alison Moore's debut novel, *The Lighthouse*, was shortlisted for the 2012 Man Booker Prize and the National Book Awards, winning the McKitterick Prize. Her fifth novel, *The Retreat*, was published in 2021. She's also published a trilogy for children, beginning with *Sunny and the Ghosts*. Her short stories have been included in *Best British Short Stories* and *Best British Horror* and broadcast on BBC Radio. She's published two collections: *The Pre-War House and Other Stories*, whose title story won the New Writer Novella Prize, and *Eastmouth and Other Stories*. She's also the author of five Nightjar Press chapbooks, her latest being *The Junction*.

Gabriella Buba is a mixed Filipina-Czech author and chemical engineer based in Texas who likes to keep explosive pyrophoric materials safely contained in pressure vessels or between the covers of her books. She writes fantasy for bold, bi, brown women who deserve to see their stories centered. Her debut *Saints of Storm and Sorrow* is a Filipino-inspired epic fantasy out with Titan Books. Its sequel, *Daughters of Flood and Fury*, was released in July 2025.

David Barnett is a novelist, journalist and comic writer originally from Wigan and now living in West Yorkshire. His most recent books are a series of interlinked folk horror novels, *Withered Hill* (2024), *Scuttler's Cove* (2025) and the third and fourth, *Scratch Moss* and *Twisted Pike*, due in March and October 2026, all from Canelo. He is on most social media @davidmbarnett.

Aveline Fletcher is a technical writer by day, creative writer by night, and fledgling baker and gardener in between (as the seasons allow). A lifetime of fascination with Greek mythology, Irish folklore, and of course, witches, led to Aveline consuming and writing stories of fantasy that built on and reimagined the dark and visceral themes of myth and folklore. She lives in the frosty state of Minnesota in the USA.

Helen Grant writes Gothic novels, the latest of which is *Jump Cut* (2023), and short supernatural fiction. Her new short story collection *Atmospheric Disturbances* was published late in 2024 by Dublin's Swan River Press. Joyce Carol Oates has described her as 'a brilliant chronicler of the uncanny as only those who dwell in places of dripping, graylit beauty can be'. Helen lives in Perthshire, Scotland, and when not writing she likes to explore abandoned country houses and swim in freezing lochs.

Lisa L. Hannett has had over eighty short stories published in venues including *Clarkesworld*, *Fantasy*, *Weird Tales*, *Apex*, *The Dark* and Year's Best anthologies in Australia, Canada and the US. She has won four Aurealis Awards, an Australian National Science Fiction Award, an Australian Shadows Award, and has twice been nominated for a World Fantasy Award. Her latest collection is *The Fortunate Isles*. You can find her online on Instagram @LisaLHannett.

Melissa Bobe is the author of *Nascent Witch*, *The Illustrated Woman*, *Season of the Witch* and *Sibyls*. Her collection *Electric Trees* won the 2023 New York Author Project, after which Melissa went on to win the Indie Author Project's 2024 Indie Author of the Year Award. She has published fiction with Whisper House Press, Intrepidus Ink, Bards and Sages, Urhi Publishing, Wyldblood Press, and World Weaver Press. After years of teaching college English, Melissa now works as a librarian. You can find her at abookbumble.com and on social media @abookbumble.

Amanda Mason was born and brought up in Whitby, North Yorkshire. She studied Theatre at Dartington College of Arts, where she began writing by devising and directing plays. Her short stories have been published in several anthologies. Her debut novel, *The Wayward Girls*, a dark and captivating story of sisterhood and family secrets, and *The Hiding Place*, a haunting novel about mothers and daughters, are both published by

Bonnier Zaffre. Her short story, 'Three Times, Lefthandwise', was shortlisted for the V.S. Pritchett Short Story Prize in 2022.

Damien Kelly is a writer and lecturer from Ireland, growing up windswept and witch-bothered in the wild Northwest. His stories have previously been published in the UK by the British Fantasy Society, Flame Tree Publishing, Jurassic London, Stone Skin Press, and in the US by Lethe Press.

Eugen Bacon is an African Australian author. She's a Solstice, British Fantasy, Locus and Foreword Indies Award winner, a twice World Fantasy and Shirley Jackson Award finalist, and a finalist in the Philip K. Dick and Ignyte Awards, and the Nommo Awards for speculative fiction by Africans. Eugen is an Otherwise Fellow, and was also announced in the honor list for 'doing exciting work in gender and speculative fiction'. *Danged Black Thing* made the Otherwise Award Honor List as a 'sharp collection of Afro-Surrealist work'. Visit her at eugenbacon.com.

Kay Hanifen was born on a Friday the 13th and once lived for three months in a haunted castle. So, obviously, she had to become a horror writer. Her work has appeared in over one hundred anthologies and magazines. Her first anthology as an editor, *Till the Yule Log Burns Out*, was published in 2024. Her first novel, *The Last Ballard*, debuted in 2025. When she's not consuming pop culture with the voraciousness of a vampire at a 24-hour blood bank, you can usually find her with her black cats or at kayhanifenauthor.wordpress.com. Instagram: @katharinehanifen

About the Illustrator

Xinyue Chen (Frontispiece and Cover Detail) is an illustrator and book artist based in New York. Their works explore emotions, memories, identities and people's connection with the environment in a poetic way. Most of their works are done in traditional media. Although coming from a fine-art background, they find narrative-driven art allows them to communicate with their audience better. Since receiving their BFA from the Central Academy of Fine Arts in Beijing and their MFA from the School of Viusal Arts in New York, they have provided editorial illustrations, book illustrations and designs for many renowned clients, including the *New York Times*, *Scientific American*, NBC News, NPR, Bloomberg, Asia Society, The Progressive, China Machine Press, Future Islands, and HAZE Sounds Beijing.

About the Editors

Marie O'Regan is a British Fantasy Award and Shirley Jackson Award-nominated author and editor, based in Derbyshire. She was awarded the British Fantasy Society Legends of FantasyCon award in 2022. She is the author of four collections of short fiction: *Mirror Mere*; *In Times of Want*, *The Last Ghost and Other Stories* and *Bleed For Me*. Her short fiction has appeared in a number of genre magazines and anthologies in the UK, US, Canada, Italy and Germany, including *Best British Horror 2014*, *Great British Horror: Dark Satanic Mills* (2017), *The Mammoth Book of Halloween Stories* and *This Way Lies Madness*. Her novella, *Bury Them Deep*, was published by Hersham Horror Books in September 2017. She was shortlisted for the British Fantasy Society Award for Best Short Story in 2006, Best Anthology in 2010 (*Hellbound Hearts*) and 2012 (*The Mammoth Book of Ghost Stories by Women*). She was also shortlisted for the Shirley Jackson Award for Best Anthology in 2020 (*Wonderland*). Her genre journalism has appeared in magazines like *The Dark Side*, *Rue Morgue* and *Fortean*

Times, and her interview book with prominent figures from the horror genre, *Voices in the Dark*, was released in 2011. An essay on *The Changeling* was published in PS Publishing's *Cinema Macabre*, edited by Mark Morris. She is co-editor of the bestselling *Hellbound Hearts*, *The Mammoth Book of Body Horror*, *A Carnivàle of Horror – Dark Tales from the Fairground*, *Exit Wounds*, *Wonderland*, *Cursed*, *Twice Cursed*, *The Other Side of Never*, *In These Hallowed Halls*, *Beyond & Within: Folk Horror*, *Death Comes at Christmas*, *The Secret Romantic's Book of Magic* and *These Dreaming Spires*, as well as the charity anthology *Trickster's Treats #3*, plus editor of the bestselling anthologies *The Mammoth Book of Ghost Stories by Women* and *Phantoms*, and Managing Editor of PS Publishing's award-winning novella imprint, Absinthe Books. Her first novel, the internationally bestselling *Celeste*, was published in February 2022, and a supernatural novella, *Resurrection Blues*, was published in May 2025. Marie was Chair of the British Fantasy Society from 2004 to 2008, and Co-Chair of the UK Chapter of the Horror Writers Association from 2015 to 2022. She was also co-chair of ChillerCon UK in 2022. Visit her website at marieoregan.net. She can be found on Bluesky @marieoregan.bsky.social, X @Marie_O_Regan and Instagram @marieoregan8101.

Paul Kane is the award-winning (including the British Fantasy Society's Legends of FantasyCon Award 2022), bestselling author and editor of over 160 books – such as the *Arrowhead* trilogy (gathered together in the sellout *Hooded*

Man omnibus, revolving around a post-apocalyptic version of Robin Hood), *The Butterfly Man and Other Stories*, *Hellbound Hearts*, *Wonderland* (a Shirley Jackson Award finalist) and *Pain Cages* (an Amazon #1 bestseller). His non-fiction books include *The Hellraiser Films and Their Legacy* and *Voices in the Dark*, and his genre journalism has appeared in the likes of *SFX* and *Rue Morgue*. He has been a Guest at many conventions, including Alt.Fiction, the first SFX Weekender, Thought Bubble, Monster Mash, Event Horizon, Edge-Lit, HorrorCon, HorrorFest, Grimm Up North, The Dublin Ghost Story Festival, IMATS Olympia, Celluloid Screams, Black Library Live, the UK Ghost Story Festival and the WordCrafter virtual event 2021 – where he delivered the keynote speech – as well as being a panellist at FantasyCon and the World Fantasy Convention, and a fiction judge at the Sci-Fi London festival. A former British Fantasy Society Special Publications Editor, he has also served as co-chair for the UK chapter of the Horror Writers Association and co-chaired ChillerCon UK in May 2022.

His work has been optioned and adapted for the big and small screen, including for US network primetime television, and his novelette 'Men of the Cloth' was turned into a feature by Loose Canon/Hydra Films, starring Barbara Crampton (*Re-Animator*, *You're Next*): *Sacrifice*, released by Epic Pictures/101 Films. Paul was also asked to pitch, along with a co-writer, for the remake of *Hellraiser* in the late 2010s. In 2023 HorrorCon UK screened a retrospective of his film & TV adaptations, and interviewed Paul in front of the live audience. His audio work includes the full cast drama adaptation of *The Hellbound Heart* for Bafflegab, starring Tom Meeten (*The Ghoul*), Neve McIntosh (*Doctor Who*) and Alice Lowe (*Prevenge*), and the *Robin of Sherwood* adventure *The Red Lord* for Spiteful Puppet/ITV narrated by Ian Ogilvy (*Return of the Saint*), plus his plays have been performed at FantasyCon and by Hideout Theatre in London. He has also contributed to the Warhammer 40k universe for Games Workshop and has been asked to pitch on projects for both DC/Warner Bros. and Marvel. Paul's latest novels are *Lunar* (set to be turned into a feature film), the YA story *The Rainbow Man* (as P.B. Kane), the sequels to *RED – Blood RED* and *Deep RED*, all collected in an omnibus edition – the award-winning hit *Sherlock Holmes & the Servants of Hell*, *Before* (an Amazon Top 5 dark fantasy bestseller), *Arcana* and *The Storm*. In addition he writes thrillers for HQ/HarperCollins as P.L. Kane, the first of which, *Her Last Secret* and *Her Husband's Grave* (a sellout on Waterstones.com and at The Works) came out in 2020, with *The Family Lie* released the following year (all three novels were Amazon sellouts). His books have been translated into many languages, including French, German, Spanish, Ukrainian, Turkish, Czech, Bulgarian and Polish. Paul lives in Derbyshire, UK, with his wife **Marie O'Regan**. Find out more at his site shadow-writer.co.uk which has featured Guest Writers such as Stephen King, Charlaine Harris, Robert Kirkman, Catriona Ward, Dean Koontz, Olivie Blake and Guillermo del Toro. He can also be found @PaulKaneShadow on X, @paulkane.bsky.social on Bluesky and @paul.kane.376 on Instagram.

Acknowledgements

And now for the important bit – our chance to say a massive thank you. Firstly, again, to all the authors for their contributions, to Nick for having faith in us once more, to Gillian and all the wonderful team at Flame Tree for their hard work. Finally, thanks to our respective families, without whom etc.

Beyond & Within

THE FLAME TREE Beyond & Within short story collections bring together tales of myth and imagination by modern and contemporary writers, carefully selected by anthologists, and sometimes featuring short stories and fiction from a single author. Overall, the series presents a wide range of diverse and inclusive voices, often writing folkloric-inflected short fiction, but always with an emphasis on the supernatural, science fiction, the mysterious and the speculative. The books themselves are gorgeous, with foiled covers, printed edges and published only in hardcover editions, offering a lifetime of reading pleasure.

FLAME TREE FICTION

A wide range of new and classic fiction, from myth to modern stories, with tales from the distant past to the far future, including short story anthologies, Collector's Editions, Collectable Classics, Gothic Fantasy collections and Epic Tales of mythology and folklore.

•